JET VI

Justice

Russell Blake

First Edition

ISBN: 978-1494974206

Published by

Reprobatio Limited

Books by Russell Blake

THRILLERS

FATAL EXCHANGE

THE GERONIMO BREACH

ZERO SUM

THE DELPHI CHRONICLE TRILOGY

KING OF SWORDS

NIGHT OF THE ASSASSIN

RETURN OF THE ASSASSIN

REVENGE OF THE ASSASSIN

BLOOD OF THE ASSASSIN

THE VOYNICH CYPHER

SILVER JUSTICE

JET

JET II – BETRAYAL

JET III – VENGEANCE

JET IV – RECKONING

JET V – LEGACY

JET VI – JUSTICE

UPON A PALE HORSE

BLACK

BLACK IS BACK

BLACK IS THE NEW BLACK

NON FICTION

AN ANGEL WITH FUR

HOW TO SELL A GAZILLION EBOOKS

Prologue

Seven days earlier, Bangkok, Thailand

Sweat trickled down the drawn faces of the men working in the harsh portable lamplight as their leader moved a heavy piece of industrial equipment into position. The hard-packed red dirt beneath their feet was damp from the torrential monsoons that had only abated the prior afternoon, leaving Bangkok rinsed clean, as though the heavens had disapproved of its debauched environs and decided to thoroughly scrub them.

The walls of the earthen chamber were lined with timber posts for reinforcement against a cave-in – a concern when tunneling under the city's busy streets, especially this far beneath the surface. The engineer who'd crafted their approach plan had assured the group that there would be no danger, but wood was cheap and plentiful, and as they'd dug deeper, it had seemed prudent to counter gravity's inexorable pull with a series of support beams running the entire hundred and sixty feet of the tunnel's length.

A string of naked incandescent bulbs hung from the cross posts along the ceiling of the passage, a procession of flickering, fading lights suspended from hastily strung wire. The cooling breeze supplied by a makeshift air-conditioning system had faltered two days earlier, a casualty of the seemingly unending rain that had plagued the city for the last few weeks, and since then, even five stories underground, the muggy heat had been oppressive, the atmosphere viscous and dank, redolent of wet earth and the sour tang of sweat.

"Careful. Careful…there. How are we doing on time?" Steven, the leader, demanded.

One of the workers checked the glowing display of his digital watch. "We're good. The alarm switchover should occur in six minutes."

"All right. It's showtime. Everyone knows what to do. Once we're through, we'll want to move fast, but carefully."

An exposed concrete slab loomed six feet above them, accessible by a vertical shaft they'd hewn from the clay-filled dirt to accommodate the drill. Preliminary testing had reassured them that the slab material had degraded from fifty years of groundwater leaching through the surrounding soil, its astringent chemicals doing much of their work for them.

The lowest part of the tunnel had been the most problematic for the same reason: water. Moisture collected at the bottom as the slope dropped beneath the enormous sewage lines that carried the city's waste from the surrounding office buildings to the treatment plants, rendering the tunnel impassible within minutes of excavation. A quick fix had been engineered involving submersible pumps and raised wooden flooring, but with the downpour, it had been tested to its limits, and everyone would be relieved when the operation was over and the makeshift drainage abandoned.

Three months of round-the-clock labor had gone into tunneling from the basement of a vacant building they'd managed to lease across the street from the target, at first down an additional three stories, and then laterally beneath one of the large boulevards that ran east to west through Bangkok's busy business district. Now, at four in the morning, traffic was virtually nonexistent, and the faint vibrations from above were absent.

"Five…four…three…two…one…go!" the man with the watch said. The powerful drill motor engaged and the long bit bored into the slab. The hardened steel-and-diamond tip tore through the material with ease. Another member of the group moved closer, a green rubber hose in hand, and directed a thin stream of water at the slab so the drill bit wouldn't overheat.

After twenty minutes of methodically coring a series of holes in the shape of a rough square, Steven brought a concrete saw into play, slicing through the remaining cement and rebar as the men readied themselves for the next part of the operation. They pulled thin black cotton balaclavas over their faces and strapped goggles into place, waiting for the inevitable drop of the slab section that was slowly disintegrating before their eyes.

Steven stopped when the saw blade shrieked against metal. "Looks like our worst-case scenario – there's a steel plate above the rebar. Get the thermite ready," Steven ordered as he handed the saw to one of his men, who placed it in the far corner, clear of the work area.

Their demolitions expert, an olive-skinned man with a gleaming black crew cut, ducked out of the chamber and returned a few moments later with a steel toolbox that he set down in front of Steven. After a hesitant glance at the slab above them, he opened it and removed a case with an array of gray cylinders.

Setting the charges in place took several minutes, during which the men prepared for the blinding flash to come, when the thermite would sear through the steel and concrete at thousands of degrees, melting the metal and the surrounding structure. They donned gas masks and filed into the passage, well away from the target area, and waited there while Steven and the demolitions expert finished his job.

The ignition created a white-hot flare, and the chamber filled with smoke. Streams of molten steel dropped from the slab. When the reaction ended, the temperature in the room was unbearable, but the top of the shaft now had a gap in it – a hole large enough for a man to crawl through. Steven neared the cavity, careful to avoid the steaming globs of metal on the dirt beneath it, and after inspecting the gap, nodded to the others. The man with the hose sprayed water onto the ground below, creating a noxious steam in the room as it cooled the molten globs of metal.

After several minutes, two others lugged an iron plate into place and set it down under the shaft as they waited for the newly created aperture to cool. Steven took the hose and directed a stream of water up into the shaft at the gap, where the edges of the metal plate were still glowing. Once he was confident it had cooled, he twisted the hose nozzle off and spoke, his mask muffling his words.

"All right. We're in. Let's do it."

A short, muscular man carried a retractable aluminum ladder to the shaft and extended it upward, positioning and shifting the uppermost rungs higher until it rose through the opening. The team of six climbed wordlessly into the vault above, silent from this point on lest they say anything that could be used to identify them. They knew from their inside contact at the bank – a vice president who tended to be talkative with his new mistress – that there was a hidden camera system in the chamber they'd penetrated, just as they knew about the alarm system and a rigged deficiency in it that would enable them to enter the safe deposit box vault between four and six a.m. without triggering it – but only through the floor.

The primary alarm on the massive steel vault door would still be engaged until manually shut off during business hours; the designers had dismissed entry from any other area as an impossibility. Steven had arranged for the motion detector system inside the safe deposit room to shut off due to a failure to adjust the timer properly – an oversight that had been expensive to contrive, but critical to their plan, and worth every penny of the hundred thousand dollars he'd paid to the technician responsible for its maintenance.

The unlucky vice president had been approached and convinced to share everything he knew about the systems, after having told his avaricious young mistress about the Caucasian client who'd stored what looked like a king's ransom in diamonds in one of the safe deposit boxes – spotted on the cameras built into the ceiling. The bank official had initially been reluctant to talk, but after his son had been abducted and he'd been assured of a safe return only if he was forthcoming, he'd seen the wisdom of sharing his knowledge with Steven's group. Of course, a half million dollars by way of gratitude hadn't hurt, either, along with the guarantee that his son would remain unharmed following his return.

The vice president's untimely death the night before from one of the city's apparent muggings gone wrong had been a necessary part of tying up loose ends in preparation for the operation, as had the hit-and-run that had snuffed out the alarm technician's life the previous afternoon.

In the vault, the men spread out and moved to the first bank of boxes they'd targeted – all but one of them decoys, so the robbery would appear to be random, not directed at a specific box. They'd estimated ten minutes per lock, and using two drills had calculated they could empty twenty of them before departing the scene, leaving the chaos of the ruined containers to be discovered when the bank opened.

Once they began working, their estimates proved painfully low, and after twenty minutes they'd succeeded in opening only one door. That dictated a change of strategy, and the third box they pulled was their target – the one that contained the diamonds. Steven verified the contents before sliding the bags containing the stones into a backpack, along with the gemstones, jewelry, and gold coins from the other boxes.

As they drilled out the seventh lock, the team member who'd stayed below in the tunnel poked his head through the hole in the floor and waved. Steven moved to investigate, and the man handed him a cell phone with a terse text message on it. Steven squinted at the two lines of information, and his heart rate spiked: the motion alarm had engaged earlier than they'd been led to believe it would, and the police were on their way.

Steven snapped his fingers and the men stopped what they were doing. He made a hand signal and dropped through the gap, and the rest of the team quickly followed. Once they were all in the tunnel, he faced them, tearing his gas mask off to be better heard.

"The silent alarm sounded three minutes ago. We got screwed. Let's get out of here. Stick to the plan. Split up as agreed and we'll rendezvous later."

The men nodded, no further explanation required. They ran down the tunnel's length, knowing seconds counted. Once they were all up the shaft that led into the vacant building's basement, the demolitions expert turned and lifted the gray plastic cover of a switch he'd earlier mounted to one of the planks. He punched in numbers on the keypad, pressed the red activation button, and watched the digits on the display count down for several seconds before he bolted for the rope ladder dangling from the shaft.

The floor trembled as he pulled himself into the basement. Dust blew from the tunnel opening as his carefully placed charges detonated under the street, collapsing the tunnel and burying it under tons of debris, eliminating any chance of pursuit. By the time it was unearthed they would be long gone, and the minutiae of the heist would be the stuff of folklore.

Steven nodded to a new arrival wearing loose black cargo pants, a black nylon jacket, and a motorcycle helmet. He handed over the backpack, and the black-clad figure spun and made for the rear exit. The wail of sirens ululating in the predawn as the police responded to the alarm filled the street, strobing lights of the squad cars illuminating the boulevard as they raced toward the bank.

A van waited in front of the vacant building, engine running, the driver tense. Its twin was parked by the building back door, out of sight of the bank. Half the men ran for the front entrance, and the other half joined the helmeted figure hurrying to the rear.

Police cruisers screeched to a halt and armed officers jumped out of the vehicles. A uniformed tactical squad with assault rifles emptied out of a personnel carrier and took up position on the street, gun barrels sweeping the area. A trace of exhaust wafting from the tailpipe of the van in front of the building across the boulevard attracted the attention of the squad commander, and he called to his men. They swiveled as one toward it just as the vehicle's rear doors pulled shut and the engine revved. After a moment of hesitation, the commander gave the signal to fire.

A hail of bullets thumped into the building façade as the van tore away, and only a few of the rounds struck its side as it accelerated down the wide thoroughfare. Several members of the assault squad ran into the street and continued shooting in the slim hope of hitting the zigzagging target – not likely in the gloom, by shooters who were themselves moving, their weapons bouncing with their strides.

Another engine roared as the second getaway vehicle wheeled from the alley at the back of the building and accelerated in the opposite direction, catching the police by surprise. The commander barked an order and clutched his radio to his mouth, issuing instructions. Several of the officers ran for their cruisers, and four of the squad cars gave chase, a pair in either direction. The heavy thump of a helicopter's blades beat the air overhead as it approached the bank. A spotlight beam stabbed through the gloom from the dark chopper and traced over the surrounding rooftops before settling on the bank entrance. It hovered there for an instant as the commander communicated with the pilot, and then began moving as the helicopter took off in pursuit of the second escape vehicle.

The squad cars' sirens followed the second van like the howling of enraged wolves as it skidded around a corner on two wheels. Inside, the driver's face was coated with a sheen of sweat, his jaw muscles pulsing, his eyes glued to the road as his companion in the passenger seat fingered the trigger guard of his PP-19 Bizon submachine gun, watching for pursuers in his side mirror.

"Two streets up on the right. Hard left. Should get us into some narrower streets where we might be able to lose them," he managed through clenched teeth.

"I thought this was going to be a milk run. Not World War III," the driver complained, doing his best to drive the gas pedal through the floorboard with a booted foot. "It's going to be hard to outrun a radio."

"We've done it before."

A police car swerved out of a cross street and fishtailed behind them before straightening out. The passenger shook his head. "Looks like we have company," he muttered.

"You going to do something about that?" the driver demanded, eyes on the rearview mirror.

"You bet. Hold it steady for a few seconds."

The passenger rolled down his window and leaned out, the Bizon clutched in his hands, and fired three bursts at the police vehicle. The car's windshield erupted in a starburst of glass as the flattened heads of slugs punched through it. The squad car veered toward the high curb. Its front wheel struck the concrete, and the front end lifted into the air as the tire burst with a pop, and then the car flipped over onto its side and slid along the street in a shower of sparks before slamming into a parked truck.

The passenger rolled his window back up and glanced at the driver, who nodded.

"Nice shooting."

The chopper's spotlight beam found them moments later, illuminating the van as it roared toward its turn. The driver blotted his forehead with his sleeve and dropped the transmission into a lower gear to slow the vehicle and get traction before the intersection. Headlights appeared from behind as it neared the cross street, and the passenger refastened his seat belt. The driver gauged the turn and yelled over his shoulder into the cargo area.

"Hang on. Grab something, quick," he warned as the van drifted in a controlled skid, nearly tipping over before righting itself and rocketing forward.

"Whooh. Now that's how we do it!" the passenger yelled, slamming his palm against the dashboard with a rare grin. His exuberance was cut short by .50-caliber machine-gun rounds stitching across the roof as the helicopter brought its heavy artillery to bear. The top of his head blew off in a bloody splatter, and he slumped against the side window, the interior suddenly spackled with crimson death. The driver slammed on the brakes and took a hard right turn. As he straightened out, he reached a hand to his chest and glanced at it, taking in the thick blood with fading eyes as he braked to a crawl in a service alley.

"I'm hit. Good…luck," he called into the rear of the van, and then his breath burbled wet through the holes in his shirt and his head lolled forward. The van coasted until it was stopped by one of the dark brick walls. The helicopter hovered overhead, its light fixed on its roof.

The two pursuing squad cars slid to a halt on the wet asphalt near the mouth of the alley, the officers shaken by the high-speed chase. The police driver unlocked the shotgun in the center console mounting and pumped a cartridge into the chamber. With a glance at the alley, his companion drew his pistol and threw his door open to use as cover. They eyed the van, steam rising from the crumpled hood, and stepped out of the car, weapons at the ready, the downdraft from the helicopter's rotors blowing a gale-force wind through the narrow space.

The officers in the second patrol car were exiting their vehicle when the rear cargo doors of the van flew open and a blast of high-velocity automatic weapon fire shredded the nearest car. The driver screamed as an errant round tore half his face off, reflexively squeezing his shotgun's trigger as he fell. The heavy double-aught buckshot pellets slammed harmlessly into the nearest wall as two motorcycles catapulted from the van bed and barreled headlong toward the squad cars. The startled officers fired at the bikes, but they stood no chance. The left motorcycle's driver leaned forward against the handlebars as his passenger strafed the officers with his Heckler & Koch MP5 on full automatic, and the 9mm rounds cut through policemen's torsos as the motorcycle roared by.

The right BMW motorcycle's lone rider soared into the air as the bike flew over the bodies of the downed police and landed with a scream of rubber. The rider swung the front tire on impact and gunned it in the opposite direction from the other motorcycle, making it impossible for the helicopter to follow them both. The rear tire smoked as the rider twisted the throttle and popped the clutch, and the BMW leaped forward like a rocket, engine revving into the redline as it streaked toward the next block, a large intersection where a few sluggish early morning commuters were wending their way into town.

Bullets pocked the street around the motorcycle as the helicopter fired a stream of lead from above, gouging divots of asphalt from the pavement. The bike hurtled forward. The staccato barking of the big gun echoed off the buildings as the first faint traces of dawn lit the sky. The motorcycle skidded, taking the turn as the rider stabilized it with a boot, and then went barreling down the main street, weaving between cars as the chopper's gunner watched impotently, forbidden to fire into a populated area no matter how hot the pursuit.

Two police motorcycles rocketed onto the main artery from a tributary and took up the chase, the officers accustomed to insane traffic at high velocity, determined to stick with the escaping bike at all costs. Word had come over the radio that the other motorcycle had disappeared, and the second van was still in a high-speed race, the police cars taking fire from at least one gunman as it tore from the downtown area in a breakneck bid for freedom.

The rider spied the flashing lights from the police bikes and slammed on the brakes, causing the BMW to skid to one side and up onto the sidewalk. A twist of the handlebars took it into a narrow walkway between two buildings, where it exploded through bags of trash awaiting early morning collection. Fruit rinds and refuse flew into the air as it narrowly avoided colliding with an old man pushing a hand cart laden with produce.

A glance at the side mirror caught a reflection of the police motorcycles behind it, and the rider instinctively gave the throttle free rein as the engine's RPMs screamed into the red. Brick walls streaked by on both sides as the bike careened dangerously, and then it vaulted out the other end and onto a small one-way street.

The ornate golden spires of a temple jutted from behind a brick and ironwork wall fifty yards away. The rider swung the bike through the nearest of its elaborate entry arches and bounced up the four stairs to a pathway that stretched through the park-like grounds. The sky glowed orange from the rising sun, high ribbons of clouds marbling the heavens as the helicopter's ugly snout appeared overhead, and the gunship opened fire again, blasting chunks of grass from the immaculately tended lawn. The motorcycle was moving too erratically, though, and the barrage missed the mark by a wide margin. At the far end of the temple grounds, the bike skidded to a halt, and then, after a split-second pause, jumped the low rear wall and landed hard in a wide culvert – a concrete drainage canal that was almost dry now that the rains had abated.

The BMW accelerated in a blur as the chopper kept up the gunfire, but with a weaving target moving erratically, the gunner had slim chance of hitting it, and the rounds struck well short of the racing bike. An overpass straddled the culvert, and the motorcycle ducked beneath it, but didn't emerge on the other side. The pilot and crew glared at the area as they hovered overhead, ready to resume blasting away when their quarry reappeared. After thirty seconds the pilot exchanged a nervous glance with his partner, who radioed in their position, requesting instructions.

"Our map shows a maintenance access point there. Repeat. There's a maintenance access point beneath the overpass," the dispatcher's voice intoned over the crackling channel.

"Damn. Where does it let out?"

"Looks like there are two alleys, one on each side."

"I see that, but the buildings are pretty close together. They don't look wide enough for a motorcycle to easily make it. Do we have any units in the vicinity?" the pilot asked.

"Negative. Closest is two minutes out. Will divert."

The helicopter rose to a higher altitude in the hopes of being able to spot a fast-moving bike in one of the alleys. When a squad car arrived, followed closely by the two police motorcycles that had been chasing the bike, there was no sign of their target. The officers dismounted, drew their weapons, and crept down the access stairs to the path that led to the underpass. There they spotted the BMW, engine still purring, lying on its side, abandoned.

Two blocks away, shopkeepers were setting out their wares on the sidewalks as pedestrians hunting for early morning bargains meandered along, many on their way to work, some finishing after a long night. A tall blonde woman with a motorcycle helmet in one hand and a black nylon backpack securely strapped to her shoulders approached a dumpster at the side of a filthy side street and tossed the helmet into the heap of trash, where it would be scavenged within the hour by one of the countless poor teeming the area.

She retraced her steps and continued to the end of the block, and found herself facing the chrome and glass exterior of a twenty-four-hour fast-food restaurant. She entered, and after ordering to go, slipped into the restroom, where she removed her jacket and stuffed it into the garbage bin, taking care to remove her cell phone from the breast pocket before burying the discarded jacket in the crumpled paper towels.

Her dark blue, long-sleeved T-shirt barely contained the swell of her high breasts. She took a deep breath and inspected herself in the mirror. She looked calm. Innocent. One of the army of tourists that walked the streets of Bangkok at all hours of the day and night. She wiped a small smudge from her right cheek, and after offering her reflection her most relaxed smile, shouldered the backpack and went back out to pick up her order. She left the restaurant, and glancing around, placed a call as she sipped her coffee and walked unhurriedly down the sidewalk. A male voice answered on the second ring.

"I've got it," she said.

"Where are you, Tara?"

She described her rough location.

The voice paused. "Can you be at the condo in an hour?"

"Maybe two. They'll be setting up roadblocks if they're smart. I'll call you when I'm clear." Tara hesitated. "I don't know how many of the others made it."

"So far it looks like we lost at least half the team."

"That's a shame."

"It is. But at least it was worth it. Take good care of yourself. No foolish chances."

Tara considered her breakneck run from the police and countless near misses, dodging machine-gun fire at a hundred miles per hour as dawn broke over the city. She smirked as she moved aside for an elderly man shambling along as though with the weight of the world on his shoulders, her blue eyes twinkling with merriment at the admonition, her smooth tanned skin creasing as the corners of her lips twitched in response to the warning.

"You bet. I'll keep a low profile."

Chapter 1

Music drifted on the evening breeze, perfumed by orange blossoms and the salty tang of seaweed. A gentle surf rolled onto the beach and pulled greedily at the sand and rocks, as though nature was trying to claw back the rarified section of coastline from its privileged residents. The last of the sunbathers had departed hours earlier, and dusk had brought with it blessed relief from the day's heat. Up the strand, the silhouette of a twenty-thousand-square-foot Italianate villa loomed like a medieval castle, every lamp in the opulent home illuminated, the lights twinkling like rare jewels as darkness descended.

A band was set up to the side of the massive pool deck, easily the rival of many luxury hotels in the area, and was playing a medley of local and international favorites as white-jacketed stewards roamed the grounds carrying trays of appetizers. A group of swarthy young men lounged around the pool in resort wear, their linen pants and silk shirts a kind of informal uniform, cigars smoldering in crystal ashtrays atop the stone tables sending pungent tendrils of smoke into the night sky.

These were the impossibly wealthy scions of Saudi oil money, the lucky offspring of families that controlled more riches than many nations, for whom no luxury was too lavish and no whim too extravagant. They'd arrived the prior day on private jets and mega-yachts for a weekend getaway from their stodgy country, where custom and the law forbid the drugs, alcohol, and female company in which they enthusiastically indulged while on vacation.

Bottles of the finest single malt Scotch sat half-consumed on each of three tables as the guests caroused and told stories about their wild times at university in Europe, where the wealthy elite of Saudi Arabia were educated while their less fortunate countrymen lived in abject poverty. None was older than twenty-five, and all were lifelong friends, frequent guests at each other's palaces, and students in the same schools.

The night's festivities celebrated the villa owner's twenty-sixth birthday, and no expense had been spared. The rarest wines had been painstakingly selected by an internationally recognized sommelier, a Michelin chef had been flown in to prepare the meal and a harem of starlets and models had spent the day lounging around the pool, providing whatever recreational diversion the young men could imagine.

Near the bar, a six-foot-tall ice sculpture of a scowling Neptune stood in the center of an elaborate display of shrimp, lobster, and every imaginable seafood delicacy, one of numerous stations where thousands of dollars of appetizers were on display for the two dozen guests. A dark-complexioned tall man stood rigidly by the seafood table in a polar-white formal chef's hat and coat, occasionally mopping the sweat off his brow with a pocketed hand towel. His clones framed the other stations, ignored by the celebrants as they joked in loud voices, their Arabic exclamations undecipherable to the local staff.

A perimeter wall ringed the property, with lush foliage to conceal all but the top. Discreet bodyguards in dark blue suits ambled along the footpaths, earbuds connected to coiled white cables that disappeared into their jackets a ubiquitous accessory. Bulges of shoulder-holstered pistols distorted their otherwise well-tailored vestments as they patrolled the familiar grounds. All were hardened professionals paid top dollar for the security duty, which routinely involved nothing more than acting as combination babysitters and bodyguards when the men tired of domestic entertainment and decided to go into town to hit one of the city's wild nightclubs, a common occurrence after a long evening of drinking and chemical fortification left the guests restless and bored.

The men's heads turned as a loud crack sounded from the bar area. Two of the bodyguards swiveled from their positions, hands on their weapons, ready to draw, and then relaxed as a statuesque blonde wearing a white miniskirt and bikini top threw her head back and laughed as her companion, a stunning brunette, held aloft a bottle of Cristal champagne, a torrent of bubbly frothing from it, the cork blown a dozen yards into the air before coming down out of sight on the other side of the nearby perimeter wall.

"Are you girls having a good time?" one of the Saudi men asked, his English unaccented, a tribute to his million-dollar education and private tutoring.

"Never better, sweetie," the blonde said, her words softened by a Texas twang that made her a requested favorite on the international hospitality circuit. She winked at her companion, a nineteen-year-old model from Rome who was already a three-year veteran of the lucrative duty, preferring the financial rewards of being a paid companion to royalty to the rigors of the runway.

"Why don't you come over here and give me a shoulder massage? I'm sore from all the swimming today," Abbas, the cousin of their host, said with his face radiating spoiled ennui.

"I'd love to, honey. Give me a second, and I'll give you a workout you won't believe," she promised, taking a sip of her champagne in preparation for her next round with Abbas, who was known to all the girls as overly rough and somewhat sadistic in his pursuits. She'd spent the morning with him and was only now walking without pain, although she did her best to hide it and would never complain – at ten thousand dollars a day, she could suffer his appetites without flinching.

"That's my Barbie," Abbas said, chuckling as the other men eyed her. He'd taken to calling her Barbie, and whatever her real name, or the one she'd chosen for her profession, it had been discarded in favor of the moniker. She didn't mind. One more year of this and she could retire in comfort at the ripe old age of twenty-two. In the meantime, she would be Barbie, or Brandi, or whatever else the clients wanted to call her. It was all the same to her. The young ones were inevitably the worst – like they had something to prove to themselves – whereas the older men tended to be gentler, and quicker to get it over with.

Three security guards watched the approach to the beach. They were more relaxed than their counterparts on the grounds; visibility was good down both stretches of sand, not a soul out now that the sun had set. The band wound down their rollicking final song of the medley and launched into a ballad, a lover's lament played to melt even the most callous heart – which went largely unnoticed by the gathering, who took everything from the spread to the band as givens, no more noteworthy than the waiters they waved off with disdainful hands.

The guard on the right side of the house reached the front corner. Two of his colleagues were smoking and chatting by a black Land Rover and a red Ferrari Scuderia parked in the large circular drive. Beyond the wrought-iron gates several stretch Mercedes limousines waited, should the guests feel the urge to go into town. The contingent of a dozen guards was typical for a low-threat location like the villa, more as a deterrent than anything, there being no threat to the guests in Spain other than the risk of self-inflicted substance abuse or overexertion with the paid talent.

He approached the two smokers and bummed a cigarette, admiring the expensive red Italian sports car with a shake of his head.

"I could retire on what that thing cost," he muttered, and one of the men lit his smoke for him with a waggle of bushy eyebrows.

"But then you'd miss the joy of standing around in a monkey suit all night while your betters frolic."

"And the satisfaction of a job poorly done," the second man said, his craggy features stony in the dim light.

The men continued the exchange, their attention riveted on the automobile, and none heard the rappelling line sail over the perimeter wall at the home's midpoint, nor did they register the small fiber-optic scope watching them over its high top from the lot next door. Seconds later a black-clad figure slid down the rope and dropped to the ground, hidden by the bushes at the wall's base. A second figure joined him moments later, and then a third, all as silent as death as they crouched in the bushes.

The guard took a long pull on his cigarette. "Thanks for the smoke. Got to get back to the party. Make sure nobody's drinks run dry," he said to his companions, who waved him away. They'd done dozens of these sorts of security jobs for the royal family and its constellation of relatives, and were accustomed to the long hours and boring duty – some of the best paid in the world.

He returned along the path, wishing for better lighting on the side of the house, and was almost to the midpoint when he heard a faint rustle behind him, as soft as a gust of wind stirring the plants.

A white-hot lance of pain shrieked up his spine as a razor-sharp carbon-fiber blade penetrated his back, his cry silenced by the vise-like hand clamped over his mouth, and then another stab sliced through his spinal cord, and he collapsed, dying even as his body betrayed him. His assailant waited until he'd stopped breathing and then expertly removed the guard's earbud and transmitter and slipped them on, removing the balaclava and dropping it on the dead guard's chest before the other two men dragged the inert corpse into the underbrush.

Leonid unzipped his black mechanic's coveralls and stepped out of them to reveal a blue suit identical to those of the rest of the guards. After a nod to the men in the bushes, he ambled toward the rear of the house, taking his time. He paused near the back corner and made a hand gesture. His two companions darted to the side service entrance and slipped inside while the suited man watched the party from his position at the corner.

The interior of the home rivaled a French royal palace, the marble floors the finest Italy had to offer, every detail and appointment the result of countless hours of deliberation by some of the most in-demand interior designers in Europe. The intruders crept on soundless feet along the hall, now with compact MTAR-21 sound-suppressed bullpup assault rifles in their hands. The first man pointed at the sweeping stairway leading to the second floor, where they knew from studying the house blueprints the master suite was located, and the other nodded, both listening for any signs of life. The servants would all be in the kitchen area, attending to the caterer's exacting instructions – if they had any luck at all, they wouldn't be molested while performing their errand.

Both gunmen mounted the stairs, rubber-soled boots silent on the polished stone surface, weapons at the ready should anyone stumble upon them as they neared their objective. The client had issued very specific instructions for the sanction, and they hoped to be in and out with a minimum of fuss, but missions could go awry quickly, and they were prepared to slaughter whomever they came across now that they were past the point of no return.

The execution could have been accomplished much more easily with a sniper round or an explosive charge beneath the owner's sports car, but that wouldn't have satisfied the contract, and this specialized group guaranteed satisfaction in the discharge of its duties. The direction had been very specific, right down to the weapon to be used, and it wasn't their role to question the whys of the client's demands. They were specialists, and they would accomplish what they'd been chartered with doing, without question – or die trying.

Not that in the group's five-year career they'd ever had a failure. True, there had been difficult escapes and some casualties within their ranks, but when this team was hired, the job was as good as done. That's why the men were among the highest paid of their kind in the world, and why they took their work as seriously as they did – they'd been casing the villa for a week, had tried bribing the caretaker of the adjacent property with a small fortune, and when he'd refused, killed him without hesitation before taking over that house for the final forty-eight hours before the party had gotten underway.

They made their way quietly down the long hallway, ears straining as they neared the master bedroom door. They knew the home had eleven guest suites and one master area larger than most beach houses, more an apartment than a bedroom. Its entrance lay dead ahead, its windows and balcony affording breathtaking views of the sea, the cost of construction enough to build a small town. The trailing man stopped at the light switch at the end of the hall and dimmed the overhead lamps until the corridor was nearly unlit – a sensible preparation for making a discreet exit, as well as to avoid alerting their quarry when they entered the bedroom.

At the door's fourteen-karat gold lever, they paused and exchanged a glance before the lead man softly depressed the handle and eased the door open. A robotic techno-beat thumped from the darkened room, and they were in with the door closed behind them in seconds. In the gloom they could make out a young woman's naked body straddling a man, bucking like a bronco as the couple neared a climax that was real for at least one of them. The lead man pushed his weapon aside and reached into his pocket as the second held his gun on the couple, eyes flat as a shark's while his partner made his soundless way to the bed.

The girl must have sensed a presence. She gave a small yelp just before her life was ended by a suppressed subsonic round that penetrated her brain from the silenced Walther PPK. She dropped against her lover, who in his arousal hadn't registered her death and was still moving even as the killer slid to the side of the bed.

When the bedbound man realized something was wrong, he pushed the dead girl off his naked body. The killer didn't wait or give him time to scream. The vicious blade of the khanjar, the curved ceremonial dagger he'd been given, stabbed into the target's throat, severing his windpipe in a single bloody swipe and silencing him. The victim clutched at his neck, and the attacker stabbed him in the abdomen, slicing upward to the base of the sternum, as directed by the client. Just before the blade could penetrate the victim's heart, he stopped, again as instructed, so the victim would endure unimaginable pain before he died, which would take several minutes from exsanguination.

The castration and butchery was to be performed while the subject was still alive. That point had been underscored multiple times. The second man stood by, now filming the procedure with his phone, using a small penlight with gauze tape over the lens for muted illumination. When the contract terms had been carried out, he approached the dying man and focused on his face as the killer drove the dagger home, finally ending his ordeal.

The dagger was to be left in place, the man's testicles stuffed into his mouth along with his phallus. This was apparently an important signal, a key step in the ritual, and it had been outlined in detail during the client meeting when they'd accepted the five million dollars to carry out the sanction.

When they finished, the killer placed a cell call, whispered in Russian, and listened for several moments. He hung up and turned to his companion.

"Time to get out of here. It's still clear, but no telling for how long. Their radio protocols are beyond amateur – only one check every fifteen minutes, and we have four left until the next one. Did you get the shot?"

"All of it. The client will be pleased."

The victim was the son of a Saudi prince, who'd raped the daughter of a rival Bedouin chieftain while the two had been getting their degrees at the Sorbonne in Paris. Five years after the horrific event, she'd confessed the violation to one of her brothers while back at home for a visit, just before she'd taken her own life. The brother had told the father, who had vowed to avenge the stain on his family's honor. Because the father was rich in his own right, he'd been able to reach across the desert and the sea and exact his pound of flesh using the Russians. With the photographic evidence of the completion of the deed, the world would now be back in balance, and the grieving father could sleep nights knowing his daughter's defiler had been dealt with appropriately.

They made their way back downstairs, the knife man's arms and chest soaked with blood, and were almost to the service corridor when the front entry door swung open and one of the guards stepped inside – his last living act as the second Russian fired, nearly silent from the subsonic ammunition, and a neat row of bullet holes stitched up the guard's chest before obliterating his face. The hapless man tumbled in a heap to the marble floor, and the two intruders now abandoned any pretext of stealth, sprinting for the service area and the door that led to the exterior, aware that the guard would be discovered at any moment.

They burst from the door just as a cry went up from the front drive. Both men ran for the rope, and the second man scrambled up as the killer freed his MTAR and switched on the laser sight. Leonid walked easily back toward him from the rear of the house, his suit unruffled, and after a whispered few words in Russian, caught the MTAR as the blood-covered killer followed the first up the wall. He was almost over it when the first shots rang out from the front corner of the house, but the range was long for the shooter, and the slugs missed by several feet. Leonid returned fire, his accuracy with the MTAR better than the guards' pistols, and the shooter went down with a scream as several rounds tore through his chest.

Once the killer was over the wall, Leonid ran for the rope. Shots rang out from the rear deck, and he spun and fired, emptying the magazine at the two men there. One fell backward as he was hit, but the other continued to shoot, causing a problem even given the distance. Leonid was drawing his pistol as he dropped the now-empty assault rifle when more fire rained down on the surviving shooter from the top of the wall. Leonid watched as the guard's body jerked from bullets ripping into him as he sprinted for the rope, pulling with all his might, climbing the steep face in seconds flat.

Two Toyota FJ Cruisers sat idling on the other side of the wall. He threw himself into the rear cargo area and pulled the door shut as the driver gunned the engine and made for the front gate. The barrier slid open in response to a press of the remote control, and the vehicles disappeared into the darkness. By the time the guards had rallied and piled into vehicles to give chase, the Toyotas were long gone, the bewildered limo drivers having watched them vanish into the night as screams of alarm and horror echoed off the villa's impeccably manicured façade.

Chapter 2

Yesterday, Mendoza, Argentina

Matt dodged past an ancient Peugeot sedan double-parked on one of the downtown streets and narrowly avoided being hit by a truck hauling beer to the neighboring restaurants. He glanced over his shoulder to ensure he wasn't going to be flattened if he changed lanes, and gave his Vespa scooter gas as he threaded the needle between two Chevrolets moving at double any reasonable speed. After nearly four months in Mendoza, he'd grown accustomed to the insane driving, much as he had in the Far East during his twenty years on the ground there. Argentines only varied from Asian drivers in degree of suicidal risk-taking, with the edge definitely going to Asia.

He saw his target destination in the middle of the block, between a travel agency and a gelato shop, and squeezed his brakes as he pulled out of traffic. He rolled to a halt in front of a massive oak tree and eased the scooter up onto the sidewalk. The freezing snow of the summer months had relented to an early warm fall, South America's equivalent of springtime, bringing with it blooming trees and blossoming flowers to line the stately boulevards of the city's heart. He twisted the ignition key, and the motor sputtered off. After hanging his helmet on one of the handlebars, he made his way down the crowded street to the internet café he'd spied – one of several he used to check his various email accounts every week.

As a former CIA head of station, he was all too aware of the deficiencies of IP-masking software and knew that the NSA had the capability to track through most of the programs to the source computer. As such, he took reasonable precautions and moved around, never using the same PC twice to check an account…just in case. Since he and Jet had taken Arthur down he wasn't worried about the cabal within the Agency finding him. Arthur's deputies would be in disarray for some time to come as their carefully crafted drug empire crumbled around them now that he'd cut the primary head off that particular hydra. But he was methodically cautious as a way of life, and took as few unnecessary chances as possible. Experience had taught him that the only thing you could truly depend on was the evil that men were willing to do in their pursuit of power and money – and the nearly two hundred million in diamonds he still had from his confiscation of Arthur's network's drug pipeline was well worth some bright lad trying to hunt him down one of these days.

Then again, that trail was cold, and had ended with Arthur. Nobody knew where he had the stones stashed in Bangkok, so he – and his fortune – were safe. Not that he needed it. Jet still had virtually all of the fifty million he'd paid her, and he had the ten he'd pulled out for his living expenses – enough for the rest of his hopefully long life – in a country where he couldn't spend fifty thousand dollars a year if he tried.

He entered the café, a large arcade with fifty computers separated from one another by blue plastic dividers, and stood in line waiting to pay for an available station. At the window, he asked for fifteen minutes of time, the minimum available, even though his trips so far had always resulted in the blinking vacant glow of an empty inbox. The young woman at the counter took his pesos and gave him a slip of paper with a numerical code, and directed him to pod number seven, adjacent to a teenage girl so enraptured by Facebook she hardly registered his presence.

He logged on and tapped in his ID and password and was shocked to find three messages, all from his bank in Thailand. He'd left this blind email address as the only way for the bank to contact him in the event of an emergency, never dreaming that the day would come when it would contain any messages, much less three.

After glancing around to confirm that nobody was paying the slightest attention to him, he opened the first message and read the polite missive with a sinking sensation in the pit of his stomach. It requested that he contact the bank president as soon as possible due to a regrettable incident the prior week – of course, omitting the critical information of what the incident had been. The second was dated a day later and repeated the request, the language slightly more strident.

The third chilled his blood. It announced in precise, legalistic language that the bank had been robbed, and that his safe deposit box had been one of several that had been broken into. Matt typed in a carefully worded response and pressed send, and then opened a browser to see what, if any, information on the robbery appeared online. A quick search brought him to the site of one of Bangkok's largest newspapers, and he read the sensationalistic account of the daring robbery and getaway with trepidation.

Stunned at how quickly his entire world had changed, he digested the news that his diamonds were gone, stolen by parties unknown. The only robbers apprehended had been killed during the escape – about which the Thai police weren't divulging any information, in the customary tradition of the secretive authorities who refused to cooperate with the media on most occasions, and rightly viewed the press as their enemy, given the massive corruption that was endemic to the system and that the papers delighted in heralding.

His time expired and he stared dully at the screen, his brain working furiously to process the ramifications. Someone had tunneled into the vault, and it had been his bad luck to be one of the handful of boxes robbed.

He didn't believe that for an instant.

In his line of work there were no coincidences. The only question in his mind was how they had tracked him to the bank, and how they'd known which box was his.

He had no doubt that it was Arthur's henchmen behind the scheme. Nobody else would have had the balls to pull it off, much less the resources. The paper had described the rental of the vacant building, the collapsed tunnel, the use of thermite to cut through the reinforced concrete slab floor...as well as the death of one of the top bank officers the day before, with all the attendant speculation in the best tradition of the yellow journalism on which Thailand seemed to thrive.

A thought flitted through his awareness and he stood, again studying his fellow computer users, now on full alert. He wiped down the mouse and the keyboard with his sleeve, drawing a bemused glance from the teen, and couldn't get out of there fast enough. Doing the internet search from the same computer had been a mistake – likely an inconsequential one, but still, a mistake. Matt mentally kicked himself for his carelessness and vowed not to make any more. If he'd gotten soft in his time out of the field, it was a weakness he couldn't afford, especially if Arthur's network was back in the game.

Matt slowed his breathing as he strolled unhurriedly to the entrance, not wanting to make an impression on anyone who might later be questioned, no matter how slim the likelihood. Once outside he paused, taking in the street: several businessmen walking with the urgency of those for whom time was money; a handful of students loitering in front of a market; a pair of women in knee-high boots and too-tight jeans that were all the rage in Argentina, taking their time about making it down the sidewalk, pausing at every other display window to consider and comment on the wares for sale. To his left, a pensioner shambling along in a navy blue dinner jacket and gray slacks, colorful cravat in place, his thin strands of hair slicked back like a tango dancer and a cigarette clutched in his hand like a smoking rosary. No obvious threats, just the citizenry going about its business in a city where wine and tourism were the main economic drivers, and the intrigue of the CIA's drug trafficking cabal was a million miles away.

He walked to his Vespa and straddled it. The realization hit that not only had ninety-five percent of his holdings been wiped out, but he was now back on the radar. He'd traveled the world to find a place where he would be safe to pursue happiness with the woman of his dreams, and reality had intruded with a harsh reminder that his enemies were out there, alive and well, and obviously active.

Matt had underestimated their drive to reclaim the riches, and now he was the poorer for it – to be sure, still rich, his life unchanged in any material way, other than to be awakened from his dream only to find that nothing was safe…just as it had never been at any point in his career. Why he'd convinced himself that this time was different seemed childishly naive in light of this newest development: because he'd fallen in love and wanted to believe that the world could be a good place, and not the snake pit he'd inhabited professionally for decades.

A harmless change of perspective that had made things seem safer.

And a conceit that he now understood carried a high price indeed.

Chapter 3

Yesterday, Miami Beach, Florida

Tara gazed out over the water. Miami's beaches stretched to the horizon as devout sun worshipers of all shapes and sizes got in their last rays of the day. She stood on the terrace of her high-rise condo, in one of the swankiest buildings in a town consumed with status, and breathed in the sweet salt air. The light breeze from the east stirred her hair, seeming to carry on it the faint scent of palm trees and coconut and frangipani from the distant islands.

Far below, a line of cars crawled along the beach road, the afternoon drawing to a close as dusk approached. A line of white thunderheads brooded in the distance as a front developed, gathering strength before making landfall, as if to remind the privileged denizens of that stretch of coast that nature was always to be respected: an unpredictable force to be reckoned with.

She inspected a shapely, well-toned leg, her skin the color of café-au-lait, bronzed and sun-kissed with a light sheen of oil, and wondered at the odd track of her life. Only a week before, she'd been a fugitive in a country she'd sworn never to return to, with a fortune in stolen diamonds strapped to her back, running from the law after masterminding the most daring bank robbery in the nation's history. She contrasted that to her present, as she contemplated the beauty of the azure sea, her biggest concern which of the countless trendy restaurants in town to grace with her cash – of which she had a seemingly endless supply, thanks to the generosity of her employers and her proficiency at her job.

Sade's atmospheric voice crooned over a seductive baseline drifting from the living room. Tara's penthouse home was a stylish contemporary unit upon which she'd spared no expense, its lavish appointments and top-of-the-line appliances worthy of the pages of one of the many decorating and architecture magazines spread on her chrome and glass coffee table.

A sound like wind chimes tinkled from the kitchen. After a final wistful look at the departing cruise ships heading to sea, she strolled inside to where a phone whose number didn't officially exist continued to ring until she answered it.

"Yes?" she said.

"We have a hit." The voice was familiar, deep and resonant, but always restrained, like a powerful animal that had learned to tame its brutality, to control itself in the presence of company. Carson Santell was career CIA, and she'd been working for him in one form or another for seven years.

"I was wondering how long it would take," Tara said.

"Good things come to those who wait."

"If you say so. Where is he?"

"Argentina. Western part of the country. Mendoza." Santell had arranged for a trace on the Thai bank's computers, and when the bank president had sent his missive to Matt, it had been child's play to have the NSA monitor the inbox for traffic and triangulate the IP address when he checked in.

"Argentina. I see." She paused for a few beats. "I have a contact there. Out of Buenos Aires. A fellow named Dante Caravatio we've done business with in the past."

"Can you get in contact with him?"

"Of course. I know he'll be willing to help us...for a price. Always for a price."

"Excellent. You have my permission to devote whatever resources are required. We're still at least sixty million short. Which means he probably split the stones up and took some with him."

"That would be the prudent assumption. It's in character." She shifted, enjoying the feel of the cool marble on her bare feet. "I'll call you back once I've touched base."

"We've already chartered a jet for you. Figure nine hours door to door, Miami to Mendoza."

She sighed, gazing at the play of sun on the sparkling waves beyond her balcony. "I suppose that's better than the twenty-seven to Thailand."

Santell grunted assent. "Can you have your team ready soon?"

"Yes. I'll call you back once I speak with Dante. I'll need to coordinate logistical support in Mendoza. Weapons and the like. Even in a private jet I suspect the customs people would get testy if we brought in an arsenal."

"Use your best judgment. You know how to reach me."

"Have the plane stand by for a late night flight. It'll take a little while to get in contact with everyone." Tara paused. "What's the budget on this?"

"There are no limitations, within reason, of course. You understand what's at stake. I trust you to be prudent. Do whatever's necessary."

"I understand."

She disconnected and went to her bedroom, where she spun the dial of her floor safe and retrieved one of several cell phones from its depths, moving ten stacks of hundred dollar bills out of the way to get to it. She powered it on and studied the display, and then dialed a Buenos Aires number.

The male voice that answered was gruff and terse, with the distinctive accented Spanish pronunciation particular to Argentina.

"Yes?"

Tara replied in fluent Spanish. "I need to speak to Dante. Is he there?"

"Who wants to know?"

"Tell him Maria. And that it's been too long." Maria was the operational name she'd always used with Dante – one of many she was known by, depending on the day and which passport she was carrying.

She waited, listening as a murmured discussion took place in the background, and then a more refined baritone voice came on the line. "Maria? I must be dreaming."

"How are things in BA?"

"Not the same without you to brighten my days," Dante purred.

"I see your charm is as polished as ever. Always the gentleman."

He laughed. "Not always. Where are you?"

"I'm thinking about coming to visit."

"Ah, yes? And to what do I owe the pleasure?"

"Business, I'm afraid." She took a breath. "Listen, Dante. I need your help."

Dante's tone changed, subtly, now all business, the patina of bonhomie discarded in favor of his customary demeanor. "How can I be of service?"

"Do you have associates in Mendoza?"

"Of course. Why?"

"I have a problem I need to attend to there. Personally."

"I see. What sort of a problem?"

"I need to locate someone who's hiding in Mendoza. A man. A very dangerous man."

"There's no place in Argentina I don't have a network, as you well know. Mendoza is no different. Tell me what you have in mind and what you require."

"Weapons. And personnel. Locals. But I'll handle the active phase. I just need some discreet support."

"Consider it done. Send me over a list and I'll make it happen. Let me give you a clean email account." He hesitated, spoke with someone, and then returned with the address.

Tara nodded as she wrote it down. "Perfect. And I'll also attach a photo of the man. I'd like you to circulate it to your Mendoza associates on the off chance they've seen him."

"Of course, my dear. But I should warn you that Mendoza is a large city. Well over a million people. And it's spread out. A good place to get lost, if that's what you're looking to do."

"I'm sure it is. But humor me."

"Your wish is my command. Now, to mundane necessities. Depending on what you want in the way of support and ordnance, the cost will vary considerably."

"Assume I want the best of the range, with top-flight assistance. Outfitting for...four."

"When?"

She looked at her watch. "I can be there tomorrow afternoon at the latest."

Dante paused, thinking. "Figure...fifty should do the trick. Unless I need to intervene on your behalf with the local authorities, in which case...eighty."

"More than fair, as always, *mi amor*. You're too good to me."

"I have a weak spot for beauty and intelligence."

"For which I'm grateful. Let's assume fifty will be the number. I'll bring cash. Can I give it to your Mendoza people?"

"Certainly. Although I'll never forgive you if you don't visit while you're in my backyard. You'll be less than an hour and a half away."

"I'll do my best. But no promises. I might be on a tight schedule for departure."

Dante's disappointed tone came back. "I see. I suppose I'll have to get accustomed to the idea of my heart breaking, yet again."

"Not if I can help it. But time may not cooperate on this trip."

"Send me your list and your photo. I'll take it from there and email you contact information and confirmation that I've sourced your requirements."

She hung up and shook her head. For all Dante's charm, he was as dangerous as a pit viper and utterly ruthless. He ran the syndicate that was responsible for most of the narcotics trafficking in Argentina, as well as prostitution, murder for hire, extortion, kidnapping, slavery, and robbery, not to mention gunrunning and money laundering for most of South America. His reach was considerable, and he was untouchable, with pockets filled with politicians, and the police at his beck and call.

In other words, perfect for her purposes.

She moved into her office and tapped out a brief list of her equipment needs and attached the last known photograph of Matt taken several years earlier – four years after he'd called their relationship off and she'd transferred back to the U.S., glad to be rid of the man who'd rejected her after learning of her affiliation with Arthur's group. And the only man who'd ever done so, for any reason…for which she'd never forgive him. That she was being sanctioned to track him down was poetic justice, and she tried not to get too excited at the idea of Matt at her mercy, begging for his life.

Mercy that would be withheld, and not simply because she was a consummate professional.

No, this was also personal, which was icing on the cake.

She sent the email and made three phone calls. Everyone would be at the airport within six hours, tops. After checking the time, she called Santell back and told him that they were game-on for a midnight departure.

"What do you want me to do with him once I have the diamonds?" she asked, wanting to hear him say it out loud.

"Terminate with extreme prejudice. How much pain he endures before he dies is up to you."

Tara smiled, her teeth even and white, her face radiating the angelic purity and calm of a newborn. A physical shiver of pleasure tingled up her spine as she nodded in agreement.

"You just made my day."

Chapter 4

Yesterday, Mendoza, Argentina

Jet stood at the kitchen island while she made a salad for lunch, keeping an eye on Hannah, who was lying on the wooden dining room floor playing with two plastic ponies, her current favorites out of the hundreds of toys she'd collected since they'd been reunited four months earlier in Uruguay. Jet tried not to spoil her too much, but the urge to lavish her daughter with everything she could think of was powerful – a function, she knew, of having been forced to leave Hannah in the care of others while cleaning up the mess that insisted on following her around in life.

Hannah was discoursing with herself in her high-pitched child's voice, engaged in some conversation known only to her, speaking a language that only she understood. Jet was used to it by now and didn't give it much thought, and was glad that her kid seemed happy and well adjusted, albeit spoiled rotten, and not just by Jet. Matt was a pushover when it came to Hannah, who had him wrapped around her little finger, a combination knight-errant and playmate. Sometimes Jet would see them sitting together on the couch, watching cartoons or one of the dozens of animated films that she never tired of, Matt patiently answering her questions with short phrases she'd understand, her brow furrowed in concentration as she absorbed his responses, and a part of Jet she thought had died long ago would swell in her chest, threatening to overwhelm her.

Jet and Matt were inseparable now, their attachment so powerful it was almost frightening at times, their connection so deep that it defied description and took her breath away some nights as she lay in his arms, trembling after making love, their bodies molded to each other, their sweat intermingled, satiated and yet wanting more. Her instinct that he'd been made for her had proven true, and now she couldn't imagine a life without him by her side. That he adored her daughter as much as he adored Jet was an unexpected bonus, one that completed her and put her mind at ease.

They'd rented a large apartment in a six-story building within walking distance of the burgeoning downtown commercial district, with its cafés and restaurants and vibrant shopping promenades, and endured a summer with abundant snowfall and more than its share of rain. After an adjustment period, they'd settled into the unique pace of the town, where all but a few businesses closed down from two until five for *siesta*, and it was considered uncivilized to suggest that anyone do much but enjoy themselves during that time, when the wine flowed like water from the plentiful neighboring vineyards in celebration of the populace's enduring spirit.

She heard Matt before she saw him, the rattle of his key in the door reverberating in the granite-floored foyer. Hannah's huge eyes looked up at Jet as if it was Christmas and Santa was about to put in an appearance, her interest in her toys suddenly abandoned in favor of Matt's imminent arrival. The front door opened, and Hannah leapt to her wobbly feet and ran toward him, screaming in glee.

"Maaaa…"

She hadn't mastered the hard consonant at the end of his name yet, but that didn't diminish her joy in saying it. Jet smiled and carried her bowl to the kitchen table, having already fed Hannah earlier. The expression froze on her face when her eyes met his, and she sat down slowly as Hannah barreled into him, hugging his leg. He lifted her and gave her a kiss, carrying her as he approached the table.

"How did your morning go?" she asked, keeping her tone even.

"Oh, you know. Traffic was terrible, but the weather's turning nice again," he said and put Hannah down next to her.

"Good to know. I was thinking about going out later to pick up some groceries."

Matt entered the kitchen and opened the refrigerator. He selected a bottle of mineral water, approached the table, and sat across from Jet as Hannah resumed her play now that the excitement of the return of her champion had waned. "We need to talk."

"I figured from your look. What happened?"

Matt told her about the bank robbery. She held his gaze with unblinking green eyes until he was done. "So the long and short of it is they somehow tripped to the box, and I'm now broke. Looks like we'll be living off your money," he finished.

"What will the fallout be?" she asked, processing furiously.

"Well, we know a few things. First is that they've obviously rallied their resources enough to be able to mount a pretty sophisticated and risky operation. Second, they're now about a hundred and eighty-five mil better off than they were a week ago, so they've strengthened versus weakened. And third, they know there are still sixty-five million more in stones floating around somewhere."

She nodded. "Which means they'll keep looking for them. For you."

"Maybe, maybe not. Bangkok was my old stomping grounds. I'm unknown in South America. The trail ends in Thailand. If you consider the amount of money that they launder every year, the sixty-five is a rounding error."

"Perhaps. But I think we need to assume the worst."

"Agreed."

"Do you think there's any risk to you here?" She didn't have to say "to us?"

"Not any more than anywhere else in the world. And there are practical limits to their reach. It's not like they have informants under every rock. They have a large network in Thailand because of the proximity to the Golden Triangle, as well as to run ops in Myanmar. In Argentina? A token presence, at most. There's just no economic driver down here. Drugs flow in the opposite direction, from Colombia north to the States. The smattering that makes it to Brazil and Argentina isn't worth their time to worry about. The real money's in supplying the Mexican cartels, who import it into the U.S."

"So you believe that if you stay low profile…"

He took a sip of his water and nodded. "That I'm just another guy in the crowd. Hell, I don't even go out very much. And when I do, it's with you and Hannah. The last thing they'd be looking for is the head of a nuclear family in Mendoza."

She took a bite of her salad. "I only let you think you're the head."

He grinned. "I know that."

"How does it feel to be a kept man now? Here I thought I'd won the jackpot, and you turn out to be penniless."

"I was thinking about asking for a raise."

Jet eyed his strong features and lean, handsome face. "We might be able to work something out. But you're going to have to up your game. Make it worth my while."

He slid his hand across the table, over hers, and grinned. "I'll wear a butler uniform if you want. Bow tie and everything."

"I was hoping for just the tie."

Matt reached for an apple sitting in a basket in the center of the table, polished it against his shirt, and took a bite. "Everything's negotiable."

રૂૐ

The last rays of the setting sun illuminated the southern sky as twilight drifted into evening, the white peak of Aconcagua glowing pink like a beacon against the darkening horizon. Footsteps echoed off the sides of the buildings in the city center, the French architecture of the large homes lending the area a European quality. The walking man pulled his long overcoat tight around him; the balmy day had ceded its warmth to a chill off the mountains, made more pronounced by the nearly three thousand feet of elevation Mendoza boasted.

When he arrived at a hulking private residence that occupied a third of the short block, he approached its unremarkable door, typical polished wood with a brass handle two stairs up from the gloomy street, and rang the unmarked bell. He fidgeted as he waited, scanning his deserted surroundings for any signs of observation. A panel at eye level slid open, and part of a heavily bearded face peered out at him.

"Yeah?"

"I'm here for the game."

"The game? I'm afraid I have no idea what you're talking about."

"I'm a friend of Julio's."

The words had the intended effect. The panel slid closed and the door opened, held by a bearlike figure wearing a windbreaker and tan slacks, his countenance that of a street fighter, the nose broken too many times to count. "And you are...?"

The new arrival cleared his throat. "Tomás."

"Very well. Welcome, Tomás. The game's in the back. I'll show you the way. Is this your first time here?"

"Yes."

"Then you're in for a treat. The girls are beautiful, the beer cold, the wine strong."

"And hopefully, the cards running in my favor."

The bouncer nodded. "Could be your lucky night. Come on."

They walked down a hall to a huge living room decorated in turn-of-the-century formal fashion, the walls covered in gold leaf and the furniture, if not antique, certainly classic. A popular tango singer bemoaned love's fickle nature over a piano and violin, the stereo speakers artfully hidden, his growling voice the perfect partner to the sweeping melody.

A dozen young women lounged on sofas and loveseats, wearing negligees and offering inviting smiles, some sipping champagne, others bottled water. Tomás took them in, and his eyes settled on a stunning blonde, no more than nineteen, with pert breasts and impossibly long legs accentuated by five-inch heels. The bouncer paused, allowing Tomás to eye the wares.

The blonde stood and sashayed over to them, her hazel eyes flashing in the light from the chandelier. "Well, hello, handsome," she said, her voice smooth as velvet.

"Hello yourself, gorgeous."

"I'm Lena."

"Lena. Tomás."

"Do you want some company, Tomás?" she asked, her tone professionally playful.

"I'm here for the game. But I wouldn't mind some companionship."

The bouncer nodded. "Come on, then. None of the boys mind the girls being in the room, so long as they stay quiet. Drink?"

Tomás smiled. "Whiskey and soda with ice. A tall one. Easy on the soda."

The bouncer snapped his fingers, and Lena went to get his cocktail. "She'll join us shortly."

They walked into another hallway and down a flight of stairs to where another door blocked their path. The bouncer knocked twice, then once again, and it opened.

"This is Tomás. Lena will be down with a drink. Tomás likes to play cards," he said in introduction to the bear's twin, who was blocking the doorway.

The big man stepped aside, allowing Tomás to enter the room. The air was thick with pungent cigarette smoke. He regarded the round table, seven players seated at it – all men, some young, others older, but all obviously well-heeled locals who enjoyed a game of chance. In a corner a small mahogany bar stood untended. Several girls sat whispering quietly near it, sipping cocktails. Tomás shook hands with his fellow gamblers and took a seat across from the dealer, a gaunt man with a cigarette dangling from his mustached mouth, his sallow expression weary but his hooded eyes rapier-sharp.

Tomás whipped out his wallet and extracted a sheaf of large-denomination bills. Lena arrived with his drink – a water glass filled to the top with amber liquid, a few ice cubes floating in it, rapidly melting from the alcohol. He took a long pull and winced as the liquid fire seared its way down his throat, almost pure whiskey with a splash of soda. The dealer slid a small pile of chips over to him and announced the rules of the game. Tomás nodded and rubbed Lena's waist appreciatively, pausing to give her behind a squeeze. She smiled and joined her friends by the bar, and the dealer flipped cards to the men after they'd tossed their antes into the pot.

Three hours later, Tomás staggered from the house, a metallic taste in his mouth from too much drink, his money lost, his tryst with Lena disappointing due to his inability to perform from all the alcohol. He shuffled along the sidewalk toward the larger boulevard where he'd left his car, and didn't register the two men approaching him from across the street until they were right on top of him.

The larger of the two, a stout man in his fifties with the square build of a door, took a puff on his cigar before speaking.

"Tsk, tsk, Tomás. I had you blackballed from all the casinos, and now you insult my intelligence by coming to a cathouse and dropping tens of thousands of pesos?"

Tomás gave him a bleary stare. "Luis, I can explain…"

"There's nothing to explain. You owe us three hundred and fifty thousand dollars. You haven't made the payments in two weeks. And yet you can come to this place and lose a small fortune, thinking I wouldn't hear about it? Do you take me for a fool?" Luis glanced at his companion, a younger man with a bodybuilder's physique, three days' growth on his face, a knit cap pulled over his head. The man moved like lightning and punched Tomás in the stomach. Hard. Tomás made a sound like a puppy hit by a car and slowly sank to the sidewalk, clutching his midsection.

After gasping for breath for several seconds, he looked up at the two men, tears of pain in his eyes. "I can get the money. I told you that."

"You're out of time. You need to do something now, or next time we're going to start cutting off your fingers. And Tomás? I'm not joking. This has gone on too long. It's not my fault you're a degenerate gambler. But it's my job to collect, and I feel like you're stalling us. This is my way of signaling that I won't be stalled." Luis kicked him in the side of the chest, and a rib snapped. Tomás screamed in pain. "Stop being a bitch. You earned this. If you don't have money for me within forty-eight hours, you'll get more where that came from. Piss me off or try to play me and you'll be walking on sticks."

"Wait. I…there's a way to…to get the money. But I need help."

Luis glared at Tomás like he'd just scraped him off his shoe. "Help? What kind of help?"

"I…it's simple. But I can't be involved."

"You are involved, Tomás."

"I can get us a half million."

Luis regarded him skeptically. "Dollars or pesos?"

"Dollars."

"Within two days? I think you're bullshitting me." Luis glanced at his companion, who drew near.

"No! No, I'm not. Please. Listen…"

"Listen? Fine. You have ten seconds."

Tomás told him what he had in mind, speaking in a low voice. When he was finished, he looked up at Luis standing over him like judge and executioner, and waited for his reaction.

Luis smiled with the warmth of a vulture circling roadkill.

"You just bought yourself two days. Now go home, clean up, and get some sleep. I'll be in touch tomorrow morning to discuss logistics. But Tomás? This better work, or you're a dead man."

Tomás nodded weakly. The two men turned and melted back into the shadows, leaving him on the sidewalk, sobbing from the pain, and what he'd finally sunk to – a far cry from the promising young winemaker who'd come to the region ten years earlier to conquer the world, his whole life ahead of him, the future bright and his fortune to be made.

He struggled to his feet and shambled toward his car, bruised and broken, detesting himself for what he'd become, and worse, for the unspeakable events he'd just set in motion.

Chapter 5

Two months earlier, Moscow, Russia

Leonid followed the comely secretary into the office of one of Moscow's most respected attorneys and took a seat across from the great man – Anatoly Filipov, a true power broker in every sense, confidante of some of the wealthiest oligarchs in Russia. Filipov looked up from the document he was reviewing, his beady eyes darting to Leonid's face, taking him in and assessing him with clinical precision, and then leaned back in his leather chair and cleared his throat.

"You come highly recommended," he said, his tone cold.

"My customers are always satisfied with my performance," Leonid acceded.

"This assignment is part of the last will and testament of one of my clients. A young man struck down in his prime. Perhaps you heard about him – Sergei Grigenko?"

Leonid nodded. "A murder, wasn't it?"

"Yes. Brutal. Grigenko and his mother, both savagely killed." Filipov fixed him with a hard stare. "The estate had a provision in the event of an untimely death. It was intended to be a deterrent; however, now it's more his final wish."

"A provision?"

"Yes. In the event of his dying an unnatural death, ten million American dollars are being held in escrow as compensation for whoever avenges him."

Leonid's eyebrow raised a quarter centimeter. "Ten million?"

"Yes. Payable upon proof that his killer has been executed."

"Do you know who killed him?"

"I don't have a name. But I do have an image. Several, actually. From a security camera at his building." Filipov slid a file across the desk to him.

Leonid opened it and flipped through the photographs, stopping at the final one – a grainy blow-up of a woman's head and shoulders. He studied it for several moments and then looked up at the attorney.

"Is this some sort of a joke?"

"I can assure you it's no laughing matter."

"This…girl…killed Grigenko? Got past his security and murdered him, and then made a clean escape?"

"Yes."

Leonid eyed the image again. "And you want her dead."

"I don't. The estate does. And it's willing to pay you ten million dollars if you can locate her, identify her, and then terminate her."

"How can I prove I got the right woman, assuming I'm able to do all that?"

"Simple. We have DNA. Blood from the scene that didn't match Grigenko's. Apparently there was a struggle. We've been able to isolate two discrete blood samples. One was his. The other…hers."

"And you have no idea who she is?"

Filipov shook his head. "No, unfortunately. But she's obviously highly competent, which would lead one to believe that she's professional."

"Russian?"

"Maybe."

"Maybe is an awfully big question mark. There are seven billion people on the planet. If you don't even know what nationality she is…"

Filipov grunted. "I'm not an expert in these matters. I'm a simple attorney. I was advised that you're resourceful, the best in your field, with connections all over the world from your days with the KGB."

"That's true. But even so."

"Here's what I propose. You distribute the images however you see fit. Do whatever detective work you feel is appropriate. At the point you get a hit, we formalize our agreement. Until then…I am managing all of Grigenko's estate, which is considerable, as you might imagine. As such, I have some discretion over how funds are allocated."

"Ah. That's more like it. So you hire me on a best-efforts basis, and assuming I figure this riddle out…"

"Exactly. Then there's another ten million in it for you."

Leonid thought about it. "I'll need half a million to do this right."

"I'll give you two-fifty."

"Four."

"I might be able to go as high as three."

"With all due respect, if she's pro, as you say, she's either with an intelligence agency, or used to be with one. That means she'll be far harder to locate, even if I'm able to learn her identity – which isn't a given, but which will require me to spread cash around, probably here, to the Americans, throughout Europe, etcetera. Three is laughably low. Do you want this done right, or do you want to waste your money but get a bargain?"

They agreed on three hundred seventy-five thousand as a retainer, and Leonid gave Filipov his wire instructions for an account in Luxembourg. He rose and shook hands with the attorney before taking the photos as he left. They agreed to communicate every few weeks, or when Leonid had something to report. In the meantime, he would begin scouring the Earth for the mystery woman once the money hit the bank.

When Leonid left, Filipov made a telephone call on his private line.

"Yes?"

"It's Anatoly."

"How did it go?"

"He took the case."

"Excellent. How much?"

"A pittance. Fifteen million."

"So there's ten left for me?"

"For you and me. I'll expect to be compensated fairly."

"We agreed on one million dollars for facilitating this."

"Yes, well, that seems reasonable. However, two million seems more reasonable."

There was a long pause on the line. "We can discuss it at the appropriate time. I'll want to meet this specialist if he's able to locate her. You can tell him I'm your representative."

Filipov bristled. It wasn't in his best interests to have Gavrel, Grigenko's former assistant, and Leonid, comparing notes – there was too much danger that Filipov's pocketing of five million of the blood money would be discovered. "Let's see how he does. It's a long shot."

"That's fine. I'm in no hurry. But Anatoly? Don't try to cut me out. Life can be very short if you do that. Remember that I am not without resources of my own."

Filipov's blood ran cold. Gavrel was as dangerous as they came, and Filipov knew he was playing a potentially lethal, if lucrative, game with the man. But for an additional five million, it was worth it. He'd just need to be clever about how he handled matters.

As with all things, outsized rewards came with risk – a situation he was used to.

He would find a way to manage Gavrel.

Because Filipov, too, was not without resources.

"Of course, my friend. You're like a brother to me. Now let us pray that this man can find her. If anyone can, he should be able to. His group's the absolute best."

"Grigenko believed his security team was the best. I don't need to remind you how that turned out."

"Very well. I'll alert you when I have something for you."

"Do that, Anatoly. It's already been too long."

Chapter 6

Present day

A warm breeze carried the smell of garlic and freshly baked bread from downtown Mendoza's bustling pedestrian boulevard to the park. Mature oak trees ringed the verdant expanse, providing welcome shade to young lovers, stray dogs, and the occasional homeless person dozing on the newly cut grass. Paths crisscrossed the area, an oasis of natural beauty in the concrete and steel city center.

Jet turned her face up and let the sun play across her features. Occasional gusts tousled her hair as she waited for Hannah's swing to return on its arc for another spirited push. Hannah kicked her legs high, squealing in delight at the unimaginable freedom of flying through space, even if strapped into a safety seat at the end of two sturdy lengths of chain, and Jet felt a tug, a long-buried memory of her own childhood, when she'd been happy…before the bad times had come to stay for good.

She banished the morose thoughts that were the inevitable conclusion to her trips down memory lane and gave Hannah another heave, propelling her forward and up into the clear blue of the autumn sky. The swing next to her with her best friend Catalina moved in tandem as her mother, Sofia, pushed again. Both girls shrieked in a combination of faux fear and exuberance, which was part of the fun, the women knew.

Jet had met Sofia a month after setting down roots in Mendoza, and they'd grown close, their daughters nearly the same age, common interests their bond. Sofia was a native, upper class but down-to-earth, born and raised in the wine country, with a large home six blocks from Jet's leased digs. Her husband worked for the family business, a prominent winery making international waves with its breakthrough Malbecs and Bonardas, garnering gold medals, high ratings, and a legion of fans who loved the highly concentrated, rich taste. Sofia was also a stay-at-home mom, doing her best to keep her daughter out of trouble as she savored their time together.

A constant topic of conversation was the private schools and the prospect of the kids going to kindergarten in a few short years – a subject that held both trepidation and relief for them, as at least a small slice of their lives would be returned to them while the children were in school. It simultaneously signaled an important threshold beyond which their offspring would slowly grow up and seek their independence in a world fraught with risk.

Catalina was Sofia's pride and joy, her only daughter, fruit of a six-year marriage that Jet intuited had gone through some rocky patches. Mother and daughter were virtual carbon copies, Catalina's high cheekbones and intelligent blue eyes the mirror image of Sofia's – much as Hannah eerily resembled Jet in not only appearance but also mannerisms. Both little girls had long hair, and could well have been sisters had it not been for their language. Hannah was beginning to absorb Spanish, easy when that age, her sponge-like brain soaking up everything around her. Sofia spoke good English, a tribute to her education and the foresight of her parents, who had insisted that she learn not only her native tongue, but also English and Italian – the first the language of commerce, the latter that of winemaking in Argentina, a legacy of several huge immigration surges from Italy a century earlier.

"They look happy, don't they?" Sofia said with a smile.

"They should be. Every day's new to them, and everything a welcome surprise," Jet agreed.

"Wouldn't it be wonderful if they could stay like this forever?"

"It would be. But that's not how the world works, unfortunately. I still can't believe how fast Hannah's growing up."

"I see the same thing with Cat. She's like a…like a little replica of me. That's what everyone says."

"I definitely agree. Two peas in a pod," Jet said and registered the puzzlement in Sofia's eyes. "I meant two nearly identical elements. It's an expression."

Sofia nodded and heaved Catalina again. "Sometimes the idiom gives me...confusion, yes?"

"Your English is very good."

"As is your Spanish. You speak like a native, Rebecca." Jet was using that name in Mendoza.

"My accent's different."

"True, but that's nothing bad."

"We can switch to Spanish if you like," Jet offered.

"No, no, like I said before, I need practice, or I'll lose my English over time."

Jet arrested Hannah's swinging to a groan of protest, but Jet was ready to go after an hour in the park. She had to get Hannah fed lunch and sufficiently napped to be up for their trip to the zoo that afternoon. Jet told her to gather up her toys and put them into her backpack, and Hannah's face looked like it was ready to explode in tears until Jet reminded her that they had a big day planned. The thought of seeing the monkeys and lions reined in Hannah's natural inclination to resist, and she trotted off to collect her things as Catalina did the same.

"So we're still on for two thirty, right?" Sofia asked as she moved to the bench to get her sweater.

"Absolutely. Hannah would never forgive me if we missed it. Where do you want to meet?"

"At the main entrance. It's up the hill in the *Parque General* San Martin. Beautiful – the entire zoo is built around the peak on a set of trails. But bring lots of sunscreen. It will be hot today."

"Okay, then. Two thirty. We'll be there."

Hannah came running, backpack clenched half open in her arms, now anxious to get her eating and sleeping over with so she could see the animals. Jet kissed Sofia on the cheek, as was the local custom, and took Hannah's hand. Hannah practically dragged her to the front park entrance, so eager was she to get home, and Jet allowed her to set the pace, her stubby little legs moving in overdrive, playtime and her swing forgotten in favor of the irresistible lure of the zoo.

Catalina took longer, and Sofia placed a call on her cell phone while she waited. Her mother's voice answered, and they chatted for a few minutes before Catalina stood with raised eyebrows, finally ready. Sofia held her hand over the phone and whispered to Catalina to go ahead, and then continued the discussion with her mother -- the topic was Sofia's brother, Carlos, who'd been in rehab three times for alcoholism over the last five years and had disappeared a week before, leaving his wife and two children to fend for themselves.

Carlos' behavior was a constant source of embarrassment for the family, and their mother was distraught that he'd apparently lost yet another round with his demon, forcing his loved ones to pay the price.

Sofia was so engrossed in the discussion she didn't notice the man on the mountain bike hurtling toward her down the path. His long, black, unkempt hair blew in the wind, his beard lending him the air of a lunatic, his clothes barely more than filthy rags. When he collided with her, she went down hard. The phone tumbled from her hand, bouncing twice on the pavement before skittering to rest near the grass, its screen dead. The rider almost lost control but managed to pull himself up at the last moment, his brakes screeching as he clamped down on them. He stopped a few yards from her, his face a filthy mask of fury, and he swore at her as she tried to get up.

"You stupid bitch. What the hell's wrong with you? Why don't you watch where you're going, eh?"

Sofia was dazed from the fall and now frightened as she realized that there was nobody nearby. "I...I'm sorry... I was on the phone..."

"You're lucky I didn't break my neck. I should sue you," the biker snarled and then spit to the side. "Idiot."

He stood on his pedals and wheeled off, leaving Sofia sprawled on the path, shocked by the sudden violence of the event and the aggressively crazy demeanor of the rider. She watched him disappear around a grove of trees and pushed herself to her feet, her hip hurting and her hand bleeding from where her palm had absorbed much of the force of the fall.

Sofia spied her phone and retrieved it, and cursed to herself when she saw the shattered display. She looked up at the park entrance in search of Catalina, but didn't see her. A flash of fear tickled her stomach as she swung around, hunting for her daughter's blue dress. Fighting down the surging panic, she hurried to the entrance, worried that Catalina might run out into the street, but when she got there, there was no sign of her. She turned, eyes sweeping the area, and gasped when she saw Catalina's dress disappear into an old van, its license plate obscured with mud.

Sofia broke into a run as she screamed for someone to help her, but the only one around was an old man sitting on a bench, a bag of stale bread by his side for the pigeons. The van picked up speed with a belch of black exhaust and lurched around the corner. Sofia stopped, hand over her mouth, eyes unbelieving, her face frozen with shock as she realized that her baby daughter, the love of her life, was gone.

Chapter 7

A crosswind buffeted the Gulfstream V executive jet as it banked on final approach to Governor Francisco Gabrielli International Airport, the Andes Mountains towering on one side of the plane, endless vineyards stretching into the distance on the other. Tara rubbed her face and took a final sip from her bottle of water as they dropped past a few scattered clouds hanging over the valley. She was tired from the flight, which had taken an hour longer than planned due to unexpectedly powerful headwinds.

The plane's tires left black streaks on the runway as it touched down. Tara peered out the window at the low terminal building, only a few commercial jets on the ground, still fewer private planes in evidence, and most of those single-engine prop jobs. The three men in the cabin with her stretched and yawned, each a hardened veteran of wet operations across the globe. Carl, the tall crew-cut man in the seat across from Tara, was the oldest at thirty-six, a geriatric by the group's standards in a business where few made it past thirty before taking a desk job or making a terminal mistake. Ken, twenty-nine, with dusty blond hair and a Midwestern look that concealed a ruthless temperament, was the resident interrogation expert, as well as being a skilled martial artist. And Isaac, a short Hispanic brawler of Cuban heritage, was their explosives and demolitions ringer, at twenty-seven the youngest of the team.

The jet taxied to the terminal, and the pilot shut down the engines once they'd parked where directed by the ground crew. The group exited the plane, carrying overnight bags and their passports, and made their way to the immigration area, where they were waved through with hardly a glance. Once inside the terminal, Tara activated a burner cell phone and called the number she'd been given. A sandpaper voice answered, and after a few terse sentences, she was told to go outside and wait for a green Chevrolet Suburban to pick them up.

Ten minutes later the vehicle arrived, piloted by a taciturn driver who remained silent for the entire trip to Dante's contact's building – an auto parts warehouse on the outskirts of town in a marginal area. Two stray dogs watched with dull eyes as the SUV pulled up to the iron gates and honked. Moments later a chubby man with a fringe of brown hair ringing his nearly bald head swung one of the oversized panels wide, and the Suburban pulled into a large dirt yard and rolled to a stop. Everyone got out, and the driver waved for them to follow him into the back of the building.

Inside, Luis sat at a makeshift conference table in a large room to the side of the warehouse area, near a thin older man with a burn scar running down one side of his gray face, who occupied a metal chair by the door.

"Welcome. Our friend in Buenos Aires told me all about you. Please. Sit. I trust your trip was pleasant?" Luis asked.

Tara would do all the talking, as usual. The men took seats while she eyed Luis, taking his measure before sitting. "Pleasant enough. You're Luis?"

"The one and only. And you must be...Maria."

"Yes."

Luis waited for her to introduce the others and, when it became obvious she wasn't going to, nodded. "So. Would you like something to drink or eat? Water? Soda? Beer?"

"No, thank you."

"Well then, let's get down to business, shall we? Armando, get the hardware."

The older man rose and disappeared, returning several moments later with two duffle bags. He placed them on the table and returned to his seat as wordlessly as a phantom. Luis stood and unzipped the first.

"As you requested. Four Beretta 9mm pistols with sound suppressors. Three spare magazines per weapon. One Ruger 22/45 threaded barrel pistol chambered for .22-caliber-long rifle cartridges with ten rounds of subsonic ammo and a custom suppressor. And in the other bag, four FMK-3 submachine guns with sound suppressors, also chambered in 9mm, with six thirty-two-round magazines per gun. A thousand rounds of subsonic ammunition, all custom loads. Enough firepower to fight a small, silent war."

Tara inspected each piece and then handed them to her men, who scrutinized the guns before returning them to the sacks. "This will be acceptable, although the FMK-3s look well used."

"They're perfectly serviceable, I assure you, even if they have a few nicks and scratches."

"Very well." Tara slid a bundle of hundred dollar bills across the table to Luis. "Fifty thousand, as agreed. For which we will require two vehicles for our stay, a safe house, and logistical support as needed."

Luis nodded and proceeded to count the money, taking his time, his fingers running through the bills with practiced familiarity. When he was done, he tossed the bundle to the older man, who disappeared again, this time not returning. Tara pointed to the color printout of Matt's photo that Luis had pinned to a corkboard on the wall behind his head.

"Have you had any luck with that?"

Luis shrugged. "I've made copies and circulated them, but nobody recognizes him right off the bat. Is it possible he changed his appearance?"

"Anything's possible. He could have different color hair, a beard or mustache, anything. But if you get a hit, I have to warn you. He's extremely dangerous and is an experienced field operative. Make sure nobody gets clever, or it'll be the last thing they ever do, and he'll disappear like a ghost. Which would make me extremely unhappy."

Luis held her gaze. "Dante assured me I was to do everything I could to make you happy."

"Dante is a wise and generous man."

"That's always been my experience."

Tara folded her hands on the tabletop. "So what are we going to use as our base? I don't want anyone watching our coming and going."

"I own the building immediately adjacent to this one, and it's vacant – very private since this warehouse is the only other tenant on this block. I would imagine that will work well for you. We also own a nearby hotel that won't disturb you with formalities like identification, and where the staff is extremely uninterested in its guests."

"That's perfect. How many minutes is it from downtown?"

"Only five by car."

"Excellent."

"The vehicles are already there. At your disposal."

"All paperwork in order?"

"Of course."

Tara stood. "Very well, then. How long do you think it will take to get something from the photo?"

"It's impossible to say. Although I have a large network, including taxi drivers, police, restaurant and hotel workers…if he's out and about around town, it's only a matter of time."

"Let's hope sooner rather than later. Much as I like Argentina, this isn't a pleasure trip."

"I understand perfectly, and I've relayed this to the field. There's not much more we can do than wait."

"Fine. Who'll take us to the hotel?"

"Armando, the driver."

"He's not very talkative. I like that."

"As I said, we aim to make you happy."

The men rose and shouldered the gun bags and trailed Tara to the door. When she opened it, Armando was sitting in the warehouse, reading the newspaper. He looked up when they left the room. Luis followed them out and instructed him to take them to the building, and he nodded.

"Don't worry. If he can be found, we'll find him," Luis said in parting.

"I never worry. I plan."

Luis nodded. "I understand why Dante holds you in such high regard."

"As I said, he's a smart and generous man."

Chapter 8

Jet stood by the zoo entry gate, the sun beating down on her as Hannah played nearby, intoxicated by the sound of the animals bleating and baying and chittering. A troop of schoolchildren led by a harried woman poured out of a private bus, and suddenly the tranquility of the area shattered as peals of laughter and shouted retorts filled the entryway. A large parrot stared at the newcomers from its perch near the ticket gate, its colorful plumage somewhat the worse for wear from the inexorable ravages of time.

Jet checked the time and watched Hannah sprinting happily after a butterfly, enraptured by the nature all around her, the city's bustle seemingly a million miles away in the lush green calm of the zoo grounds. The skyline seemed to shimmer in the distance; the sunlight reflected off the towering buildings' glass in a blinding display, the high-altitude atmosphere crystal clear. After waiting another few minutes, she fished out her cell phone and dialed Sofia's number, but received an out-of-service message. Annoyed, she thumbed to Sofia's home and called.

Her housekeeper, Isabella, answered. "Hello?"

"Hello. This is Rebecca. Is Sofia there, or has she already left for the zoo?"

Isabella hesitated. "One moment, please."

When Sofia came on the line, her voice was hoarse and she sounded...odd.

"I'm sorry, Rebecca. I completely forgot about..." she said, trailing off as though she'd lost her train of thought.

"No problem, Sofia. Is...are you all right?"

"I'm...fine. This is just a bad time."

Jet frowned. This wasn't the Sofia she knew. "What's wrong? You don't sound fine."

"It's nothing. I...I don't want to talk about it."

"Sofia, is there anything I can help you with? We're friends. All you have to do is ask. Is it Catalina? Is she sick? Hurt?"

Sofia began sobbing softly, and her next words rushed out in a jumbled torrent. "Oh, God. I don't know what I'm going to do…"

"Sofia, what is it? Tell me."

"I'm not allowed to talk about it."

"Allowed? What does that mean? What happened?"

"It's…I…" Sofia gasped for breath, now in a full-scale meltdown. "They took her."

"Took her? Who? What happened, Sofia?"

"At the park. Kidnapped…"

The blood drained from Jet's face as she watched Hannah, now skipping to a song only she could hear.

"Kidnapped! No. How? Why?"

Sofia sobbed again. "Money. Of course. Isn't everything about money?" She broke down, crying, unable to continue.

"I'm coming to your house, Sofia. I'll be there in ten minutes. It'll be okay. I promise."

"No…I…no…"

"I'm not leaving you to deal with this by yourself. I'll see you soon." Jet hung up and called to Hannah. "Honey, come on. Aunt Sofia has an emergency. We have to go help her."

"But…soo…the…maminals…" she protested. How could her mother have forgotten about the zoo and the animals?

"I know, my love. But first we need to go see Aunt Sofia. Come on."

Hannah shook her head and, when Jet gave her a steely stare, began crying and stamping her feet. "No…no…no!"

Jet took a deep breath as her mind raced over Sofia's bombshell, and tried not to overreact to Hannah's tantrum. She could understand her disappointment – she'd been promised a trip to a miraculous place filled with unimaginable wonders, and now it had been snatched from her when she was literally only feet from the entrance. Jet moved to her and held her shoulders as tears rolled down her red face, allowing her to vent before giving her a light shake.

"Hannah. Enough. Sofia's in trouble. Catalina's in trouble. We need to go to their house. The zoo will still be here. I promise."

Hannah registered her mother's serious tone and snuffled, her nose running, her eyes radiating betrayal, but she gradually quieted as she took in Jet's expression.

"Pro...meth?" she said in a tiny voice.

Jet nodded solemnly and knelt so she was eye to eye with her daughter. "I do. Now come on. Be a brave girl and help me with Catalina. We need to go."

Hannah wiped her eyes with the back of her sleeve while Jet felt for a tissue and blotted her nose. This particular crisis over, Jet took her hand and led her to their car, a newish maroon Chevrolet compact sedan with absolutely no distinguishing qualities – the anonymous styling a deliberate choice, forged by a lifetime of tradecraft, where her training placed a premium on avoiding being memorable.

Jet's thoughts raced as they rolled down the hill toward the city and Sofia's huge home in the Quinta district – one of the most upscale, old-money neighborhoods in Mendoza. When they arrived, she parked across the street and led Hannah to the ornately carved entry door, where she rang the buzzer and waited. Footsteps on hardwood sounded from within, and then Isabella swung it wide, her face tight.

"I'm here to see Sofia," Jet announced in Spanish, and the woman nodded and stepped aside so they could enter. After pushing the heavy door closed behind her, she escorted Jet and Hannah into the living room, where Sofia was sitting with red eyes on one of the expensive sofas, clutching a handkerchief. A bottle of water sat in front of her on the polished coffee table. Sofia stood, and Jet rushed to her, greeting her with an embrace. Sofia was trembling and looked to have aged several years in the last two hours.

"You...you shouldn't have come..." she whispered. "But thank you."

"Tell me what happened," Jet said, taking the seat next to her. Hannah sat cross-legged on the floor in front of them and gazed up at Sofia with wide eyes.

"It...it all...happened so fast..." Sofia began and then gave a rambling account of the events at the park.

"Oh, my God. I can't even imagine what you must be feeling," Jet said.

"It's...the worst violation I could imagine."

"But why is it a secret? And where are the police?"

"The kidnappers called an hour ago and warned us not to contact the police or tell anyone. They said if we did, they'd know, and they'd...they'd kill Catalina." Sofia began crying again at the mention of her daughter's name.

"Of course they did. They're afraid of the police. Which is why you need to go to them."

Sofia shook her head. "We can't take the chance…"

"I disagree. These are criminals. Thugs. They can't be trusted. Their word means nothing."

"I know. But my husband feels that we're best off doing as they say."

"Your husband. What about you?"

"I…I don't know what to think."

"Are kidnappings common here?" Jet asked, thinking furiously.

"No, not like in Buenos Aires. And certainly nothing like in Mexico. That's why it never occurred to me there might be any danger…especially in that park…in the best area of town…"

"I know. It surprised me when you told me."

"It's…it's unbelievable."

"Did the kidnappers give you a ransom demand?"

"Yes. Half a million dollars."

"That's a lot of money. Do you have that much liquid?"

"I called my parents. They do. They've made arrangements to have it available at the bank before closing time, and then he's supposed to meet and trade the ransom for–"

The sharp rap of footsteps approached from the rear of the house, and a man appeared, his face angry, Jet could see.

"Sofia." His eyes settled on Jet for a second, then swiveled back to Sofia. "What's she doing here?" he demanded.

"Tomás. You remember my friend Rebecca? And that's Hannah."

Tomás ignored the introduction. "What's she doing here?" he repeated.

"I'm here to help," Jet said simply.

Tomás' eyes narrowed to slits as he glowered at Sofia. "What have you told her?"

Jet kept her tone neutral. "She told me about the kidnapping."

Tomás focused his barely constrained fury on Jet. "This is none of your business. You should leave. And tell no one."

"I think you're making a huge mistake not bringing the police into this. You can't trust criminals to keep their word, even if you give them the money."

"Rebecca, with all due respect, this isn't any of your concern. We have to do what's right for our daughter, not what my wife's friends think or don't think is appropriate."

"I adore Catalina, and I'd hate to see something happen to her because the police were never notified."

"Your sentiment is noted, but again, your opinion is only that. This is our affair, not yours, so I'll tell you one final time. Keep your nose out of it," he growled.

Sofia patted Jet's hand. "I'm sorry. He's right. I shouldn't have said anything."

"He's not right. He's gambling with Cat's life here, and he's making the wrong call." Jet turned to him. "What guarantee do you have that if you give them the money, they won't kill your daughter?"

Tomás waved her away. "These thugs want cash, not to be hunted for the rest of their lives for murder."

"And if you're wrong?"

"I'm not."

Jet took a deep breath and struggled to remain calm. "I believe you are. And I have some experience with crooks from a past life. It's a coin toss as to whether you get her back, even after you hand over the ransom. Remember, these are the lowest of the low, to kidnap a helpless child. They can't be trusted in any way, and you're trusting them. That's a bad idea."

"Look, Rebecca. I don't care what you think. I have to make this decision, and I'm saying we do this their way. End of story. Now please leave. I don't want you causing more stress to my wife than what she's already dealing with."

Sofia shook her head. "Tomás. Please. There's no need to be rude. She means well, and she's my friend."

Tomás looked like he was going to take a swing at her, but then bit back his anger with a visible act of will. "Fine. I need to finish what I was doing. I'm going to the bank in fifteen minutes. Rebecca? My wife is right. I'm sorry for snapping at you. But this is not my best moment."

Jet turned to Sofia. "This is a very difficult situation. A lot of emotion. It's nobody's finest hour. But I do want you to reconsider your decision. I can't tell you how strongly I feel that you're making a dangerous choice."

Tomás cut her off. "I heard you the first time. But it's my choice to make, and I've made it. Now please don't interfere with our private matters.

Your unsolicited opinions are duly noted, for whatever they're worth." He paused, sizing her up. "If Sofia wants you to stay, that's her business, but I've heard about enough of your thoughts. Good day," he snapped and spun on his heel and stalked out.

Tomás' departure left a tension thick as a fog hanging in the room, and Hannah, who had remained quiet through the entire exchange, began to cry. Sofia rushed to her, beating Jet off the couch by a second, and hugged her as she cried herself. Jet watched them, realizing that the act of comforting Hannah was itself cathartic for Sofia, and rose.

"I have to use the bathroom. Would you excuse me?" she asked.

Sofia nodded with a sniff. "It's down the hall, first door on the right."

Jet followed her direction, and when the door locked behind her, slid her cell phone from her back pocket and called Matt.

"Well, hello, stranger. How's the zoo going?" he answered, his voice light, filled with good cheer.

"Change of plans," Jet whispered. "Something happened."

Matt's tone instantly became serious. "What? Are you okay?"

"Yes. But I need you to do me a big favor. I need some help."

"Help? You got it. What do you need?"

Jet explained what had happened, and Matt listened without comment. "I'm getting a really bad feeling from the husband. Something's wrong there," she finished.

"Like what?"

"I don't know. But something's off."

"Fine. What would you like me to do?"

"Get over here, wait outside without being obvious, and follow the husband. He's supposed to head to the bank, and then I'm assuming he's going to meet with the kidnappers to exchange the ransom for Catalina."

"Stupid bastard. That's a great way to get himself killed."

"Exactly. So I want an insurance policy in place, and you're it. Shadow him, and if anything looks sketchy, take action. Catalina's the same age as Hannah…"

"I get it. This hits close to home. What's the address?"

Jet gave it to him and described the house. "You probably have no more than ten minutes."

"That's not very far away. I'll be there in five."

Jet paused. "Thank you, Matt. I'm sorry to get you involved. Hell, I don't want to be in the middle of this, either. It's just that…she doesn't have anyone else. She's all alone, and her husband's a first-class asshat."

"So you're making it your problem," Matt stated flatly. "I understand. Let me get going. I'll call you when I get a chance."

The line went dead. Jet switched the phone to vibrate and slipped it back into her pocket, and then flushed the toilet and washed her hands. She wasn't sure what about Tomás had rubbed her so wrong, but she'd long ago learned to trust her instincts, and they were telling her that he was a weasel.

Or something worse.

Chapter 9

Matt coasted to a stop twenty yards from Sofia's house and left the motor of his Vespa running so he'd be able to move quickly. He knew from experience that a reasonably well-dressed man on a scooter wouldn't draw any attention in Mendoza, where the two-wheeled conveyances were common for shop owners and office workers on their way to work, with gasoline expensive and money hard to come by.

He slid off the seat, keeping his helmet on, and crouched down as though examining his motor, eyes hidden behind his sunglasses as he watched the huge brick home's driveway. Several minutes later his vigilance was rewarded as the wooden garage door slowly rose and a white Mercedes 300 series sedan backed out and pulled onto the street. Matt swung onto the scooter and pushed away from the curb, letting the car gain some distance, confident that he wouldn't be spotted as they moved into downtown traffic, which was always congested, even during the late afternoon when most shops shut down.

Tomás was jittery from too much coffee. So far his plan had unfolded as anticipated: Sofia's parents had coughed up the ransom money without protest at the prospect of losing their only granddaughter. It had been a brilliant plan, and so easy to pass off as a genuine threat as to be laughable. Sofia had bought it without question, and she'd sold her parents – he hadn't even had to do much talking, preferring to let her heart-wrenching terror at her daughter's mortal danger carry the day and persuade the old tightwads to cut loose the cash.

He felt remorse at using his daughter to settle his debt with Luis, but only a little. He'd been a reluctant parent, her birth unplanned, and had only decided to stay with Sofia once she'd announced her pregnancy because he'd figured the parents could be depended upon to contribute to his and Sofia's lifestyle – a good bet, as shortly before Catalina was born they'd bought the house and given it to Sofia so their daughter, and her child, would have a comfortable place to live.

Her father had rubbed it in when he'd handed them the keys, underscoring that it was a shame that their daughter's husband hadn't met with sufficient success to afford something decent on his own. Just another in a series of slights they'd directed at Tomás, whom they'd grudgingly brought on to run one of their wineries after he and Sofia had married. His prior engagement as the winemaker at a mediocre label had run its course by then, as all of his jobs did when his arrogance with his subordinates and his frequent absences due to too many late nights caught up with him. So now he had his winery – 'his' only because the family had decided to throw a few crumbs their way. He earned enough after expenses to cover their living, but couldn't keep up with his secret life of gambling and mistresses.

Which is how he'd wound up so badly in debt to Luis – married to a woman he despised and stuck in a life where he was little more than an indentured servant to her parents, who contained their dislike of him only out of respect for Sofia's choice. This had been the perfect scheme to clear his slate once and for all, reset his accounts to zero, and win himself a new lease on life. From his perspective, the kidnapping had been nothing more than self-preservation. He had no real idea of how connected Luis was, but he obviously had enough pull with the casinos to get Tomás' credit shut down, and sufficient reach with the private games to be alerted when Tomás appeared.

It was an insulting state of affairs, and he was relieved that it was almost over. The money would pay off his chit and show he was willing to do whatever it took to honor his obligations, restoring his standing with the clubs and proving that he was a man of his word. Besides which, the parents wouldn't miss it – five hundred thousand dollars was a drop in the bucket to them, with their holdings of land, wineries, and housing developments, in both Mendoza and Buenos Aires.

When his phone rang, he nearly jumped out of his seat and fumbled in his jacket pocket for it before pulling it free and answering it.

"Hello?"

"Tomás, how are we doing?" It was Luis' second-in-command, Javier, with whom he customarily dealt. Luis' appearance in his life had represented an undesirable escalation – his debt was owed to Javier, who apparently had some affiliation with Luis.

"Good. I'll pick up the money within the hour, and it will be in your hands shortly afterward."

"That's promising. But listen. There's been a little change of plans. Luis and I have been thinking, and with all the risk falling on our side, we're going to change the terms of our arrangement. We want half as our cut for pulling this off."

Tomás sputtered, his color climbing in his face. "What? No! That's unacceptable. We had a deal. Seventy-thirty. You get thirty for your part; I get seventy. Which goes to you anyway, but clears my tab."

"I know that's what you proposed, but now that we have your daughter and the full extent of the risks involved have become obvious, Luis said no. Fifty-fifty."

"But that will still leave me owing you another hundred grand!"

"Which you should have no problem winning back now that your luck has changed."

"You can't change the deal now," Tomás protested.

"'Can't'? I'd be careful what you say, Tomás. We can always release your daughter downtown, and you still owe us the three-fifty…and have twenty-four more hours to come up with it, or your world comes caving in on you. Your choice."

"I want to talk to Luis. This isn't going to fly."

Javier's voice hardened. "Tomás. You don't dictate terms. This isn't a negotiation. The word came down from him, and that's final. This is as good a deal as you're going to get. So suck it up, go get the money, and meet me as planned. You don't want to anger Luis. Trust me on that."

"I never agreed to this. I wouldn't have done it if I'd–"

Javier cut him off. "Spare me, Tomás. Now stop wasting my time. Go to the bank and then make the delivery like a good boy, and be happy that Luis didn't decide to cut some fingers off…or let the boys have some fun with little Catalina. Who's cute as a button, by the way."

"You bastard."

"I'm not the bastard, Tomás. I didn't come up with the plan to use my daughter to extort money from my wife's parents. Stop being a bitch, and do as you're told. I'm tired of this conversation."

Tomás listened to the dead line with mounting rage. How dare that small-time punk try to change the deal once Tomás had done all the hard work and shouldered the risk! That was typical of a street thug like Javier, who immediately tried to jockey for the upper hand once he thought he was in the stronger position. Luis probably hadn't even changed the deal – it was more likely that Javier had decided to stick an easy hundred grand in his pocket by bluffing Tomás. Yes, that was more likely. A guy like Luis couldn't develop a reputation as a cheat, or nobody would want to do business with him. This smacked of Javier.

And there was no way Tomás was going to let him get away with it.

Tomás thought hard as he drove, and then an idea sprang to the forefront of his mind. He knew exactly how to deal with Javier and have him begging to go back to the original deal. All it would take was a single phone call.

Tomás punched in the familiar digits and waited for his brother to pick up.

"Yeah?"

"Bruno. Long time. You busy?"

"I'm still on duty, so make it fast. What's up?"

"I've got a problem."

"Welcome to the world."

"No, I mean a real problem. And I need some help."

Bruno's tone became cautious. "Tomás, what have you gotten involved in this time?"

Bruno had been saving Tomás' bacon since they were children, and was sick of his brother putting the arm on him when the going got especially rough. But family was the ultimate bond, and he couldn't refuse his younger brother. Blood demanded they stick together, no matter what stupidity Tomás had embarked on – no doubt another one of countless ill-advised adventures he'd undertaken, where Bruno had been forced to intercede.

"It's bad, Bruno. I...I didn't have any choice." Tomás' voice cracked on the last words.

"I can't talk right now. I get off at five. Can you swing by the station then? Or call me back closer to quitting time. Maybe fifteen minutes before."

"Just promise me you'll help me, Bruno. I'll never ask for anything again."

"Gotta go. Call me later."

Tomás hung up, the gears meshing in his head. He knew he could count on Bruno, even if he would be furious about Catalina. He probably wouldn't want to talk to Tomás for a year, but Tomás would deal with the fallout later. Right now he needed to do damage control, and to do that, he needed Bruno at his back.

So engrossed was he in his drama he never noticed the black Vespa a half block behind him. He'd already moved on to how to put the fear of God into Javier so he would never mess around with him again.

He made a lazy right turn on a major artery that led to the bank, glancing at his watch as he did. He had a half hour to kill before the money would be counted and ready for pick-up. Just enough time for a few fingers of whiskey to calm his frayed nerves and dull the pain in his rib from where Luis had savaged him.

An insult he wouldn't soon forget.

After two stiff drinks he felt restored, if not invigorated, and when he walked out of the bar he had a spring in his step. He'd arrived at some conclusions as he steadied himself with his good friend Ballantine's. Javier was trifling with the wrong man, trying to play him for a fool, but he'd put a stop to that. Tomás was nobody's bitch, as Javier had called him, and he'd soon regret his insolence. Tomás had suffered from a bad streak with the cards, but he was still a player, the head of a winery, married to a socialite, residing in a mansion. Javier was street scum who had to live by his wits, and this time he'd bitten off more than he could chew.

The bank welcomed him into the president's private office, where two armed guards flanked the door as the manager ran the stacks of hundreds through a bill counter to verify for Tomás that he was signing for the full amount. Twenty minutes later the guards were escorting him to his car, hands on their pistols, eyes roving over the street, alert. They stood on the sidewalk until he'd pulled away, and then returned to the bank, done with their final chore for the day.

Matt watched as Tomás slid behind the wheel of his car, and called Jet, figuring he'd soon be on the road again.

"He just picked up the money."

"This is where it'll get dicey. Anyone tailing him?"

"Besides me? Not that I've seen."

"That was one of my fears – that they'd hit him outside the bank, or on the road."

"What's the point if he's heading straight to the exchange?"

"Crooks are crooks. Haven't met one yet I would trust to wash my car."

"Fair point. Damn. I'll call you back once I figure out where he's headed."

"Perfect. My phone's on."

Matt dropped his cell into his windbreaker pocket and took off after Tomás, narrowly avoiding the errant fender of an ancient Ford Falcon that sounded as though it was running on kerosene and a prayer. Tomás drove at a moderate pace, making it easy for Matt to track him as he headed north along Avenue San Martin.

Eight blocks later, he made a right, and Matt followed him down a smaller street with older tenements lining its sidewalks. Tomás' brake lights flashed ahead of him and he turned his flashers on, double-parking in front of a large building flying the blue and white Argentine flag. Matt slowed to a crawl and was easing up onto the sidewalk when he realized where he was – in front of one of Mendoza's police stations.

Tomás watched the entry as the day-shift officers left, and saw Bruno's rugged features in the crowd. He lowered the passenger window and leaned toward it and shouted his name.

"Bruno. Over here."

His brother saw him and patted his companion on the shoulder as he shook his hand, and then turned to where Tomás was parked and moved unhurriedly to the car.

"Come on. Get in," Tomás said.

Bruno eyed him distrustfully. "Where are we going?"

"I'll tell you on the way."

Bruno sighed and pulled the door open. Once he was seated, Tomás pulled out, and Bruno glanced at him.

"Have you been drinking?"

"Just one."

"You said you were in trouble?"

"Bad trouble, Bruno. Worse than anything before."

"Christ. What did you do, kill someone?" he asked, only half-joking.

"Almost." Tomás told him about the fake kidnapping, his gambling debt, and the double cross. When he was finished, Bruno closed his eyes.

"Stop the car."

"Bruno. I need your help. For real."

"No, you need a psychiatrist and an attorney. And probably a priest. What in God's name were you thinking?"

"I had to do something. They were going to escalate it. Cut fingers off. They already broke my ribs."

"I wish they'd broken your neck. You deserve it."

They stopped at a red light, and Tomás hung his head. "I know. It's all gotten so…crazy."

"That's the tame version. Does it get any lower than what you've done?"

"I'm not excusing it, Bruno. And if I could take it back, I would. But right now I've got a real problem. They've got Catalina, and they changed the deal so I'll still be a hundred large into them even once I give them the money."

"That sounds like the least of your worries. I'd be more concerned about burning in hell for eternity."

"That's a given. But I need you to help me, Bruno."

"How?"

"I want you to go with me. Push them around a little. If they see I'm with a cop, they'll think twice about screwing me."

Bruno shook his head. "You're insane. There's no way I'm going to do anything while in uniform."

"No, think about this. They'll assume you're in on it with me. My partner. I'll tell them you're a cop, you show them your badge, and it sets them straight. They won't want to bite off trouble with the cops on a nice clean transaction. All we want is for them to honor the original deal. You tell them that I'm partners with you, and that if they renege on their deal, they're reneging on a deal with you, too. Puff out your chest some. They'll fold. These are low-level street scammers. They'll take the money and run."

"And what if they don't?"

"There's no way they're going to go to war with the police over trying to screw me. Besides, I'm pretty sure their boss doesn't know what they're pulling. Once they see they're in over their heads, they'll honor the deal, I'll get Catalina back, and nobody gets hurt."

Bruno sighed. "How well do you know them?"

"Pretty well. They run a lot of the loan sharking in town. And some card games."

"Local, or connected?"

"I think they're small fry, although they have some pull with the local casinos – but only to lend money. It's not like they run them or anything. I wouldn't get you into something you couldn't get out of. I'm telling you, these guys are punks."

Bruno watched two young women in tight jeans walk by as they pulled away from the intersection, their hair glowing in the dimming light. He bit his lip and touched his pistol, then nodded.

"You'd better be right. You carrying?"

"Carrying?"

"Are you armed?"

Tomás looked shaken. "No. Of course not."

Bruno gave him a sidelong glance. "Okay. Go to my house. I have an extra piece there."

"What? I don't want a gun."

"I'm not asking you what you want. If this gets ugly, you're going to wish you had one. Now go to my house. No more bullshit. I've had about enough to last me a lifetime."

"But the meet's at a casino."

"You told me. I know that place. There aren't any metal detectors at the doors like the more upscale joints."

"I don't know, Bruno..."

"Tomás? You wanted me involved. I'm involved. Now drive to my house, or do this on your own."

Chapter 10

Matt followed the car to a middle-class residential neighborhood, all single-story homes built from exposed brick, and watched as the cop got out and dashed into the house. He returned five minutes later dressed in civilian clothes – black slacks and a blue windbreaker. As the Mercedes lurched forward Matt gave his scooter some throttle, remaining almost a block behind now that he knew Tomás' plodding driving style.

The afternoon light was giving way to dusk, the sky streaked with a rainbow of color as the sun drifted behind the mountains, the mature trees lining the downtown streets rustling in a light wind that carried with it the smell of freshly tilled earth and vineyards as Matt eased to a stop a hundred yards from where Tomás was parking. The only obvious destination was a low-budget casino – a small type that catered to the locals rather than the tourist trade, its neon sign as shopworn as the pavement on the street. Matt watched as Tomás retrieved a suitcase that probably had the money in it and raised his cell to his ear.

Jet sat with Sofia on the sofa, looking through a photo album filled with shots of Catalina, while Hannah lay on the carpet and played with some of her friend's toys. When her phone vibrated, she glanced at the number and excused herself before moving down the hall to the rear of the house for privacy.

"Hey," she said.

"They're at a casino five blocks from Sofia's house. They just walked in. This must be the meet. I'm going inside so I don't lose them." Matt gave her the location.

"I can be there in five minutes. Stick to them."

"This is getting weird. He stopped and picked up a cop at the police station, then drove him home so he could change. I don't like the direction this is going."

Jet thought furiously. "I agree. This is sounding more and more like amateur night. I'm on my way. Don't lose them."

She hung up and rushed back into the living room. "Sofia, I'm so sorry, but that was kind of an emergency. Can I leave Hannah here for a few minutes? No more than a half hour, tops?"

"Of course. I enjoy her company. She's such a good little girl…"

"Thanks."

"Is everything all right?"

"Oh – yeah. I just forgot I need to take care of something at the apartment. Pay a worker."

"No problem."

Jet sprinted down the sidewalk to her car and leapt in. She cranked the ignition, flicked the headlights, then tore down the empty street, anxious to get to the casino. Catalina's life hung in the balance, with a father who seemed determined to make poor choices. Why he would bring a cop to the tradeoff defied reason – unless he was part of the kidnapping plot. But then why would Tomás be playing taxi for him?

When she arrived, she called Matt as she parked.

"I'm here. Outside."

"Stay put. I'm inside. The two of them met a guy by the slots and they just disappeared through a door in the rear."

"Damn. Why wouldn't they stay out in the open? Their safety odds just dropped through the floor when they walked through that door."

"Agreed, but I don't know what I can do."

Jet sighed. "Just wait, I suppose. Hopefully they'll return in a minute with Catalina in tow and we can all go home."

Tomás and Bruno entered the casino, which was nearly empty, most of its patrons still at work earning the income they would come to squander later in the evening. Tomás saw one of Javier's men standing at the end of a row of slot machines and walked over to him. A short man, balding but with long strands of black hair combed over his scalp in an unsuccessful attempt to forestall the inevitable, he gave Tomás an ugly look.

"Who's your date?" the man growled.

"None of your business. He's with me. I have the package. Let's do this," Tomás said.

The man looked Bruno up and down and turned back to Tomás. "Where is it?"

"That's none of your business."

"You better know what you're doing," he warned.

"Thanks for the advice. Now are we going to do it, or not?"

The man shrugged and moved to a door at the rear of the gaming area and knocked twice. The door opened and the man motioned for them to go in, choosing to remain in the casino, his beady eyes darting around the floor like a bird of prey.

Tomás entered the room, Bruno by his side, and approached the desk where Javier was sitting, a smirk on his face. Four of his bully boys lounged on chairs and sofas that lined the walls. The men stiffened when they saw Bruno, and the atmosphere became tense. Javier's expression changed as he took in Bruno and then he fixed Tomás with a cold stare.

"What the hell is this?" he hissed.

"This is my associate. He's my partner in several of my endeavors, and I asked him to come along."

"Your *associate*. I see. And what does your…associate…have to do with our transaction?"

"He's very concerned that you changed the terms. Very."

Javier sat back, the situation completely different from the one he'd been prepared for, and glanced at his men.

"You're on very dangerous ground, Tomás. You don't want to bring anyone else into this," he warned, his voice quiet.

"My associate is involved in my affairs. Your changing our deal creates considerable hardship for him, so he's in this, whether you like it or not."

"Is that so?"

Bruno shifted. "That's right. You need to stick to the original deal," he said gruffly.

"You're about three seconds away from getting bones broken, tough guy," Javier said.

Tomás laughed with false bravado. "I don't think so. My friend here is a police officer. You want trouble with the police? Screw me over, you're screwing them over." He gave Javier his best tough-guy glare. "You obviously have no idea who you're dealing with."

The men put down their newspapers and drinks and slowly slid apart, putting space between each other. Bruno registered the movement and tensed, aware that things were spinning dangerously out of control, that his brother had misjudged the level of professionalism of the group he owed money to. The men looked street-hardened and older than Bruno had expected – hardly punks or amateurs, as Tomás had assured him.

"Tomás. Ease up. Now," Bruno whispered, his hand clutching his pistol in his pocket.

Javier nodded. "Listen to the man, Tomás. You owe me money. This is a simple deal. I don't care who else you're in bed with. I want my money. The deal you get is the new one I told you you'll get – and bringing your boy here to the party has only served to annoy me."

Tomás whipped the little P380 pistol Bruno had given him from his pocket and held it up for Javier to see. "Time to rethink that, Javier."

Bruno caught movement on the periphery of his vision. One of the men went for his gun and then everything fell apart in a matter of seconds as he pulled his Beretta free, cursing Tomás' recklessness as he instinctively dropped into a crouch.

Matt was moving to the change booth near the rear door to exchange some of his bills for coins when gunshots exploded from the room. A woman screamed, and an old man who had been feeding one of the machines stood abruptly and tottered to the exit. The little weasel who'd shown Tomás and his cop friend to the door jerked a pistol free from his jacket and bolted toward the door to the back room. Matt had to make an instantaneous decision and didn't hesitate. He covered the distance between himself and the man in three long strides and sweep-kicked his legs out from under him just as the door flew open and the cop, still shooting, fell across the threshold, blood streaming from his chest and down his face as he fired.

Jet was nearing the casino entrance when she heard muffled gunshots, followed by a hysterical woman and a pensioner bursting through the double doors with panicked expressions. Jet paused, and when more shooting sounded from within the building, she swore under her breath and darted into the casino.

Pandemonium greeted her. She took in the terrified gamblers huddled behind whatever cover they could find and saw Matt at the far end of the room knocking a man with a gun to the floor. Two security guards in gray uniforms were running toward him. Jet threw herself headlong down the aisle between two banks of slot machines in an effort to cut them off before they reached him.

Gunfire blasted from the room as she reached the end of the aisle and hurtled at the first guard, his partner a dozen yards behind him. She caught him in the chest with her shoulder, just as he was bringing his revolver to bear on Matt, and his breath blew out with an *oof* as she followed through with a strike to the pressure point on his neck, instantly disabling him. His gun tumbled from his hand as he fell. Jet went down with him, using his bulk to shield herself from the second guard as she groped for the pistol.

Her fingers found the cold blue steel and she brought it up, pointing at the second guard's head as he struggled to get his gun free of his hip holster. Seeing the weapon aimed at him, he stopped and slowly raised his hands.

"Keep them up," she warned, getting to her feet.

A volley of shots echoed from the doorway, where Matt was firing into the room. The guard cringed as she moved to him. He slumped into an inert pile at her feet when she brought the revolver down on his head. She ran to where Matt was lying next to a blood-covered body, a gun in his hand trained on the room beyond the doorway.

"Are you hit?" she whispered, her pistol also pointed into the room.

"No. But he's a goner," Matt said, indicating Bruno, who wasn't breathing.

"Where's Tomás?"

"Inside."

They exchanged a look. "You ready to do this?" she asked.

"Let's go."

She rolled through the doorway with her weapon as Matt swung his gun around the doorjamb, sweeping the room. Inside was a tableau out of a nightmare – five men lying in pools of their own blood, two with their brains blown against the wall, one still spasmodically twitching on the floor, another moaning. Tomás was face down near a file cabinet, blood soaking his shirt. She moved to him and turned him over, then checked his pulse. Faint, but steady. A quick look showed he'd been hit in the chest and the shoulder, and the bloody hole in his lower trousers showed a flesh wound.

Matt caught her eye. "Looks like it didn't go as planned."

"No, that's safe to say."

"What now?"

"I don't see any more rooms to search for the girl – and the police will be here any second. Let's get out of here. Go on. I'll be right there."

"Where do you want to meet up?" he asked.

"I'll call you. Now go."

Matt didn't need any further coaching, and dashed for the casino entrance as Jet reached down and dragged Tomás clear of the room. She checked his pulse again before sprinting for the doors, even as sirens wailed their approach.

When she came out onto the sidewalk, Matt had already gone. She hurried to her car and started the engine just as the first police vehicle swung around the far corner. Jet punched the throttle and the Chevy leapt into the street. She watched more squad cars arriving at the front of the casino in her rearview mirror and thanked providence she'd gotten away when she had. As to Tomás, the police would get an ambulance there for him faster than she could.

When she pulled to a stop in front of Sofia's house, she debated how to handle the situation and decided to play dumb. As far as her friend was concerned, Tomás was taking care of business and hopefully getting their daughter back safe. Reality was that something had gone badly wrong and now the little girl's safety was a question mark. She dialed Matt's phone. When he answered, she could hear his scooter motor in the background.

"Where are you?" she asked.

"On the way back to the apartment. I'm at a red light. Talk fast."

"I'm not going to tell my friend what happened. If Tomás was carrying ID, she'll get a call soon enough."

"Good thinking."

"What the hell happened?"

"My guess is Tomás and his buddy, for whatever reason, tried to take them."

"Bad idea. And no sign of Catalina."

"Maybe that's why he freaked out."

"Could be. But now he's a pincushion, and she's still kidnapped."

"Bad situation all around. Oh – light turned. Gotta go."

"Stay at home until I get there. And Matt? Sorry I got you into a shootout."

"I was just beginning to think hanging with you might be nice and boring."

"You should know better."

"I do now."

Chapter 11

Luis looked up as his second-in-command entered with a dour expression. Luis finished scribbling in his ledger, closed the heavy leather-bound book, and set his pen down on the desk.

"What do we have?"

"Footage from the casino. As you know, we get the security cam feeds real time. I had our boy run us a copy of the relevant sections."

Luis shook his head, fuming. "How did a simple cash collection turn into a bloodbath?"

"There were no survivors to tell the story, which was why I brought the footage."

"I don't have to tell you what a black eye this is going to give the place."

"No. It's pretty clear." The second-in-command handed the flash drive to Luis, who slipped it into his computer. An icon popped up on the screen. He double-clicked it and then maximized the window as it loaded up.

The footage showed two views – inside the casino and inside the room. Luis watched in grim fascination as Tomás and his mystery companion entered, exchanged some words, and then pulled guns.

"What the fu–"

The shootout was over in thirty seconds, Tomás' companion killing Javier and one of the other men almost instantly, the other two of Javier's gunmen throwing themselves to the ground as they fired at Tomás and his friend.

"What a nightmare," Luis murmured. His eyes narrowed as Matt appeared, firing at his men, killing the final two. "Who the hell is that?"

The second-in-command shook his head. "I have no idea. He just sort of showed up. But on the other view, you can see him attack Sergio and take him down. That's where he got the gun."

"So he didn't arrive with a weapon?"

"Not that we could see."

"And who's the woman? She took out two guards in as many seconds."

"Unknown at this time."

Luis replayed the video again and, after studying the two minutes of relevant footage, played it yet again. "Damn. She's a machine," he muttered, watching her disable both guards with ease. He switched his attention back to the mystery man who had finished the fight. Something nagged at him, but didn't register.

"How long until the police put this out to the public?" Luis asked.

"Probably not until tomorrow morning's news at the earliest. Possibly not until tomorrow evening. We've delayed getting them the footage, claiming it would take a few hours to pull it up with only a skeleton night crew working. I figured that would buy us some time. But we can't stall forever."

"Drag your feet as long as possible so I can think this through and start running interference. I want a story in place. Our official line will be that we have no idea why anyone would come in and shoot up the casino. Probably a robbery gone wrong. We aren't missing a dime, so our receipts will balance with the actuals when they check," Luis said.

"Then that's what we'll go with." He paused. "But what are we going to do about the ransom?"

"That's an interesting question. We still have the little girl. But now we're in the kidnapping business and whenever the mother tells the police, without her idiot husband to dissuade her, the stakes go up considerably. I don't want to risk having a regional manhunt for the kid, especially since the husband was shot up in one of my establishments. It wouldn't take a rocket scientist to put that one together."

"So...what? Do we release her? Or do you want to..." The second-in-command ran his finger across his throat.

Luis appeared to think for a moment. "Do nothing for now. Let's see how this plays. After all, if the mother still has the half million..." He trailed off, lost in thought, then stood and moved to his corkboard to retrieve the color printout of the photo he'd distributed to his network. "Damn. I knew it. I knew he looked familiar."

He sat down in front of the monitor and played the footage one last time, freezing the screen when he had a decent shot of Matt's face. He held up the picture and compared it to the image on the screen before lifting his telephone handset to make a call, smiling to himself as he listened to Maria's line ring.

"Gotcha," he muttered to himself, waiting for her to answer.

When he hung up, he eyed his subordinate, who was waiting for instructions. "She wants the feed delayed as long as possible. She feels it would complicate matters if there was a citywide search for the man – it would cause him to go to ground or change his appearance. Pay our contacts with the police to drag out getting the footage somehow. Perhaps we can cite technical difficulties that require a technician to come in tomorrow morning. With any serious effort, we should be able to kick this can down the road until tomorrow lunchtime. Which hopefully will be long enough."

Luis' second-in-command nodded and left to put the necessary pieces in motion. Luis sat back in his chair, looking at the image frozen on his display, and punched the playback. Whoever this man was, he was good – and the woman was even better. He wondered to himself what they'd done to draw the wrath of Maria and decided that what he didn't know wouldn't hurt him.

But the child was a potential wrinkle that he'd have to deal with soon. She was all liability at this point, unless he wanted to risk demanding the ransom again from the wife, who probably had no idea about her idiot husband's disastrous stunt.

A definite possibility, he supposed, but one he needed to carefully consider. Kidnapping wasn't his usual stock in trade and he didn't need the heat it would bring down on him, even though the half million would be the easiest money he'd ever made, and he'd already done the hard work.

A big part of Luis was leaning toward having the troublesome child killed and buried in a shallow grave far from the city, although his business sense was saying to do the deal with the mother.

He'd have to think about it some more. If he decided to have her killed, he could always do it in the morning, he thought.

Death had collected enough tribute for one evening.

⭐⭒⭒

Jet was sipping tea with Sofia when the phone call from the police came in, advising her that her husband was in the hospital. Sofia gasped when she heard the news and nearly fainted, dropping the telephone as she clutched at the nearby wall to steady herself.

"What's wrong?" Jet asked, retrieving the phone. Sofia collapsed onto the sofa, staring into the distance in incomprehension.

"It's Tomás. He's in the hospital. They…they said he's been shot."

"Shot! No! How?"

"I don't know. That's all they said." Sofia looked around the room as though in it for the first time. "I need to get down there."

"Of course. I'll drive you. You're in no condition to be driving, Sofia."

She nodded like a child. "You're probably right. Oh, God, I wonder what went wrong? Catalina…"

"Did they say anything about her?"

"No. Just that Tomás had been in surgery for the last hour and was in stable but guarded condition."

"Which hospital?"

"Hospital Central. The big one."

"I know where it is. I'll take you as soon as you're ready."

"I…give me a few minutes to straighten up," Sofia said absently, rising.

"Of course."

"And thank you for staying with me. You're a true friend."

"I'm sure you'd do the same for me. Go get what you need. I'll be waiting."

As Jet watched Sofia shuffle off, like a woman twice her age, a part of her heart broke. Jet had tried to save her husband from himself, but he wouldn't listen, regardless that she'd risked her own life – and Matt's – to do so. To no avail. Now he was lying in a hospital with tubes sticking out of him for his reward, his daughter still missing and a room full of dead men who would tell no tales. A total loss, as far as she could see. And a totally unnecessary one, if he'd just listened to her.

Hannah pushed a small plastic train on the hardwood floor, but Jet knew from long experience that if she didn't get home and fed fairly soon her daughter would have a meltdown. Isabella had brought some fruit and cookies, but those would only go so far and Hannah didn't do well when you interrupted her routine. Jet checked the time and calculated that she'd need to be sensitive about that when she was at the hospital.

Sofia returned wearing slacks and a fresh blouse and seemed, if brittle, a little more together. Jet had Hannah gather up her things and prepare to leave, with Sofia supervising, while she used the bathroom. She studied her reflection in the mirror with the usual sense of disbelief – she'd been in a gun battle a short time earlier, had subdued two armed men and looked like she'd just taken a long, restful nap. Good genes, she supposed.

The drive to the hospital took fifteen minutes. Jet pulled into the emergency room parking area after slipping some pesos to the attendant and found an empty space. They entered the sliding glass doors and approached the desk, where a fatigued admissions clerk was processing paperwork. Jet inquired about Tomás. The woman made a phone call and told them that he was in the main hospital on the fifth floor. They made their way to the elevator, the harsh overhead fluorescent lights making everyone look slightly pale and ill. At the fifth floor they were greeted by a carbon copy of the downstairs clerk, who checked her sheet and announced that Tomás was in room five-twenty, down the hall on the right.

Jet remained behind while Sofia went to see her husband, holding Hannah's hand as they took a seat in the waiting area. Half an hour later Sofia appeared at the door, her face tense, visibly shaken. Jet stood and went to her.

"How is he?"

"He…he looks dead. The nurse said he's lost a lot of blood, but he's stable and the prognosis is positive."

"Well, that's something, then."

"Yes, but a police detective also stopped in while I was there and said he wants to talk to me. I…I don't know if I can deal with that right now. And I don't want to say anything about Catalina…"

"Sofia, I think the time has come to acknowledge that Tomás made a serious mistake somewhere in all of this by not telling the police. I really don't recommend you continuing to make the same mistake."

"I…I don't know what to do…" she said. Tears rolled down her cheeks and she began sobbing. Jet hugged her as she cried, aware of Hannah staring at them both, and tried to offer what comfort she could.

"And I need to get home…what if the kidnappers call again?"

"You need to get the police involved."

"I…they said they'd kill her if I did. Rebecca, I'm sorry, I know you think I should, but I…I just can't take the risk. Please don't hate me for that."

Jet decided to forego arguing. Her friend was clearly not thinking rationally and the only thing any further insistence would achieve would be to alienate her at a time when she needed all the support she could get.

"I could never hate you, Sofia."

She looked at Jet like a child, trusting and needy, and sniffed. "Would you stay with me while I talk to the police?"

Jet glanced at the time. "I need to get Hannah home."

"You're going to leave?" Sofia asked, fear in her voice.

Jet thought hard and offered a wan smile. "No, I just need to make a call. Go do what you need to do and I'll see what I can manage.'

"Thank you, Rebecca. Thank you so much."

Jet led Hannah back downstairs and called Matt. "Can you do me a huge favor?"

"Last time you asked me to do one I wound up in a gun battle."

"This one's a little easier."

"That's what they all say. How's your friend?"

"Not so good. Tomás looks like he'll live, but she refuses to bring the police into this."

"That's her choice to make, I suppose, even if it's a dumb one."

"Which it is. Just look how well doing it that way has worked so far."

"You know, I was thinking, though. Tomás wasn't carrying a bag or a briefcase. So it could be that was the problem – maybe he tried to get cute with the kidnappers."

"Really? Then there might be hope. That means the money must still be in his car."

"Makes me want to take up auto theft. Now that I'm broke."

"Back to my favor…"

Matt sighed good-naturedly. "What is it this time?"

"I need you to come to the hospital and pick up Hannah. She needs to eat and be put to bed. I don't know how long this is going to take and I can't leave Sofia alone."

"I thought you were going to ask for something hard. Sure thing. But can I use your car? It's got the car seat…"

"Deal. We can take a cab back to the house, assuming she doesn't want to spend all night here."

"And where is here, again?"

"Hospital Central. I'm in the ER."

"Give me fifteen minutes."

Jet hung up and slipped her phone into her pocket, then smoothed Hannah's hair. A woman came through the doors holding a bag of ice against a teenage boy's head, blood caked on his face, followed by two uniformed police officers. Jet decided to get some fresh air rather than expose Hannah to a parade of horror. They stepped outside, where the weather was cooling. Jet explained that Matt would be taking her home and cautioned her to be a good girl and follow Matt's instructions. Hannah assured her that she would with the sincerity of an angel.

A blond woman carrying a satchel strode purposefully up the walkway before moving through the entrance doors. Jet noted her posture automatically. A tingle of apprehension played through Jet – the woman had the gait of a professional that she would recognize anywhere. Probably part of the police assigned to the hospital, she supposed, the Hospital Central ER being the primary delivery point for those injured during the commission of violent crimes. Still, something about the woman bothered Jet, and she was uneasy for the remainder of her wait.

Matt strolled up five minutes later. Hannah ran to him and gave him a hug. Jet did the same, savoring the smell of his skin and hair as she held him for an extended moment, before disengaging and handing him the keys. She indicated the car at the far end of the parking area.

"It's over by that SUV. You can just see it. If you hear something bouncing around in the trunk, it's the guard's gun I tossed back there."

"Good to know. I've still got the other piece from the casino. We can start a collection at this rate." He smiled. "How are you holding up?"

"All in a day's work, I suppose. But I'll be glad when today's over."

"I hear you."

"When you get her home, she really wants mac and cheese. That was the request."

"I'm sure I'll hear all about it on the drive." He looked down at Hannah. "Come on, kid. You ready to go eat?"

Hannah nodded, her eyes sleepy. Jet knelt and kissed her. "Okay, sweetie. Be good. I'll be home soon."

"O-tay," Hannah said in a small voice and took Matt's hand.

Jet watched them walk to the car, he so tall, she so tiny, and felt something shift inside her, as she always did when she had to leave Hannah with anyone. The Chevy's headlights blinked on and Matt pulled out of the lot. Jet watched them go and then turned and reentered the ER and made her way back to the main hospital, resigned to supporting her friend through her ongoing ordeal.

Tara's cell phone vibrated as she left the fifth-floor intensive care wing, too many police around for her to get into Tomás' room to question him about Matt, and she answered as she moved back to the bank of elevators. It was Ken from his position outside the ER parking lot.

"Yes?"

"Abort. I just saw the target in the hospital parking lot."

She pressed the down button and watched as the floor indicators for the four elevators blinked their positions. "You did?"

"Yes."

"Where is he?"

"He got into a car with some kid and took off."

"Shit. Wait – what did you say? He had a kid with him?"

"Correct. But don't worry. Carl's got him. He took the car and is tailing him."

"Perfect." She paused, thinking. "What was he doing here, with a child?"

"Looks like he just came to pick the kid up. He met some woman, gave her a hug, and took off in a car. He arrived on a motorcycle."

Tara recalled the mystery woman from the casino Luis had described on the security tape and nodded to herself. "Seems like our man has taken up with a local."

"Could be."

"I'll be down in a minute. Tell Carl not to lose him under any circumstances."

"Roger."

Tara didn't mind terminating her foray into the hospital – the whole point of slipping into Tomás' room and interrogating him would have been to find out what he knew about Matt and the woman. But now that they had Matt in their sights, the only thing that mattered was keeping him there until they could take him and find the diamonds. Tara had no interest in the woman, Tomás, or any of the rest of it, and she was relieved she didn't have to subject herself to any undue risk to learn Matt's whereabouts.

The elevator arrived with a ping and the doors slid open. Tara stepped inside and pressed the ground floor button and disconnected. The doors closed just as another elevator arrived from the lobby and Jet stepped out. She moved down the hall to the wing and asked the nurse where Sofia had gone and was told that she was in a vacant room with one of the police detectives. Jet decided to avoid that part of the experience – there was nothing she'd be able to do to help Sofia lie to the police, and she wanted no part of it. She returned to the waiting area and settled in for what she hoped would be a short wait, her mind poring over the day's events with a distinct sense of unease.

Chapter 12

Hannah was quiet on the way home as Matt wound through the streets toward the apartment. Aggressive drivers flew past him on both sides, the notion of defined lanes a laughable concept to most. When they arrived at the building, he punched the button on the garage door remote and waited for the iron gate to slide open. Hannah stirred when he parked in their slot and turned the engine off – she'd dozed off on the short ride home.

"Hey, Hannah. You ready for some mac and cheese?"

"Yeth…"

"All righty then. Let's get you fed."

They trudged up the stairs to the fifth floor. Matt fumbled with his keys, as he always did, before getting the lock open. He switched on the lights and moved into the kitchen, where Hannah had run and was standing, dutifully waiting for him to make her meal. Matt smiled at her look of concentration, as though without her oversight he might ruin the macaroni and cheese – which reminded him very much of her mother, who could get the same expression.

He dumped the noodle packet into a bowl of water and popped it into the microwave. Hannah was very particular about which brand she ate and fortunately favored one that was sold all over Argentina and Uruguay. He entered the appropriate time and started the oven, marveling how much his life had changed in just a few short months. He'd gone from living in the wilds of Laos and Myanmar, with no electricity, running water, or food besides what he could catch or hunt, to a domesticated existence with the most remarkable woman he'd ever met.

Jet had entered his life with the velocity of a meteor and, even after having to disappear following the attack in Ko Samui, he'd thought about her daily. When they'd reconnected in Washington, he'd correctly viewed that as a second chance he wasn't going to let slip by, and he was glad he'd pursued the relationship. Sure, it was an odd pairing, but for whatever reason, it worked, and worked well. They were good together. He'd never felt as powerful an attraction for a woman before – and from what he could see, the feeling was mutual.

Hannah was a stabilizing factor, grounding them both and normalizing their lives, which left to their own devices could have been a circular exercise in paranoia. The world was filled with Jet's powerful enemies and Matt would never be completely safe from the narcotics cabal at the CIA, so they would always have something legitimate to worry about. But they'd settled into a routine in a place a million miles from their old lives, where their priority was Hannah. She'd already bonded completely with Matt and now adored him like the father she'd never known – a heavy responsibility for him, but one he gladly shouldered.

The oven chime went off. He removed the bowl of noodles, setting it on the counter to cool.

"Hannah? Go potty and wash your hands. Dinner will be ready in a few minutes."

Hannah nodded and padded off to attend to her necessities, having mastered potty training early, relieving Matt of at least one challenge that evening. He moved to the kitchen window and popped it open, then walked to the rear balcony and opened the sliding glass door. Below, at the pool area, one of the neighbors had half the city over for a *parrilla* – the obligatory weekend grilling of beef that was a badge of honor for Argentine males. Every home, every apartment complex, had a large outdoor wood-fired covered grill, where many evenings and every weekend a dizzying variety of steaks would be cooked while the admiring celebrants drank wine and quaffed beer.

Matt watched the gathered crowd: a mixed bunch, easily thirty people, varying from old to young, a cross-section of the population, mostly working class judging by their clothes. It was too cool for the children to be swimming, so the pool was empty, but several were running along the perimeter of the large deck, laughing uproariously as the adults focused on grilling the long slabs of meat waiting in marinating trays. As the rich smell of wood smoke drifted up from the grill's chimney, Matt reflected that things could have been much worse than finding the love of his life and living in the epicenter of the Argentine wine country.

He looked up at a stippling of stars glinting in the night sky, more visible than almost anywhere he'd been due to the altitude. Things had certainly taken an interesting turn and, even though he'd just lost a hundred and eighty million dollars in diamonds, he felt strangely ambiguous about it. It wasn't like he'd planned on spending the money anyway, so it was just a number, although the ramifications of his old CIA foes being back on his trail were somewhat alarming. Apparently he'd misjudged them – he'd believed that scrambling to salvage their global trafficking network from the ravages of a competitive market would keep Arthur's subordinates busy until the scent had long grown cold.

Now that they had the diamonds, he figured, most of their incentive to keep up the hunt would fade. True, they'd think he still had seventy million, but they made that in a few weeks, so he couldn't see it keeping them in the game for long. Plus, he'd disappeared and there was nothing to lead anyone to him. He had a different passport with a different name, had dyed his hair darker brown, and was living in a relatively small town on the opposite side of the globe from Thailand. It was hard for him to imagine being any more removed from his old operational life, and he and Jet had agreed that while they'd be vigilant, there was no need to take immediate action.

Feminine laughter rose from the party, and Matt waved at the assembly when his neighbor gazed up at him. The man and his wife waved back, but wouldn't invite him over, he knew. Argentines tended to be a close-knit bunch and, even if he had been living there for years, from their standpoint he would still be an outsider.

Which was fine by him.

Last thing he needed was more beef, he thought, patting his stomach.

෨෧

Tara met Carl and Ken down the street from the building, where they'd parked the car for a quick getaway. The sidewalks were empty, ancient streetlights throwing faint illumination from opaque lamps. They huddled near the vehicle as Tara listened to Carl's account of his pursuit and surveillance.

"You're sure it's the fifth floor?" she asked.

"Absolutely. They pulled into the garage, and a couple of minutes later the lights went on up there. It's not a huge complex – looks to me like one apartment per floor. I'd bet a month's wages that's his."

"You've reconnoitered the building?"

"Yes. There's a doorman in the lobby. But I've been watching people go in – judging from the arrivals, there's some kind of an event taking place. If someone were to show up who looked harmless, they'd easily be able to get in, I'd think. I've watched at least ten people enter since I've been here. Mostly couples, by the way."

Tara looked down the street. "I have the perfect solution. There's a wine store on the next block. Carl, you stay in the car, engine running. Be ready to get out of here on a moment's notice. Ken, come with me. We're going to playact a little."

"I love playacting. You want to do 'prisoner and the warden's wife'?"

"Very funny. Come on. Let's go get a bottle of vino and crash this party."

Chapter 13

Dante's Mercedes rolled to a stop at the end of the alley, the buildings on either side crumbling, the industrial façades deteriorated from decades of neglect, the docks of the old port a hundred yards away deserted. His driver unlocked the doors with the press of a button and Dante exited the car and walked unhurriedly toward the two men framing the metal warehouse door – both older, wearing pea coats and black knit caps pulled tight in spite of the warm weather. Clouds of aromatic smoke drifted slowly away from them in the dead air, the black tobacco of their Parisiennes cigarettes as distinctive as that of hand-rolled Cuban cigars.

Dante nodded at the shorter of the pair, a muscular man with three days of salt-and-pepper stubble on his dark face. The man pulled the door open and Dante entered, his eyes requiring a few moments to acclimate to the gloom of the cavernous expanse. Water dripped from a leaky overhead pipe, one of many crisscrossing the ceiling. He moved across the empty floor of the abandoned warehouse until he reached another door. He knocked, and it opened as though by magic, pulled by a portly bald man in his fifties with the ugly white puckering of an old knife scar running down the left side of his paunchy neck.

"Gilberto. Always good to see you," Dante said, his voice soft.

"Likewise, *Jefe*."

"Where are they?" Dante asked.

"Over there, in the corner," Gilberto said, pointing to where two small boys were chained.

Dante walked over to their position and stared down at them. "So, you thought you could compete with me, snitch about my operations and live to tell about it?"

The younger of the two, perhaps eleven, burst into tears. His older brother, more like thirteen, glared defiantly at Dante.

Dante gave him a disgusted look. "You liked making money selling the Paco, huh? But you thought it would be a good idea to rat out my people to the police so you could have their territory? Not very smart. You've caused me a substantial headache. And you will pay the price."

Dante nodded at Gilberto, who approached carrying an axe handle. Dante took it from him and swung it at the older boy, cracking his arm with an audible snap. The child screamed in agony. Dante continued his assault, beating the boy until he was an unrecognizable pulp. He turned to Gilberto and wiped a fleck of blood from his chin, panting from the exertion, as the surviving sibling wailed in horror at the sight of his brother, now dead beside him. Dante held out the wooden staff and his expression changed. He slowly pivoted until he was facing the crying boy again.

"You want to be a tough guy, eh, *cabron?* Make big-man money the easy way? Then you can expect to pay adult prices for your behavior."

Dante swung the axe handle at the child's legs, shattering his left kneecap. The boy fainted from the pain. Dante tossed Gilberto the blood-smeared length of wood. "Toss him back onto the street. Find his family and tell them that they owe me double whatever we lost in that raid."

Gilberto nodded. "They live in Villa 31." Villa 31 was the most notorious and dangerous slum in Buenos Aires, where the police refused to go and where the murder rate was astronomical – killings for over as little as the equivalent of a dollar, as well as for all the usual reasons: turf warfare, passion, revenge. "A big family. Two more boys and four daughters."

Dante smiled. "Good. Tell them that if they don't pay up, we'll sell their daughters to raise the money. Any idea how old they are?"

"From seven to fifteen."

"We'll start with the seven-year-old. Give them one day. If they try to run, we'll take all the girls and kill everyone else. Make that clear." Dante turned to the unconscious boy. "Now get this garbage out of my sight. What else do we have for me to deal with?"

"We got in twenty new girls for the brothels."

"From where?"

"Mostly Brazil. Four from Paraguay."

"What quality?"

"Sixes and sevens. Two eights."

"How old?"

"Thirteen to sixteen."

"Start them on heroin – that'll make them compliant. We can put them to work this weekend. And wash the two eights up and have them brought to my house tonight. Might as well see what our associates to the north are supplying."

"Yes, *Jefe*."

These sorts of chores were a necessary part of the day-to-day operations of Dante's empire. He was a big believer in setting a strong example for his men, so attended to many of the more unpleasant disciplinary tasks himself, as well as availing himself of the perks of dealing in underage human flesh for sex tourists who seemed to have an endless desire for youngsters. He didn't understand the fascination with adolescents, but he didn't have to. He was merely supplying a market. Now, when the girls began to mature, especially when they were in that coltish youth of puberty...*that* he understood, preferring to be the first to defile many of the girls who would be his slaves, burned out and used up within two years, infected with AIDS and hopelessly addicted to drugs by the time they were too broken to earn for him anymore.

Again, not his problem. The world was an ugly place; if he wasn't supplying what it demanded, somebody else would.

He returned to his car, energized by the prospect of new talent for the evening, and sat back into the butter-soft leather seat as his driver negotiated his way out of the seedy district and back to his home in Palermo Chico, one of the most exclusive neighborhoods in Buenos Aires, where his two-story French-inspired mansion was on the same block as several embassies.

҂ର

When Sofia returned to the hospital waiting area, she looked shaken. Jet approached her and they hugged, words unnecessary. Eventually the moment was over and they moved apart, Sofia tentative as she walked to the water cooler and dispensed a cup.

"How did it go?" Jet asked, watching as Sofia gulped the water like she'd been lost in the desert for days.

"So-so. I don't think the inspector believed me about knowing nothing about why my husband was involved in a shootout in a casino. But what's that old saying? The wife's the last to know? I played dumb and it seemed to work well enough to get me through it."

"What kinds of questions were they asking?"

"Why he had a gun when he doesn't have a license. I told them, honestly, that I had no idea. Then they wanted to know why he was at the casino. Again, I don't know why he went there. It was all along those lines."

"And you really still feel it's best not to tell them the truth?"

Sofia sat down on the shabby couch as though she'd run a marathon. "The police here are…they aren't always trustworthy. Often, they're part of the criminality they're fighting against. It's not unheard of for them to have been participating in robberies, kidnappings…even murder. Many are honest, but enough aren't that I can't risk it. I have no faith that if I told them, that information wouldn't go straight back to the kidnappers, and then Catalina…"

"I understand."

Sofia gathered herself and rose. "Come on. Let's get out of here."

"Sure. But we'll need to take a taxi. Greg took Hannah home." Matt used the name Greg in Argentina.

"Ah, of course. Oh, Rebecca, I'm so sorry to have put you out like this. I know it's an imposition."

They walked to the elevators and, as they were waiting for a car to arrive, Sofia leaned in close to Jet. "The detective said that there was another man with Tomás. His brother, Bruno. He's a policeman, which I think complicates matters for everyone. He…he didn't make it."

Jet feigned surprise. "Why would he have met up with Tomás and gone to a casino?"

"That's another thing I have no answer for. I'm guessing he wanted his brother along in case something went wrong. Maybe they were supposed to hand the money over at the casino and get Catalina and there was a double-cross. I'll know more once he's out of critical condition."

"That raises another question. A big one."

"What?"

"Where's the ransom money?"

Sofia shook her head like it was no problem. "Oh, I know where it is. Tomás told me. It's still in his car, which is parked a block away from the casino."

Jet eyed her. "Really?"

"Yes. He said he didn't have it with him when he went inside."

The elevator arrived. Jet pressed the lobby button before turning to regard Sofia. "Did he tell you why he was there?"

"No. He was fading in and out of consciousness. But he made me promise I would get the money…in case the kidnappers called."

Jet's eyebrows rose. "Those weren't the kidnappers at the casino?"

"He didn't say. But I gathered they weren't. At least not the ones actually holding my daughter. Might have been part of the same gang or something."

"Then I agree we need to get the money. Let's take a taxi and get his car. Do you have a key?"

Sofia nodded. "I have a spare."

The admission nurse called a cab for them, which arrived a few minutes later. The drive to the casino was mercifully short. When they arrived, there were still police cars everywhere, emergency lights blinking off the surrounding windows. The uniformed officers were mostly standing around while the crime scene technicians went about their business inside.

"Take us around the block," Jet instructed the driver. When they saw the white Mercedes, Jet had him stop and let them out.

Sofia popped the trunk and they saw the briefcase. Jet opened it, confirming that it was filled with hundred-dollar bills. Sofia seemed uninterested in the money, having retreated back into her shell on the ride over, and merely handed Jet the keys after she closed the trunk.

"Will you drive?" Sofia asked.

"Of course."

Jet started the engine, a puzzled expression on her face. "I still don't understand why Tomás would have agreed to meet anyone in a casino unless it was to do the exchange. If we assume that's what happened, then the question is why he didn't go in with the money. That would be a huge risk, assuming the kidnappers were on the level. Which they apparently weren't…" Jet's voice trailed off, the situation not adding up, and then shook off her unease and put the car in gear.

"Once he's in better shape, I'm sure Tomás will tell us what happened. He was just so…so weak… I didn't have the heart to tell him about Bruno. They were very close."

"There'll be plenty of time to talk once this is over."

"I know it's horrible, but all I can think about is Catalina. It's not that I don't love Tomás, it's just that Catalina has got to be so scared, all alone… I can't imagine what she must be going through…" Sofia began quietly crying again as Jet negotiated down the street and onto the larger boulevard.

Jet wanted to say something comforting, but no words came to her. The truth was that this was every parent's worst nightmare and anything she said would sound hollow. The most respectful thing she could do was to let Sofia grieve in peace while Jet tried to figure out what was really going on.

She pulled her phone from her pocket and dialed Matt, the car suddenly feeling claustrophobic with the two of them in it. When he answered, she almost gasped in relief.

"So? How did it go?" he asked.

"Good, I think. We're on the way back to Sofia's. How's Hannah?"

"Fine. I'm just finishing up the mac and cheese."

"Thanks again."

"No problem. When do you think you'll be home?"

"Probably not for a while. Will you put her to bed for me?"

"I kind of figured. Of course I will. But you owe me big time for that."

Jet smiled for the first time in hours. "I'll see if I can figure out some way to reward you for your chivalry."

"I have a list."

"Sounds interesting. But we need to get at least a little sleep tonight."

"Sleep's for wimps."

"That's my big, strong, red-blooded American he-man."

"Give me a call when you're headed home and I'll slip into something more comfortable."

Jet hung up and dropped the phone back into her pocket, noting with relief that Sofia had stopped crying. Part of the problem they faced was that the woman wasn't equipped to deal with this situation, which was why Jet didn't feel comfortable leaving her. If the kidnappers contacted her again…there was no way she'd stand any more of a chance than her husband had.

Jet slowed to a stop at a red light and looked over at Sofia. "Don't worry. I'll do everything I can to help you. You're not going to have to do this alone."

"If they don't call…I'll never forgive myself for not contacting the police…"

Sofia was obviously having second thoughts about handling the affair now that she realized she was on her own, with Tomás out of the picture. Jet wanted to chide her and point out that she'd seen it coming, but elected to leave Sofia to her thoughts. There was no need to rub anything in. She was suffering enough.

Still, Jet figured she'd try one last time. "Water under the bridge, although it's never too late..."

Sofia didn't say anything, preferring to stare through the window at Mendoza flashing by as they made their way back to her house, the inviting city now anything but, every shadow containing a threat, every doorway an enemy. Jet recalled when Arthur had blackmailed her into going after Matt, holding Hannah as leverage, so she more than knew what Sofia was going through. There was nothing she could say to improve the situation, so instead she concentrated on avoiding colliding with the slaloming cars on the road, all moving at double any sane speed, her heart breaking for Sofia and the ordeal she was going through.

Chapter 14

Tara and Ken swayed drunkenly up the sidewalk, laughing easily as they approached Matt's building entrance. The doorman looked up as they knocked on the glass. Tara held up a bottle of Malbec with a smile, Ken's arm around her as he nuzzled her neck. The doorman buzzed them in and they approached the reception counter where he was seated.

"We're here for the party," Tara said, offering a dazzling display of gleaming white dentistry.

"The Renaciers?" the doorman asked, eyeing Tara after a brief glance at Ken.

"Who else?"

The doorman pointed to an olive metal door. "Through that door, straight to the one at the end of the hall. Out by the pool. Can't miss it."

The sound-suppressed .22-caliber pistol in Tara's hand was so quiet that the only noises it made were a muffled crack and the clacking of the slide as the weapon ejected first one shell and then another. The initial shot caught the hapless doorman in the right eye, the lead slug tumbling through his brain, instantly ending his life. The second was to ensure he was dead even as he slumped forward.

Ken rounded the counter and lowered the corpse below the desk level so his body would be out of sight, while Tara cleaned the blood off the tabletop with a rag she'd brought for that purpose.

She slipped the gun back into her purse as he returned to her side. Ken glanced at her and they both eyed the ceiling area for a camera.

Nothing.

Executing the doorman had been a risk, but they weren't planning on being in the building for very long and the likelihood that he would be discovered while they were still there was low, considering the late hour and the fact that most would assume the man had gone to use the bathroom and would return shortly. Luis had been able to source a syringe of animal tranquilizer that would knock Matt out in seconds and the plan was to carry him out, explaining that he was drunk if they were stopped, and if that didn't work, shooting whoever asked.

Tara pointed to the door. Ken darted to it and did a quick reconnoiter of the area. When he returned, he whispered to Tara.

"Big group. A barbeque. Loud. They'll be there for a while."

"Good. Hopefully that will cover any noise we make." She glanced at the stairs leading up. "Let's go."

At the fifth floor Tara extracted a lock-picking kit and went to work on the keyhole, brushing the curved pick while twisting with moderate pressure on the flat one. After half a minute the mechanism clicked and she turned the knob, opening the door. Ken withdrew his suppressed Beretta and leaned against the jamb as Tara eased the door open.

It stopped abruptly, a brass security chain in place, leaving a three-inch gap to tantalize them. Tara cursed under her breath and glanced at Ken before stepping away from the door, a look of cold determination on her face.

Matt stirred the macaroni and cheese, confident that it was now the consistency Hannah favored, the patently artificial orange-yellow of the cheese like nothing found in nature. Satisfied that it would meet with her approval, he unwrapped a loaf of coarse Italian peasant bread and cut a chunk off with a long-bladed serrated knife as the echo of laughter drifted up from the party five stories below. His neighbors sounded like they were having a hell of a time and he hoped that Hannah's room would be quiet enough for her to sleep. He glanced down the hall at the bathroom, where Hannah was still attending to her necessities, and called out.

"Honey? Dinner's ready. Come and get—"

The front door blew in with a crash and a gunman entered, his weapon clutched in front of him in a two-handed grip. Matt instinctively ducked behind the kitchen island as the intruder swung the pistol's ugly snout toward him.

"Matt. It's no good. We know you're in here. Come out and we won't hurt the girl," the man said, his voice quiet and evenly modulated.

Matt realized he'd been fast enough and the man hadn't spotted him. He slowly felt along the knife edge until he'd reversed his grip and was holding it by the blade. He listened as the man's footsteps neared and, after taking a deep breath, tensed every muscle in his body and threw himself from behind the island and flung the knife at the man's crouched form.

The blade hurtled at the gunman and caught him in the chest as he tried to draw a bead on Matt, who had never stopped moving, ducking into a roll before leaping to his feet. The attacker squeezed off a shot that narrowly missed, then Matt rushed the intruder, eliminating any advantage he had with the gun.

Matt slammed into him, driving the knife deeper into the man's body, and delivered a series of brutal blows to his eyes and face with his right hand while he grappled with the gun with his left. The gunman grunted in pain and dropped the pistol, then a woman's voice called out.

"Matt. It's over. Stop this, or I'll shoot."

Matt instantly recognized the voice, and that recognition threw him for a critical instant – just long enough for his attacker to rally and push him backward. Matt clutched him, knowing his only chance was to use him as a human shield, and pulled the bloody knife out of his chest before stabbing into the side of his abdomen again and again as they stumbled like drunken dancers toward the open balcony doors.

"I'll shoot," the woman screamed as the two men wrestled like grizzlies. And then they both tumbled over the terrace railing, carried by their momentum, as Tara watched her quarry drop out of sight.

Matt's body hit the surface of the pool a split second before Ken's. The impact of his back slamming against the water followed by Ken's body landing on top of him knocked him out. If it hadn't, he would have been blinded by pain when his arm snapped like a twig from Ken's bulk striking him a glancing blow, most of the force of the fall absorbed by Ken's head and shoulder striking the pool steps, which Matt had missed by scant inches.

A geyser of water shot into the air and drenched the bystanders. A woman screamed as the pool turned crimson from Ken's blood. A quick-thinking former soldier dove in to save Matt, who was slowly sinking, face up, as though asleep beneath the garnet water.

Tara gazed down at the scene, considering her next step.

She spun at the sound of the bathroom door opening, her gun in her hand. At the end of the hallway a figure stood, so small she could barely reach the doorknob, long hair lending her the appearance of an angel in the shadows. Her eyes locked on Tara's for a long second, then Tara slipped the gun into the waist of her jeans and slowly stepped forward, avoiding the blood on the floor as she crossed the living room.

Tara stopped at a bookcase where a recent photo of Matt, Jet, and Hannah, standing in front of a fountain, was framed. She slid the photo from behind the glass and slipped it into her pocket. After glancing around the room, she approached the coffee table. Matt's cell was sitting next to a Spanish-language television magazine. She scooped up the phone before smiling at Hannah with as friendly an expression as she could muster.

"Honey, don't worry. Everything's going to be okay from now on."

Hannah tried to back away, but the bathroom door blocked her escape route.

Tara took measured steps toward the toddler and extended her hand. "I need you to be a good girl and come with me, okay?"

Hannah shook her head. "Maa..."

"Matt had to leave, honey. But your mommy sent me to take care of you."

"Hungry."

"Of course you are. We'll get you something as soon as we can, okay? Come on. Let's go."

Hannah drew back, trying to make herself even smaller as Tara moved to her and took her arm. "I don't have time to argue with you. You need to do as I say, all right?"

Hannah started crying, large tears flowing down her cheeks as Tara led her out of the apartment, the girl near panic as a woman she didn't know led her from the safety of her home into an uncertain future.

Chapter 15

The streets in the Quinte district were dark as Jet and Sofia rounded the corner of her block and rolled into her driveway. She depressed the garage door opener button and they sat in silence waiting for the wooden barrier to raise, the longest day of Sofia's life threatening to stretch on indefinitely. Once inside, Isabella met them in the kitchen with a worried face.

"*Señora*, someone has been calling every twenty minutes. A man. He asks for you and, when I tell him you haven't made it home yet, hangs up," she said.

Sofia and Jet exchanged a look. "Thank you, Isabella. Don't worry about anything. I'm home now, so I can take the call the next time."

"Very good, *señora*. I made some empanadas and tea. If you're hungry."

"Thank you, Isabella. We'll have them in a minute in the dining room."

"I'll see to it."

Sofia waited until Isabella was out of earshot and turned to Jet. "That has to be them."

"Probably. That is a good sign."

Sofia sighed and smoothed her hair with a trembling hand. "Will you excuse me? I want to use the facilities. And anything you want, you have but to ask. Isabella is a wonderful cook and can whip up whatever you like…"

"I'm sure the empanadas will be fine, Sofia. Go do what you need to do. I'll be here waiting."

The phone rang, startling them both. Isabella picked up and, after a few murmured words, appeared at the kitchen door holding a wireless handset. "*Señora*, it's…him."

Sofia took the phone from her. "Thank you, Isabella. That will be all." Sofia waited until Isabella had ducked back into the kitchen before raising the handset to her ear. "Hello."

"Finally. I don't need to tell you who this is."

"No."

"Your husband is a very foolish man. This was a simple exchange. You're lucky I'm patient. But that patience only goes so far. Listen carefully. I want you to go to La Gaviota Park at ten o'clock – in one hour. At the northern side of the park there's a statue of a general. Bring the money. We'll bring the girl. Do you understand?"

"I understand…but how do I know you won't shoot me, like you did my husband?"

"I don't know what happened there, but I can assure you that we didn't shoot first. Your husband is an idiot. He had a gun and brought a stranger with a gun. That wasn't the arrangement."

"But I–"

"No more discussion. Be at the statue in an hour. Under no circumstances tell anyone, or your daughter dies. There will be no further chances. Do as I say and you'll have her back in an hour. Try to screw me and they'll be finding pieces of her around the valley for weeks."

The line went dead. Sofia stared at the phone like it was a live snake, then collapsed onto one of the dining room chairs like her bones had liquefied.

"What is it?"

"They want me to bring them the money in one hour. At a park in the town center." Sofia told her the details.

Jet considered their options, disliking all of them. "You're in no shape to do this, Sofia."

"I have to."

Jet shook her head, having arrived at a decision. "No. No, you don't. I'll go instead."

Sofia's eyes widened. "I can't ask you to do that…"

"Sofia, I can do it."

"It's too dangerous."

Jet sat across from Sofia and took her hands in hers. "Listen to me, Sofia. Before I moved to Argentina, I was in law enforcement. I have experience with this sort of thing. Believe me when I tell you there's nobody more qualified to do this than me."

"You were?"

"Yes. Which is why I was trying to convince your husband to bring the police into this earlier. The way you've gone about handling this is…it's not good, Sofia. It's way more dangerous for all concerned to let the kidnappers dictate terms."

"I…I can't take chances with Catalina's life. You don't know the police here…"

"I know. You already told me, and I understand. But that doesn't change things."

"Then what should we do?"

"Two things. First, you need to go somewhere safe. This house may not be. They knew you were at the park, so it's likely they know where you live, too. I don't like that one bit. Until this is resolved, you need to stay somewhere else. Do you have any place like that where you can go? Maybe a summer home or a weekend cottage?"

"No. The only place I could go is my parents' house. It's about twenty minutes out of town – they own a number of wineries and they live on a compound on the grounds of one of them."

"Is it secure?"

"Oh, yes. I mean, it's a big place and they have a caretaker and a guard. They aren't in town right now – they're in San Andres visiting friends, but they should be back tonight or early tomorrow."

"Is there any problem spending a few days there, just in case?"

"Of course not. But…do you think that's really necessary?"

"There have been enough foolish chances taken today. Let's start playing it safe. Making sure you're where they can't get to you if there's another unexpected twist seems like an excellent idea."

"What about Isabella?"

"I can't see anyone wanting your housekeeper, unless she keeps a half million dollars under her mattress. But if she has a friend, she should have him come over. Again, just in case. Criminals don't like crowds. Tell her to call the police if she sees anything suspicious. This house is built like a fortress, with the bars on all the windows, so nobody's going to get in easily. Do you have an alarm?"

"Yes. The most expensive they make. It's wired in to an operator with a guarantee the police will be here within five minutes of it triggering."

"Then I wouldn't be too worried. But until we know more about what happened with your husband, you should make yourself scarce. I don't like surprises and a shootout at a casino with armed men is about as big as they come."

Sofia nodded. "Are you sure you want to do this? It's not your problem…"

"I adore Catalina. I want her back with her mom, where she belongs."

"Oh, Rebecca, I don't know how I can ever thank you."

"You don't have to. Wait until we have Catalina and then we can break out the champagne."

Sofia paused, looking off into empty space. "Do you think we'll get her back?"

"Realistically, they have no reason to keep her. But having said that, people who kidnap children are the scum of the earth. There are few things lower in my book. So we can't get our hopes up too high. I wouldn't trust a word they say. Especially after the casino."

"Then what do you intend to do?"

"There's not a lot I can do, Sofia. But one of the things is to get to the park early and scope it out. Make sure that it's not a setup. I'm leery of believing they're going to take the money and hand her over. Don't get me wrong – I have no reason not to believe it, other than the entire situation. Frankly, the one thing working in your favor is that even though five hundred thousand dollars seems like a lot of money, in the scheme of things, it's amateurish. Which is both good and bad. Amateurs can behave unpredictably. They could be drug addicts. That wouldn't be a first. What I'm saying is that there's no telling what their true intentions are."

"How will you protect yourself?"

Jet hesitated. "Do you have a gun?"

"No. There's never been any need for one."

"No matter." Jet checked the time. "I want to get going. We've already burned ten minutes. With travel time, I've only got a half hour or so to familiarize myself with the layout. Which reminds me… You have a computer?"

"Of course. Why?"

"I want to see a satellite image of the park so I understand what I'm walking into. Where is it?"

"In our office. Come on."

After five minutes studying the park's orientation, Jet was ready to leave. She had Sofia go to her bedroom and pack a bag, then led her to the car, where she explained what she intended to do.

"I'll take you to one of the big hotels. Catch a taxi to your parents' place. Give me the address and directions and a phone number, and hopefully I'll see you, with Catalina, sooner than later."

Sofia scribbled down the information and handed it to Jet, who slipped the paper into her pocket and nodded. "Let's get out of here. The clock's ticking."

Jet dropped Sofia off at the nearby Hyatt hotel and watched her step into the taxi in the front of the queue at the entrance. Once she was confident Sofia was on her way, she plowed into the sparse night traffic and made for the park, turning over possible strategies in her mind as she drove off in Tomás' Mercedes. She hadn't told Sofia everything – she didn't need her losing it at the thought of what Jet was contemplating.

She dialed Matt's cell, but it went to voice mail. He was probably in the shower, or reading Hannah a bedtime story – another endearing habit he'd developed since they'd become a couple. Or rather, a family. Something she'd never believed she'd have.

The guard's revolver, still in the trunk of her car, would have come in handy, but there was no time now to stop by the apartment and get it. A shame, but not a deal breaker, because she more than knew, as someone who had killed with as innocuous an item as a credit card or a pencil, that a gun was more of a convenience than a necessity after dark.

She felt the wooden handle of the boning knife she'd lifted from Sofia's kitchen next to her in the center console, and smiled. No, a gun was just one way of leveling things. There were other, equally effective methods.

Which the kidnappers were soon going to find out, with any luck at all.

Chapter 16

Jet parked two blocks away on a quiet residential street, the only illumination coming from occasional porch lights. A shaggy form slunk into the gloom at the sound of her door closing – one of the many street dogs that occupied the downtown, using the complexly interwoven network of irrigation canals to move around the city, where they fed on steak offered to them by outdoor diners who were suckers for begging canine eyes.

She left the cash in the trunk. There was at least a fifty-percent chance that the kidnappers had no intention of ever returning Catalina, especially after the gun battle. Jet checked the time as she moved along the sidewalk, thankful that she was wearing her black running shoes in preparation for the now-distant walk at the zoo instead of her customary boots. The rubber soles left no footsteps, so she had silence in her favor.

The park loomed ahead of her, a dark rectangle surrounded by mature trees, the longest sides two blocks long, the shorter, one block, she knew from her time on the computer. The streetlights, like many, had long ago burned out and never been replaced, affording her even more shadows to move between – and more cover for the kidnappers to stage an ambush.

She walked the perimeter and, other than a few vagrants loitering in its depths, didn't see anyone that looked like a threat. As she rounded the corner on the side nearest the statue, she saw movement in a car at the far end of the block, across the street. Her watch said she still had ten minutes before the rendezvous, so she continued on her way and then circled the block to get a better look at what had attracted her attention.

Jet neared the intersection and glanced, seemingly uninterested, down the thoroughfare. She caught a glimpse of two men in a dark sedan with the unmistakable shape of a child's head between them. Her heart rate increased as she considered her options, but she continued walking, just a woman on her way to dinner or to meet a friend.

At the next block she cut over to the park and entered its inky grounds, giving the three bums sharing a bottle a wide berth. The last thing she needed was an unplanned-for distraction from her objective and, while she had not the slightest worry about walking away unscathed if attacked, a mugging attempt would consume valuable time.

There was only one direction the men would be coming with Catalina. She knew from her walk that there were several oak trees along the sidewalk leading to the section with the statue. She eyed the closest tree and took a run at it, her feet pushing off the trunk and propelling her higher, as she'd learned to do with her Parkour hobby. Her hands grabbed the lowest of the thick branches and she pulled herself up, and, once standing on a thick one, steadied herself with others using her hands. She glanced down at the caliginous sidewalk below.

It could work.

⤙⤚

The lights of the critical care ward had dimmed now that visiting hours were over. Only a skeleton crew of nurses manned the floor, gathered at the central station where their patients' vital statistics displayed on a bank of blinking monitors. The rooms were three-quarters full, but if tonight was like most others, the ward would lose ten percent of the patients overnight as they succumbed to whatever trauma had brought them there. Most were victims of traffic accidents, the number one killer of the adult population under sixty and, due to the high velocity favored by motorists, the ward never wanted for admissions.

An orderly padded on crepe soles from the emergency stairwell at the end of one of the corridors, listening for any signs of movement from the staff. Satisfied that they were all at their consoles gossiping or having a late night snack, he counted the rooms until he came to his destination.

The door opened soundlessly and he stepped inside the dark room. The only lighting came from the heart monitor tracing an unending jagged graph beside the bed, where a figure lay still, snoring softly. The orderly crept to the bedside where an IV bag was suspended, half full with clear fluid, and withdrew a syringe from the breast pocket of his dark green smock. With a glance at the patient, he unhooked the IV drip and emptied the amber contents of the syringe into the line, taking only a few seconds before reconnecting it.

The stairwell door was closing behind him when he heard an alarm sound from the front of the ward. He smiled to himself at how easy it had been to make five thousand dollars. If only all his contracts were that straightforward.

An ambulance with its emergency lights flashing off the hospital's windows pulled into the driveway with another casualty as he pushed through the doors and made for the street, unnoticed by anyone, an unremarkable man in his thirties, his face in need of a shave, dressed in hospital scrubs, heading home after another long and thankless stint caring for the infirm and the hopeless.

☙❧

Raul coughed, the habitual hack of a lifelong smoker. A nicotine stink rose from his clothes, his hands stained from a two-pack-a-day habit. He glanced at the dash clock, turned to his partner, Arturo, and tapped the car window.

"It's time. Let's get this over with."

Arturo placed a call on his cell phone to the vehicle at the far end of the park, there to prevent an ambush. Luis' instructions had been clear – they were to get the money and kill the mother and daughter, ending any chance of his being implicated in a scheme that had gone disastrously wrong. Of course, there would be outrage at the senseless violence in the usually safe city, another example of how the deteriorating economy or the decline in moral values had led to ruin, but it would all be forgotten in days and he would be back to business as usual, one more threat effectively eliminated.

Neither Raul nor Arturo had the slightest qualms about executing the pair. This was their chosen line of work. It was just a job – another in a long string of assignments unremarkable except for the method of extermination. Luis had instructed them to simulate a robbery gone wrong, using knives, like the street people that populated the city's nocturnal haunts would if someone had tried to steal their valuables. They'd flipped a coin: Arturo would slice the girl's throat with a practiced hand that would result in practically no pain. Raul would take the mother. It would be over in a matter of seconds and they'd be long gone by the time anyone arrived to help.

Both had dressed in rags, the anonymous uniform of the homeless, dark and dirty, indistinguishable from the silent army prowling the nocturnal streets. The only difference was that both men wore latex gloves and had Glocks in their waistbands, in addition to the sheathed bone-handled hunting knives they would use for their chore – knives that could be purchased in any of countless curio and tourist shops in town.

"Okay. They're in position. There's nothing on the police frequencies and nobody around but some drunks hanging out in the park. So we're good."

Raul grabbed Catalina's arm and pulled her roughly out of the car. Her face was swollen where he'd cuffed her several times to show her he meant business when he told her to stay quiet. She'd quickly gotten the message, reduced to a state of steady snuffling as silently as possible, quaking in fear, instinctively understanding that the men holding her captive meant her nothing but harm.

They crossed the cobblestones, dragging the little girl as they moved, just an object in their eyes, not a human being – a distinction they couldn't have articulated if asked, but part of the professional insulation they'd learned in their teens when they'd first taken to murder-for-hire as their vocation, the economy then, as now, in freefall, no jobs available for even those with educations. Not that either had spent more than a few years in school, preferring to make easy money in the drug trade, seeing no point in pretending to try to learn anything when their real education took place on the streets.

Their footsteps echoed off the sidewalk as they moved down the block. Catalina had begun bawling again, quietly, her fear increasing as they approached the park.

Arturo drew back his hand to strike her. "Shut up, you little bra–"

Jet dropped behind him from the branch above and plunged the boning knife between the C2 and C3 vertebrae, severing his spinal cord. He collapsed in a heap as Raul spun, groping for his Glock. Jet slashed at him with the bloody knife and sliced his ribs through his soiled jacket, but it wasn't enough to stop him and she followed it up with a strike to his eyes, trying to blind him.

The blow missed by scant millimeters. He bellowed in rage and pain as he whipped the gun free. Jet head-butted him with the top of her skull, shattering his jaw even as she kneed him in the groin, putting all her might into it. His finger spasmodically pulled the pistol's trigger, and a detonation shattered the silence. The bullet ricocheted harmlessly off the concrete a yard away. Jet spun and leveled a kick at his profile. It connected with his ruined face and snapped his head to the side, his neck broken like a dry twig from the force of the blow.

Raul tumbled to the sidewalk, his weapon clattering by his side, the entire exchange over in under ten seconds. Jet knelt to bring her eyes to Catalina's level.

"Are you okay, Cat?" she whispered.

The little girl nodded, wide-eyed, shocked by the sudden violence but obviously relieved to see a familiar and trusted face.

Jet touched Catalina's face where she'd been hit. "Let's get out of here. I'm going to carry you so we can run faster, okay?"

Another nod. Jet rose and retrieved Raul's gun, and then moved to Arturo and felt in his clothes for his. She found it and slipped one in her front waistband and the other in the back, then hoisted Catalina and took off at a sprint, staying to the shadows thrown by the park foliage until reaching the corner and bolting across the street.

Luis' men were running through the park as fast as they could, alerted by the shot, their weapons in their hands. When they reached the sidewalk, they stopped at the lifeless bodies lying in a pool of blood as lights flickered to life in the surrounding apartments. After scanning the street and seeing nothing, they erred on the side of prudence and retraced their steps to the other side of the park and their waiting car, dreading the report they'd have to make to their boss, but driven by the sirens keening only a few blocks away, attracted by the gunshot.

Jet reached Tomás' car and strapped Catalina in before starting the engine and pulling away. As she neared the closest intersection, the night was split by two police cars, lights flashing and sirens blaring, headed to the park. Jet waited for them to pass and took in the bruising and swelling on Catalina's face. She glanced at her clothes to ensure there was no obvious blood splatter on them. The light changed. She returned her eyes to the road and gave the car gas, glad that this chapter of the little girl's life was finally over.

She thumbed her phone on and made a call, but got voice mail. She left a message and returned her full focus to the road, on her way to Sofia's parents' estate nestled among the vines in Lujan de Cuyo, one of the premier wine-growing regions in the country. Jet didn't think there was any threat to Sofia now, but she couldn't predict any backlash from the kidnappers and, until the police were involved and had tracked them down, Sofia was best off remaining well away from the menace of the city's predators.

Behind her, a motorcycle kept its distance, its headlight jittering in the night as Jet rolled toward the road that would take her south.

Chapter 17

Luis sat at his desk in the warehouse, a bottle of single malt Scotch in front of him, two fingers still left in his glass, and eyed the man delivering the report about the disastrous encounter at the park. The speaker was clearly rattled. When he finished, Luis took a long pull on his drink and set the empty glass next to the bottle.

His words held the warning hiss of a snake. "How could this have happened?"

The man hesitated. "I don't honestly know. By the time we made it to the front, they were gone. The only good news is that Armando is tailing the Mercedes the woman's driving so we'll know where she's headed."

Luis rose and shook his head. "I knew we shouldn't have gotten involved in this scheme. It felt wrong when that dolt proposed it, and it's done nothing but go from bad to worse. Now we're out the money, we have no girl, and I've lost more men in one day than I have in the last five years."

The subordinate stood with his head bowed, his body language contrite.

Luis' second-in-command cleared his throat. "The question is what we do now. Do we leave it, or continue to pursue the ransom?"

"With Tomás dead, we'll never have another chance to get paid. I don't like the idea of walking away."

"But the situation has also changed. We have a random variable that we didn't know about that's altered the game. Armando saw her take down our men — alone."

Luis nodded. "True. But she's only one woman. We may be guilty of underestimating her, but we won't make that mistake again."

"What do you want to do?"

"Let's see where she's going. And get some of the boys ready. Our best."

The second-in-command rose. "I'll get right on it."

Luis sat back down and poured another healthy dollop of Scotch. "Do that. And you?" he said, addressing the gunman. "I want you to be part of the group that goes after her. I'm holding you personally responsible if there's another screw-up. I don't need to explain what that means, do I?"

The hapless man shook his head. "No, sir."

Luis waved him away with his glass.

"Get out of my sight."

❧

Carl drove at a moderate pace as Tara recounted the situation at the apartment. Hannah was in the back seat, sitting quietly, watching them both as they talked.

"Then you have no idea whether he's dead or not?" Carl asked.

"No, but it's a fairly safe bet after a five-story drop into a pool. Don't get me wrong – I'm hoping that's not the case, but I'm not betting on it."

"Then why the girl?"

"Insurance. If he does survive, she'll be instrumental in leading us to him."

"How can you be so sure he won't just disappear, assuming he made it? Why would he stick around and endanger himself with some mystery woman?"

Tara patted the pocket with the photo in it. "Call it a hunch. He has snapshots in the apartment of the sweet little family together. Looks like our boy has gone native." She paused, thinking. "I know Matt. If he's bonded with someone, he'll do everything possible to protect them."

"What do we know about her?"

"Nothing, except that she looks pro, based on the casino footage. I have to admit, when I saw it, it was almost like watching me…"

"Except nobody's as good as you are."

"If you're angling to be promoted into Ken's position, you're going about it the right way."

Carl shook his head. "Poor bastard. I'll bet he never thought the end of the road would be in a swimming pool with a kitchen knife sticking out of him."

"Just goes to show you the importance of keeping on your toes. That could have been avoided. He should have taken his time. He rushed it and paid the price." Tara frowned, her disgust evident. "I don't need to tell you that headquarters isn't going to be happy if we had Matt in our hands and killed him. We're not going to get the diamonds back from a corpse."

"What do we do if he's dead? And how will we find out?"

"I'm sure Luis has contacts with the local police. I'll have him put out feelers. If there were two bodies picked up, it's game over."

Carl's eyes swiveled to Hannah in the rearview mirror. "What do we do with the kid if he's dead?"

Tara shrugged. "She's of no use to us in that case. I say we give her to Luis and let him deal with it. Maybe he can sell her and make a few bucks. I know that Dante's big in that market, so it should be worth something to them."

Carl nodded. "What a world, huh?"

"Don't hate the playah, hate the game, isn't that the saying?"

"True dat."

A ringing trilled from Tara's pocket. She felt for the phone and stared at the screen before allowing the call to go to voice mail. A notification flashed at her a few seconds later, and she selected the speed-dial button Matt had programmed for voice mail and punched it. She listened intently to the message and smiled as she searched for the button that would put it on speakerphone so Carl could hear it. When she'd found it, she pressed another button to replay.

Jet's voice sounded from the speaker. Hannah's ears perked up when she heard her mother, which Tara caught.

"Matt. It's me. Call me back as soon as you get this. I've got Catalina."

⥼⥽

The highway was nearly deserted as Jet barreled down the four-lane, the Mercedes eating up the miles, its big tires thrumming on the uneven pavement. Once they were out of the city, the surrounding countryside was pitch black, with only occasional faint lights from distant farmhouses. Jet had tried to engage Catalina in conversation, but she'd shown no interest, which she couldn't blame her for. God knew when she'd last been able to sleep, or eat and drink — and Catalina hadn't volunteered any information, silent as a sphinx, her skin white with shock.

Jet supposed the trauma of the kidnapping, not to mention having her captors killed before her eyes, would scar her, but there was nothing Jet could do about that. With enough love and care from her mother, she'd

108

probably get over it – children tended to be resilient at that age. Jet hoped she'd soon forget the entire experience as she occupied her mind with other, more pleasant, memories. Hannah was happy and well adjusted and showed no ill effects from having been snatched at birth, raised by a surrogate family, and held by Arthur while Jet had been in Thailand. She'd adapted to her new life and Jet was sure the same would happen with Catalina.

Jet watched the signs blur past. When she saw one announcing the road she wanted, she pulled into the right lane and took the off-ramp, unaware of the motorcycle that had been tailing her from a safe distance, its headlight turned off since turning onto the empty highway. She slowed and made a left, taking the overpass over the freeway, and soon found herself on a rural strip of asphalt leading nowhere, with not even a dividing line to keep traffic straight.

Exactly two miles from the main road she spotted the placard announcing Sofia's parents' winery and turned down a dirt track with vines on either side. Two more minutes and she saw lights and a compound appeared out of the darkness. The home was huge, with a low wall running around the perimeter of the property. She could make out several people inside, behind the curtains in the downstairs section of the house.

Jet pulled to a stop at the gate and buzzed the intercom mounted on the wall. A gravelly male voice answered and she announced that she was there to see Sofia. The gate whined and slid aside. She rolled through, down the long drive, and parked in front of the big home's entry door.

Sofia threw it open, framed by backlighting from the interior, and squinted against the glare of the headlights. Jet killed the engine and turned to Catalina.

"All right, sweetie. You're safe now. There's your mommy waiting for you. Are you ready to get out of the car?"

Catalina nodded, her face animated for the first time since they'd gotten underway. Jet slid from behind the wheel and pulled the rear door wide so Catalina could climb out. The little girl practically vaulted onto the large paver tiles and ran to her waiting mother as fast as her legs could carry her, long hair blowing in the breeze.

Mother and daughter embraced on the porch seemingly forever before Sofia stood, carrying Catalina, and regarded the approaching Jet.

"How can I ever thank you…" she began, her voice tight from emotion.

RUSSELL BLAKE

"All's well that ends well, right? Let's go into the house and I'll tell you all about it." Jet studied Sofia's relieved face. "You know, I'll bet Catalina needs to use the bathroom and would love something to eat."

"Is that it for guests, *señora?*" the same male voice from the intercom called from a *casita* at the side of the drive. Jet peered into the gloom at an older man wearing an oversized peasant sweater and corduroy pants, his shoulders stooped, standing by the cottage's door.

"Yes, Valentine. I'm not expecting anyone else."

"Very good, *señora*," he said and shuffled back inside.

Sofia turned to Jet. "That's Valentine. He's the groundskeeper and what passes for a guard when my parents aren't here."

"Ah. And when they are?"

"They have three full-time bodyguards that go everywhere with them. Since things have gotten more difficult in Argentina, it's the prudent thing to do. Believe me, after this episode, I'll have at least one as well."

"That makes sense if you're a target."

"I didn't think I was, but this has convinced me otherwise." Sofia gestured to the door with her free hand. "Come in and tell me what happened. I want to hear everything."

Jet accompanied her into the house, which was opulently furnished with antiques of every description and spoke to the considerable hereditary wealth the family had accumulated. Sofia led Catalina into the depths while Jet took a seat on one of three couches. A woman in her fifties materialized in the dining room and introduced herself as Bella. She asked what Jet would like – wine, cocktails, soda or water, food. Jet's stomach growled as she realized that she hadn't eaten anything since lunch, the empanadas having been left forgotten after the call from the kidnappers. She agreed to a sandwich and water, and the woman left as silently as she'd appeared to prepare her meal.

Sofia and Catalina returned several minutes later. Sofia sat on a different sofa, Catalina beside her.

"Those sick animals beat her," Sofia spat angrily.

"Yes, it looks like they did. Fortunately, it doesn't seem like it's anything that won't heal in a few days."

"I'm going to take her to the doctor first thing in the morning to make sure that's all they did to her."

Jet nodded. "That's probably wise."

JET VI – JUSTICE

Sofia fumed for a few more moments and then snapped back to the present. "So tell me everything."

"It looks like they were planning to ambush me. I managed to get the upper hand and deal with two of them, and got Catalina free before the rest could show up."

"How do you know they intended to ambush you?"

"Both men were carrying guns and knives. As far as they knew, I was an unarmed housewife. What does that sound like to you?"

Sofia shook her head. "I can't believe you were able to escape that."

"Yes, well, it was close, but I surprised them."

"And you were able to subdue them?"

"That used to be my job, so yes, I was able to without too much fuss."

"And the money?"

"Still in the car. They didn't get a penny, so this was all for nothing."

"Good. I hope they rot in hell. I'll be going to the police tomorrow as well as the doctor. There's no reason to keep this secret anymore."

"Well, actually, there might be. I left two bodies in the park."

Sofia's eyes widened and she did a double take, as though she'd misheard. "You...what?"

"They were going to kill me. And Catalina. So I neutralized the threat."

"Neutralized...?"

"They're dead. It was either us or them. I chose them."

"Then it was self-defense," Sofia pointed out.

"Of course. But I have my reasons for not wanting to be in the system, Sofia, so it would be best if that part was left out of this. I'd just tell the police that Catalina was kidnapped, you paid a ransom and got her back, and that you suspect that was what the shootout in the casino must have been about. Let them figure it out from there. No need to mention the attack in the park and complicate matters."

Sofia gazed at her with new respect. "No, I don't see how that would help anything, now that you mention it. And I wasn't even there, so I'd have no knowledge of it if you hadn't told me."

"Which I didn't."

"I understand. Are you...are you okay? No injuries?"

"I got lucky. They didn't. Today the good guys won a round."

Sofia smoothed Catalina's hair. "They did indeed."

Bella returned with a sandwich and a crystal decanter of water on a tray. She set it down on the coffee table in front of Jet and moved to an armoire in the dining room to get glasses. She placed one in front of each of them and poured the glasses three-quarters full. Sofia softly questioned Catalina and then told Bella to make her some food and get her some juice. Jet rose during the exchange and moved to the window to look out over the grounds. The blood drained from her face as she saw headlights turning off the distant road and rolling down the track toward the house.

"Sofia. Do you have any neighbors? Is there any reason three vehicles would be approaching from the road?"

"Three vehicles? No. My parents only have two…"

"Damn. We have a problem. Are there any guns in the house?"

"Guns? I…I think so. In my father's study. I believe he has some hunting rifles."

"Where's the study? Quick."

"This way." Sofia led Jet to the small room.

Jet hurried to the cabinet. Inside were several shotguns and a bolt-action Remington 700 rifle. She quickly pocketed two handfuls of shells and then loaded the box magazine, as well as the only spare she could find, and handed Sofia a box of ammo and held up a shotgun.

"This is a double-barreled gun. This lever opens the breech, see? Like this." Jet demonstrated. "Put a shell into each chamber, like this…" Jet opened the box in Sofia's hands and slipped two into the gun. "Then close it like this." She shut the breech and handed Sofia the heavy gun. "There's no safety on it. You have to cock the hammer on each barrel and then pull the triggers. The good news is it will blow a hole in anyone you fire it at if you're close enough. Now take Catalina and go into the basement and wait there. Lock the door. If anyone but me tries to get in, shoot them, and keep reloading and shooting until there are none left. Do you understand?"

Sofia nodded, numb.

"What about you?"

"I'm going to make them wish they'd never been born. Now go. We're out of time."

Sofia did as instructed and raced to take Catalina and Bella into the cellar. Jet ran to the front door and shut off the lights in the house, plunging the interior in darkness as her cell vibrated. She thumbed it on as she watched the approaching headlights and whispered into the phone.

"Matt, thank God…"

"No, it's not Matt."

Jet started at the female voice. "Who is this?"

"My name doesn't matter. What does is that I have your daughter. Hannah. If you ever want to see her again, you'll tell me where Matt is."

"What are you talking about? Matt's with Hannah," she blurted, instantly regretting it.

"Not anymore. He took a fall from your balcony and landed in the pool."

Jet paused. "What do you want?" she snarled, her tone now completely cold and dispassionate.

"I told you. I want Matt."

"I have no idea where he is. But if you so much as harm a hair on Hannah's–"

"Yeah, yeah. Stop wasting my time. I want Matt, and I'll do whatever I have to in order to get him. Do you understand?"

"Yes. The only problem is I have no idea where he is. Or even if he's alive, if he fell off the balcony."

"If he's dead, I'll know soon enough. But if he's not, he'll get in touch with you, and I need you to tell me when he does. Either that or your daughter won't live to see morning."

"I can't work miracles–"

"I suggest you start. I obviously have his phone. Call me when you hear from him, or she's dead. You have four hours."

Tara hung up.

Jet slipped the phone into her pocket. The vehicles were thirty yards from the gate, and she needed to deal with that immediate threat before focusing energy on the call. She retrieved the two Glocks from her purse and slipped them into her waistband as the first truck rammed the gate, blowing it inward. She used the rifle barrel to shatter one of the living room windows and knelt, thankful that the house was built out of concrete block and not sheetrock – bullets wouldn't penetrate the walls.

Valentine emerged from the *casita* with a shotgun of his own and fired at the last vehicle pulling through the gate, a sedan with four gunmen in it. His shot blew the rear window out and vaporized one of the men's heads. He got off two more shots before automatic weapon fire spat from the bed of the lead truck and cut him down.

Jet squinted, sighted on the driver of the truck through the rifle scope, and fired. A neat hole appeared in the windshield, and she saw the cab explode with a spray of the driver's blood as the head shot found its mark. She slid back the bolt, ejecting the spent cartridge, and chambered another, then fired again, this time hitting the passenger. The truck slammed into the low wall that ran in front of the house and stopped. Jet picked off another shooter in the truck bed as he tried to jump out, then she ran for a different window as slugs pounded into the walls around her, the attackers concentrating their fire on the location of her muzzle flashes.

She kept low and slid one of the dining room windows open a crack, then shot the driver of the second car as it rolled to a stop. The doors opened and four men poured out. She was able to hit one of them before they directed their shooting at her new position. She retreated into the kitchen and, after a split-second appraisal of her plight, cracked the rear door open and slipped into the night, foregoing the illusory safety of the house in favor of maneuverability and stealth as rounds tore into the wood-paneled walls and priceless antiques.

The gunmen were still shooting at any and all of the windows, vindicating her decision to exit, the din that of a pitched battle, the weapons chattering and booming as the shooters brought their full fury to bear on the house. Jet ran to the perimeter wall and climbed over it, the rifle slung over her shoulder, then dropped onto the other side and ran along it until she reached the mangled gate. The men were crouched behind the cars, but now fully exposed to her as they concentrated on the building. Jet knew that all the gunfire would provide a brief window of opportunity where she'd be able to take out the three firing from near the last car in the line without alerting those in front of her.

She swung the rifle off her shoulder and trained the weapon on the nearest of the men, who was firing a submachine gun from beside his motorcycle. The rifle barked, and his head tore apart. She loaded another round, which caught his companion in the throat, then punched a round through the third man's back.

Jet reloaded and ran flat out to the car, praying that the remaining shooters continued to blast at the house. She made it and pulled a gun from one of the dead men's hands – a Steyr TMP that was good for about 850 rounds per minute. She ejected the box magazine, pulled the spare from the gunman's back pocket, and slammed it home before cocking the evil little weapon and peering at where six shooters were still firing, their backs exposed to her, unaware of the threat behind them.

She opened up and stitched the nearest three with a series of controlled bursts, killing them all within seconds. One of the remaining three must have intuited that something was wrong, because he yelled and turned toward her just in time to get four rounds through the chest. The last two dove for the ground, as slugs pounded the side of the truck, and switched their fire to her position.

Her advantage now evaporated, she threw herself down and emptied the weapon at where she was sure they would have landed, and heard a scream as her reward. But the final shooter was smarter and had rolled beneath the truck by the time Jet tossed the machine pistol aside and whipped out the two Glocks, one in each hand. The night was suddenly still, the shooting stopped. She listened for any sign of the last man, her ears ringing from the unsuppressed fire.

Motion stirred near the front fender, and she blasted at it. The ground around her erupted as the gunman fired back. She aimed at the flashes and carefully squeezed off two rounds, more selective this time, and rolled as more rounds shredded the dirt where she'd just been lying. Her foot struck one of the dropped weapons, and she crawled to it, using the dead man's collapsed form for cover. She was about to return the Glocks to her belt when she heard a rustle nearby. She twisted, but she was too late and found herself facing a swarthy-complexioned man in his twenties aiming a gun at her. Their eyes locked, and he pulled the trigger. His gun fired its final round, which struck the dirt so close to Jet's head it parted her hair. She fired a split second later and her slug fared better, hitting him squarely in the abdomen. Her eyes never left his as his pupils contracted to pinpoints from the sudden pain. He dropped his gun, his mouth open as if he was trying to say something but couldn't catch his breath.

Jet sat up, the barrels of both pistols trained on him as his knees buckled. He toppled over in slow motion, both hands clutching his stomach. Even in the dark she could see blood streaming between his fingers, so she held off on firing again. She rose and moved to where he was now crumpled in a fetal position, gasping in agony, and stood impassively over him.

"Who are you?" she demanded, her voice low.

The man struggled to speak. "Luis...sent us..."

"Luis? Who's Luis?"

"Runs…Mendoza…"

"And he kidnapped the girl?"

"Yes…but…gnnn…" He convulsed, unable to finish.

"Where can I find him?" Jet asked, kneeling next to him. "Just so you know, you can survive a stomach wound, although it hurts like hell. It's always a question of time. Tell me where this Luis is located and I'll call an ambulance. Otherwise, you'll be lying here bleeding out as your bowels contaminate your bloodstream, and whenever I get around to calling one, you'll probably die of sepsis over the next day or two – but in pain like you've never imagined."

"He's…got…a building…" He spat blood and then murmured an address.

"Why did you kidnap my daughter?"

The man's fluttering eyes were genuinely puzzled.

Jet decided to try a different approach. "Who's the woman who called me just now?"

"Who? I…I don't…know…"

"Why is she after my boyfriend? She says she kidnapped my daughter."

"I…maybe…Luis…guests…foreign…"

"Is one of those guests a woman?"

"I…think…"

Jet ran her hands over the man's jacket and found another Glock – which seemed to be the mandatory weapon for Luis' thugs. She rose and moved cautiously to the other bodies. One other gunman was still alive, holding his throat as if he could stop the bright flow of arterial blood with his hand. He'd dropped his weapon several feet away and was lying in a red pool, so no threat, but she still frisked him, removing a fourth Glock as a trophy before she turned with the weapons and walked to the entry door.

She set all but one pistol on the dining room table, which had been shattered in three places by stray rounds, and moved to the rear of the house, where the door to the cellar stood locked. She knocked, taking care to do so from the side in case Sofia's frazzled nerves had her shooting at the slightest sound.

"Sofia. It's me. Open the door. It's over."

Several seconds later the sound of a bolt sliding free greeted her. Sofia pushed the door open, the shotgun clenched in her hand, her knuckles white – and thankfully, her fingers not on the triggers. Jet nodded, maintaining eye contact, and took the weapon from her, easing the hammers back into place so the gun wouldn't go off accidentally.

"Is it safe?" Sofia asked, her voice hushed.

"For the time being. But the house is going to need some repairs…"

Bella joined them with Catalina in tow and they moved into the living room, Sofia's expression of shock at the destruction not unexpected after several hundred rounds had been fired through the windows.

"Oh…my God…"

"God has very little to do with this."

"And the gunmen?"

"Dead. Except for one or two. You need to call the police and get ambulances out here. And Sofia… Valentine didn't make it. He got at least one of the bastards, though."

Bella's face fell and tears streamed down her face as she absorbed the news, her eyes roaming over the walls, bullet holes everywhere. Sofia was about to say something when lights washed over the room through one of the gaping windows. Jet moved to the side of the window and peered out at the drive, where several SUVs were pulling through the gate.

"Sofia. Hit the lights. This isn't finished."

"But…"

Jet pulled the Glock from her waistband and held it at the ready.

"Do it. Now."

Chapter 18

Sofia switched off the lights and the house plunged back into darkness. Jet moved to the dining room and grabbed two more Glocks, sliding one into her waistband, leaving one gripped in each hand. She ran in a crouch to the nearest window and stopped, peering out into the darkness for several seconds before turning to Sofia.

"What kind of cars do your parents and their bodyguards drive?"

"Toyota Land Cruisers. Both white."

Jet relaxed and tossed the weapons back onto the table. "False alarm, then. It's them. Better tell them what happened before one of the bodyguards starts shooting at us."

Sofia turned the lights back on and strode to the entry door, her eyes lingering on the damage the torrent of bullets had done to almost every surface. She pulled the heavy wooden slab wide and gasped when she saw the three vehicles parked there, corpses strewn around them, her parents' security men standing by their SUVs with their weapons drawn.

She raised her hands over her head and took a cautious step onto the porch. "Dad? Mom? It's me. Sofia. Carlos, it's Sofia. It's okay. They're all dead."

Carlos, a tall man with a fighter's build, thick black hair, and a serious expression, was the most senior of the bodyguards and had been with Sofia's parents for a decade.

"Sofia! What happened?" Carlos called. "Step out here so I can make sure nobody's holding a gun on you."

"Okay. Just don't shoot me." Sofia walked down the stairs, keeping her hands in the air. "Better?"

Carlos slowly lowered his weapon and the other two bodyguards did the same. He glanced at the bodies on the ground and made a hand signal to the other vehicle. The door of the second Toyota opened to reveal an older man with gray hair gelled straight back off his regal forehead, wearing a double-breasted navy blazer and wheat slacks.

"Sofia!"

"Papa!" she said and ran to him. They embraced, then he held her at arm's length.

"What is this? Are you all right? And Catalina?"

The passenger door opened and Sofia's mother stepped out of the truck, managing to look glamorous even in a sweater and khaki pants as she rounded the front fender to hug her daughter.

Sofia shook her head. "Everyone's all right. These men were part of the kidnapping ring." She told them what had happened. "They came to finish the job."

"But how? How did you…"

"I didn't. My friend Rebecca did."

"Rebecca?"

"Yes. We wouldn't be alive if it wasn't for her. None of us. She got Catalina back, and she killed these men. Single-handedly."

Her father took in the bullet-riddled vehicles and contorted forms of dead men. He scowled. "A woman did all this?"

Jet appeared in the doorway, brushing dirt off her sleeves as she eyed the new arrivals. "Not all of it. Valentine gave his life protecting us." She descended the three stairs from the porch and approached the group. "I'm Rebecca."

Sofia's mother stood, apparently unsure of how to respond to the apparition of the woman who'd saved her daughter's and granddaughter's lives, and then hugged her in a burst of emotion while her father looked on, his face somber.

"Rebecca used to be in law enforcement…" Sofia started.

Jet nodded. "That's right. And I got very lucky with your hunting rifle. I was able to flank them."

Her father's eyes narrowed. "Lucky, eh? How many men were there?"

"Looks like they sent a dozen," Jet said.

"And you were able to defeat them with my rifle?"

"Not all of them. I got my hands on one of their machine guns, which made it a more even fight." Jet paused. "I'm afraid your house is a mess, though."

Sofia's father glanced around at the carnage. "I thought I'd seen everything in my army days, but this…this…defies description."

Jet frowned and lowered her voice. "I'm afraid I have bad news for you. I questioned one of the survivors. The man behind this is some kind of local criminal boss. A thug named Luis. I don't think there's any way he's going to stop coming for Sofia." Jet paused. "I don't know why, but look around you. He planned to flatten the place, and her with it."

Sofia cut in. "My father's a senator. He can get the army mobilized if he has to."

"That's not going to work. A man like that will have contacts everywhere. There's only one way to deal with him," Jet countered. "A surgical preemptive strike."

Sofia's father eyed her and moved away from them. Jet took several steps as well and waited. "You have something in mind?" he asked.

"Yes. But you need to know something I just learned. My daughter was kidnapped tonight while I was saving Catalina."

Sofia overheard, and her expression changed to shock as she rushed forward. "What? Hannah? No."

Jet nodded. "I've got powerful reasons to want to take Luis down, and do it before there's any word on the street about this mess. My daughter's life depends on it."

Sofia's father nodded. "What can we do to help?"

"For starters, I was never here."

He cleared his throat. "Fair enough. Valentine fought the good fight, as did my daughter."

"And there has to be a complete communications blackout, even within the police force, for at least the next few hours. Until morning, preferably."

"That's easy. I know the chief of police. One phone call handles that."

"There can't be any leaks," she warned.

"It will be arranged. What else?"

"You should get a small army here, just in case."

"Done." He regarded his daughter. "Would you excuse us, Sofia?"

"Of course, Papa," she said, returning to where her mother was standing, surveying the slug-pocked walls in shock.

He waited until she was out of earshot and leaned in to Jet. She could smell his cologne, which was undoubtedly expensive, as was everything about him. "What can we provide you with, young lady? Name it. Whatever you can think of, it's yours."

"I don't need anything. I'll take some of the weapons they brought. That's it." Jet hesitated and her eyes darted to Tomás' car. "Oh, and your five hundred thousand dollars is in the trunk of the Mercedes."

Sofia's father shook his head and studied her untroubled expression with amazement. "I…don't think I've ever met anyone like you in my entire life."

"You've been lucky."

Jet's phone vibrated. She excused herself to take the call, moving to the corner of the house as she thumbed the line to life.

"Hello?"

Matt's voice echoed on the line. "We've got a serious problem."

"Matt! You're alive!"

"Barely. I've got a broken arm, and my bruises have bruises. But I'm ambulatory." He sounded worked, but his usual self, she thought with relief.

"Where are you?"

"I was just released from the hospital half an hour ago. That's not important. Listen to me. I was attacked at the apartment."

"I know." She paused. "They got Hannah."

"What?"

"They took her. Who are they, Matt?"

"CIA-affiliated black ops. Arthur's colleagues must have traced me somehow – I would have thought that was impossible, but with technology changing daily, I guess you never know." Matt hesitated. "The woman heading the team…we have some history. She's the best they've got, and completely ruthless. If she's got Hannah…"

"She called. She wants me to do a trade. You for Hannah."

"That bitch. I can't believe–" He explained his history with Tara, culminating in the attack and his interview with the police, whom he'd fed a story about an attempted robbery of the apartment.

"She's working with the gang that kidnapped Catalina, Matt. I know where their headquarters is." She told him about Luis' warehouse and described the battle she'd just fought at Sofia's parents' estate. Matt took it all in without comment. When Jet was done, an uncomfortable silence hung on the line.

"What are you planning to do?" he asked softly.

"What do you think?"

"I'll help you."

"With a broken arm, after a five-story fall? Are you kidding me?"

"I can still hold a gun."

"No offense, sweetheart, but you're a liability now. I can't afford a liability. I'll have one chance to take these scumbags out, and it's got to go flawlessly."

"You don't know Tara."

"She doesn't know me."

She could practically hear him scowl through the phone. "I can't let you do this alone."

"Matt. Listen to me. I need you to think for a second. I appreciate that you want to help, but I don't need any. I'm going to find this Luis and wipe the floor with him. And I have very little time to do it. He's working with Tara, and she's got Hannah, so every second I delay is another that this psychopath could be hurting her." She sighed. "I don't want to argue, okay? Just please stay out of it and I'll call you when I'm done."

"You can't take on a mob stronghold by yourself."

Jet surveyed the drive, a sliver of tangerine moon rising in the sky, the bodies of dead men lying everywhere, the vehicles shot to pieces, Sofia's parents standing by the bodyguards, whose weapons were still clutched in their hands. She smiled humorlessly.

"Wanna bet?"

Chapter 19

The wind off the Andes had increased, carrying with it a chill redolent of year-round snow and wet stone chasms, and it rocked the Land Rover as Jet accelerated onto the highway back to Mendoza. Six minutes into her drive, she passed a line of police vehicles racing in the opposite direction. Sofia's father had sworn to run interference for her until she could either complete her errand, or die in the process. On the passenger seat beside her was an Uzi one of the gunmen had been using, three spare magazines, and two of the Glocks, now reloaded, a spare mag for each in her pocket.

She had no idea what she'd be walking into at the industrial building that Luis used as a headquarters, but she was confident that whatever it was, she'd prevail, as she had so often before. This time the stakes were as high as any mission she'd ever embarked upon, and she would not fail. Luis was as good as dead, as was the elusive Tara, who was going to learn before the night was through that she'd taken on far more than she'd bargained for.

At least Matt is in one piece, she thought. Although it was more than obvious to Jet that their idyllic life together in Mendoza had come to an abrupt end and they'd need to get out of Argentina immediately if they wanted to be safe.

The off-ramp to the industrial area where Luis' compound was located was dark, the streetlights nonfunctional. Graffiti covered the light poles as well as every visible section of gray concrete embankment. Squat homes, tiny rectangles of brick with iron bars crisscrossing the windows, lined the road. The cars parked in front were relics, most of them rusting heaps from the sixties and seventies. As she continued on, the neighborhood degraded, until she crossed a small river and was among the warehouses and office buildings.

Jet parked several blocks from the building and studied the approach – a desolate thoroughfare plunged in gloom, no sign of life other than a few lights brightening her target's grimy windows. She slipped the Glock into her waistband and shouldered the strap of the Uzi, taking care to pull the windbreaker she'd borrowed from Sofia's father over it as a cover. That was one of the positives of the small size of the submachine gun, the negative being that its effective range was only two hundred yards.

Jet was the only person on the street, not surprising given the hour and the district. She crossed to the block next to Luis' building, sticking to the shadows along the other properties, her rubber soles soundless on the concrete.

A furry black form shot from a crevice and ran across her path followed by another, larger animal, startling her. She realized it was a rat being chased by a cat even as her finger found the gun's trigger. She forced her breathing back to even, her pulse throbbing in her ears. Up at the next block she saw a cloud of smoke drift lazily from the front of Luis' building, where two men were standing, their cigarettes a giveaway to their position – for which Jet was thankful, because it not only told her where the guards were, but also meant they weren't expecting trouble.

Jet turned the corner and rounded the block, taking her time on the perimeter, watching for more guards but seeing none. A frontal approach was to be avoided given her army of one, so she was depending upon stealth to penetrate Luis' defenses. She studied the concrete wall running along the sidewalk. Spray-painted gang tags marred nearly every inch and it was topped with barbed wire. After confirming that the large, flat-roofed, single-story structure beyond the wall was Luis' building, a tentative plan gelled. It would be a difficult way to get in, but she'd done harder.

She stopped at the base and listened. Every nerve was raw, on high alert for any evidence of movement on the other side – dogs, a patrol, a lone guard. Several minutes of complete quiet convinced her that there was nothing there. After adjusting the submachine gun strap so it was secured to her back and rolling up the windbreaker and stuffing it partially into her pocket, she ran toward a large tree growing along the sidewalk no more than seven feet from the wall. Momentum carried her several yards up the trunk and she pushed off with her right leg, propelling herself higher as she spun in midair, arms stretched above her head.

Jet hit the wall hard, which nearly knocked the wind out of her. Her fingers locked onto the top with a vise-like grip and she used the energy from the jump to bounce upwards. At the top of the wall, balancing like a gymnast, she whipped the windbreaker free and draped it over the coils of barbed wire. After a long glance at the inky ground on the inside of the compound, she shifted the gun to her chest and hoisted herself over the razor-sharp metal before dropping to the ground, tucking and rolling as she landed.

She was on her feet in seconds, the Uzi in her hands, scanning the yard. No alarms sounded, no gunfire erupted from the darkness, no warning cries echoed through the grounds, so part one of her incursion had gone as well as could be hoped.

Jet edged along the brick surface of the warehouse, peering into the gloom as she took cautious steps, weapon at the ready. Three-quarters along the building's rear, she came to a single steel door, its knob marred with a dusting of corrosion. She tried twisting it, but the deadbolt above it was locked. She eyed the keyhole and reached into her pocket, pausing to listen before setting the gun down next to her and kneeling, two primitive lock picks fashioned from hair pins in her hand.

Thirty seconds of work and the deadbolt opened with a soft click. She replaced her picks and retrieved the submachine gun, senses tingling as she readied herself for the most difficult part – locating Luis in a building that occupied the better part of a block. The interior would be black as pitch, judging by the few high, barred windows near the roofline.

When she pushed the door open, a klaxon sounded in the cavernous space. Any thoughts of subterfuge fled as the intrusion alarm alerted the occupants that the building had been breached. As expected, the interior was shrouded in darkness, the only illumination the moonlight filtering through the grimy glass above her head. She worked across the warehouse floor, dodging pallets heaped with wooden crates, aware that she had only moments before she was attacked by guards. Across the expanse glimmered a bar of light below what she assumed was a door. She ran toward it.

As she neared the door, it swung wide and the silhouettes of three men appeared. Jet didn't hesitate. She squeezed off burst after burst at the men, the chatter deafening in the warehouse. The lead man jerked like a marionette as her rounds slammed into his torso, his scream dying on his lips as he tumbled to the floor. The men behind him fired at her, but she stayed in constant motion and their pistols were no match for the stream of death issuing from the Uzi. The second grunted as a bullet thudded into his chest and the third was turning to run when her slugs cut him down with a cry. She paused, ears ringing from the gunfire and, seeing no more gunmen, continued to the door, where one of the bodies had blocked it from closing.

A shotgun's baritone boom sounded from down the brightly lit hallway. A chunk of cinderblock tore from the wall she'd been standing near an instant before she threw herself to the ground. She used the corpses for cover as she brought her weapon to bear on the shooter, who was leaning around a corner, into the hallway, the gun barrel pointing at her even as he pumped another cartridge into the weapon. She fired two bursts where she calculated his torso would be, watching with satisfaction as her rounds ripped through the sheetrock, and thanked providence that the construction wasn't concrete throughout the complex. The shotgun dropped to the ground, followed by the man's inert form. She waited for more shooting and, when it didn't come, ejected the magazine and slapped a fresh one in place before rising and running down the hall in a half-crouch.

The downed gunman's breath burbled in his throat as he struggled for air, his inhalations choking him. Jet ignored him, toeing the shotgun well out of reach before she continued down the hall toward a set of double steel doors. She made it three-quarters of the way when they burst open and four more men filled the doorway and began firing. Jet's submachine gun burped as she dived for the ground, the walls around her shredding from the gunmen's bullets, the whistle of near misses in her ear as she dropped.

She hit the cement and rolled, all the time firing at her assailants, and watched two of the men slam back into their companions as her shots pounded into them. One of the survivors had the presence of mind to duck, almost avoiding her fire. She lowered her aim. He screamed as three of her rounds blew half his face off. She squeezed the trigger, the last gunman in her sights, but her weapon clicked, empty. The final shooter drew a bead on her as she whipped the Glock from her waist and fired four shots in rapid succession. Two of the slugs struck him in the chest as he fired, his rounds missing her by a hair's breadth as she continued to roll.

At a final shot from her weapon, the top of his head disappeared in a spray of bloody emulsion. He tumbled backward and Jet scrambled to her feet as she felt for another magazine and slammed it home in the Uzi, dropping the spent one on the floor next to her as she sprinted for the doorway.

She found herself inside another warehouse, this one with illumination from overhead fluorescent lights in metal housings high above, and she ran through it, gun at the ready in front of her. A large office occupied most of the far corner. The door flew wide and automatic weapon fire opened up on her as she sprinted nearer. She lunged behind a forklift as slugs pounded into the metal housing. When the shooter paused, she fired her own volley at him from the cover provided by the engine. More of his bullets ricocheted off the steel before one of her rounds caught the gunman and he went down, his gun clattering against the cement slab as he fell.

The siren continued to blare as she emerged from behind the forklift and approached the door. Once near it, she ducked to the side and grabbed a pair of coveralls from a nearby rack and threw them across the doorway. Four shots sounded from within the office but she held her fire, preferring to let the occupants come to her.

Ten seconds stretched into a full minute, then the sound of running footsteps approached from the other side of the warehouse. Two men wielding pistols materialized from near the huge metal cargo door. She cut them both down before they had a chance to get off a shot. A gun barrel poked from the office – she sprayed the enclosure with the remainder of her magazine. An older man fell through the doorway onto the warehouse floor, his face contorted in agony, his shirt soaking through with blood. Jet waited to see whether anyone else appeared and, when no further threats presented themselves, she approached the office, her Glock in hand.

A quick scan of the interior revealed no other occupants. She knelt by the dying man.

"I'm looking for Luis."

The man's lips worked, but no sound but a rasp came from his mouth. Jet tried again.

"Where is he?"

The man's eyes swiveled to the side, glazed with pain. He said one word before shuddering and lying still. Jet rose in a fluid motion and headed for the door. She led with the barrel of the Glock, holding it in a two-handed grip, keeping low in case there were any more heroes that wanted to take her on. Out of the corner of her eye, she saw the iron stairway to the roof in the far corner. She ran silently, another sound now cutting through the siren – the whump of rotor blades beating the air above her on the other side of the steel roof door.

She was up the flight of stairs in seconds. When she threw the door open, she wasn't surprised by the gunfire that pummeled the doorframe. She waited until it waned and rolled out onto the roof, firing at the figure crouched thirty yards away as a helicopter dropped from the sky. Another shot echoed off the slab. She fired four times and was rewarded for her marksmanship when the shooter fell against the roof, his pistol tumbling uselessly from his wounded arm.

Jet approached and kicked the weapon away as the helicopter touched down, the area too dark for the pilot to be able to make them out. Jet nudged the man, who was holding his shoulder where one of her bullets had shattered his scapula.

"Luis, I presume," she said. The man's eyes opened and regarded her with a combination of fear and fury. "Where's my daughter? Where's Hannah?"

Luis appeared to not understand the question, so she put her foot on his chest and pushed. He screamed as a lance of pain seared through him.

"Where is she?" she repeated.

"I don't know…what you're…talking about…"

"The woman took my daughter. You're helping her. Where is she?"

"I…woman?"

Jet regarded him, noting the recognition in the last word. "That's right. The woman. A foreigner. She took my daughter. Where is she?"

"I…don't…know…"

"Do you want me to shoot your other shoulder? I will. You've caused me a lot of trouble today…"

Luis looked terrified. "No… Please. I don't know anything about her."

"Yes, you do. Your men said you were providing her with help."

Luis nodded. "That's right. But I…I don't know her."

"How did you get tangled up with her?"

"My boss. Dante…Caravatio. In Buenos Aires. Said I…was to…help…her."

He screamed as Jet increased the pressure on his chest.

"Last chance. Where is she?" Jet demanded.

The top of Luis' skull vaporized as a single dum-dum round blew it apart. Jet spun and found herself facing Tara, who was holding Hannah, a pistol against her head. Her daughter's face was a mask of terror.

"Drop the gun. Now. Or she's dead. I'm only going to give you one chance," Tara warned, her voice cold as the grave.

Jet wavered and then dropped the Glock to her side, her eyes locked on Hannah's. She slowly raised her hands. "Now what?"

"Now you tell me where Matt is."

"I don't know where he is."

"Liar."

"I really don't," Jet insisted.

"I'm about two seconds from shooting your daughter to pieces, just for fun. I was thinking we can start with her feet. Is that how you want this to play out?"

"No. I swear I don't know where he is!" Jet's voice sounded panicked for the first time.

Tara moved away from the doorway, her gun still at Hannah's head, and dragged the little girl toward the helicopter. "That's a shame. She might have been a brilliant ballet dancer or ice skater. It'll be hard to do that hobbling on stumps because Mommy's a liar."

Jet shook her head. "I really have no idea where he is. You have to believe me."

"Say goodbye to your foot, sweetie," Tara said, her eyes narrowing as she neared the chopper.

"Hold it right there," Matt's voice called from the doorway. Tara's attention swiveled to Matt, who slowly emerged, a pistol trained on her, his left arm in a sling, the plaster of the cast a ghostly white in the moonlight.

"Well, well. Isn't this sweet," she said.

Jet took advantage of the momentary lapse by scooping up her weapon and drawing a bead on Tara's head. Tara glared hate at Jet. "If you don't lower that weapon, now, I'm going to blow the little girl's brains all over this roof."

"Tara, you don't have any business with her. It's me you want, not the kid. Let her go," Matt said, refusing to lower his pistol.

"You're really trying my patience. Put the gun down, now, or she's dead."

Matt glanced at Jet, who had Tara in her sights, and then stepped from the doorway and placed his pistol on the roof beside him. "Tara, let's not make this ugly. I'll come with you. A swap. Me for the girl."

Tara appeared to consider his words before nodding. "That seems fair. Now tell Mama Bear over there to drop her gun and we'll be in business."

"That's not going to happen. I want my daughter back. I'm not going to let you shoot us," Jet called across the roof. "Matt, you can't do this."

Matt shook his head. "And I can't let Hannah pay any more than she already has. This isn't your fight." He took a few cautious steps toward Tara. "Here's what we'll do. You release the girl; I'll come to you. You keep your gun on me, and her mom will keep hers on you. If you keep your word, nobody gets hurt. You shoot at the girl or her mom, she'll kill you." Matt looked to Jet. "Take cover. Now."

Jet moved to the doorway and disappeared into the darkness. Her voice called out from inside. "Fine. Let's do it."

Tara moved to the helicopter and stood by the nose. "I'm taking cover here. Same deal. Anyone shoots at me, the girl gets it."

Matt nodded. "All right. Everyone just stay nice and calm. Tara? Let her go. I'll walk to your position. Hannah? You go to Mommy, okay?"

Hannah appeared petrified, but then she nodded her head.

Matt tried a half-hearted smile. "Hannah, sweetie, listen to me. Don't run. You come meet me in the middle, okay? Just come on." Matt began walking toward the helicopter. Hannah started slowly, but then picked up her pace as she neared Matt. They stopped between the helicopter and the doorway, where Matt knelt and gave her a long hug. Hannah was crying as Matt held her tight. "Be brave for me, okay, honey? I love you, Hannah. Be a brave girl."

"Enough with the soap opera. Get over here, Matt. I'm tired of waiting," Tara snapped.

Matt gazed into Hannah's eyes. "Run straight to Mommy. Don't turn around, and don't slow down, no matter what you hear, okay?"

Hannah nodded.

Matt stood. "This looks like the end of the road," he called. He turned and watched as Hannah ran toward the doorway.

"Matt, get your ass over here, or I'll pop a cap in her for target practice. You know I'm serious," Tara threatened.

"Yeah, I know." Matt took long strides toward Tara's position, his one good arm held aloft. "Hold your horses. I'm not going anywhere."

Tara held her pistol on him as he approached. "Nothing tricky, lover man."

"I don't have anything. I'm clean."

"I'll be the judge of that. When you get here, face the helicopter, legs spread. Nice and easy, all right?"

Matt nodded. "You got it."

Hannah was shuddering, gasping for breath as she reached the doorway, where Jet crouched inside, her pistol unwavering on Tara – a difficult shot at almost fifty yards, but not the most impossible she'd ever made. Hannah threw herself at her mother. Jet took her in her arms, her eyes never leaving the helicopter, where Matt had just arrived and rounded the cabin, now out of sight.

Tara moved behind the chopper, so she evaded Jet's wrath. Matt had used their agreed-upon code in his last words – the end of the road signaling that she wasn't to interfere, and that he was to be considered lost to her.

Only Jet had no interest in playing that game. Tara wanted the diamonds. Matt had his ten million worth in a vault in Buenos Aires, at one of the largest banks in the capital, so that would be where they would be going. Of course, Tara couldn't know that Jet had fifty million in stones, nor would she know her background, so that gave Jet two advantages – with the third being that she knew which bank they'd ultimately have to go to.

Jet watched as the helicopter lifted from the rooftop and rose into the night sky, the whine of the rotor and the roar of the turbine deafening, even over the sound of the siren in the warehouse. She watched it drift over the city, fading into a dot, just another in the glittering constellations in the night sky.

"Come on, Hannah. Let's get out of here. Now. Close your eyes and grab my neck while I carry you, and don't open them until I say it's okay."

Jet lifted her, gun clutched in her right hand, and Hannah complied, her eyes screwed shut as she sobbed. Jet came down the stairs into the warehouse and moved along the wall toward the entry, ignoring the bodies, keenly aware that she was racing the clock now to escape with her daughter before the police got there and all hell broke loose. She arrived at the entry and paused, remembering the two guards smoking outside. What were the odds they wouldn't have been among those who had rushed her downstairs? Slim, she thought, with Luis' life on the line – and Matt had been able to get in, so there was little chance they'd survived.

She pushed open the steel door next to the loading dock and peered out. Nobody there. After listening for a few seconds, she edged outside and shifted Hannah the better to be able to maneuver the gun and hurried across the pavement to the door in the perimeter wall. Jet swung it wide and slipped through it. She took off at a dead run, Hannah clutching her like flotsam following a shipwreck, and was rounding the corner when the first police cars screeched to a halt in front of the warehouse gate, a ghost disappearing into the night, leaving no trace other than a trail of the dead and dying and faint rust-colored footprints memorializing her passage in blood.

Chapter 20

Jet loped along with a fluid stride as she melted from shadow to shadow on the way back to the Land Cruiser. More sirens pierced the air as she moved and Hannah's little arms hugged her for dear life. Only once they were halfway back to the car did Jet tell her to open her eyes and, when she did, Jet could see the worry and uncertainty in her gaze, even as her tears dried on her face, reservoirs of sadness exhausted.

The Glock rubbed against the base of her spine as she ran, her breathing easy, practiced. When they arrived at the car, she strapped Hannah into the back seat and slid behind the wheel. The big V8 cranked over with a muted rumble and she eyed the empty street one final time before easing the SUV onto the road, away from the warehouse and its carnage.

She checked the time and saw that two hours had passed since she'd left Sofia's parents' estate – barely enough time for the forensics team to have done their cleanup. But she had no other options than to return. The apartment wasn't safe, Sofia's house was still a question mark and the only people she could rely on for help were Sofia and her father, who'd made it clear there was no limit to what he was prepared to do out of gratitude for saving his daughter's and his granddaughter's lives.

Jet keyed in the phone number Sofia had given her and waited as the phone rang. Sofia picked up on the sixth ring, sounding exhausted.

"Yes?"

"Sofia. It's me."

"How…how did it go?"

"I was able to rescue Hannah."

"That's wonderful! Congratulations. You must be so relieved!"

"I am. But I have another problem."

"What?" Sofia asked, sounding cautious.

"I need you to watch Hannah for a little while. A day, at most."

"Of course. But what's wrong?"

Jet gave her sparse details about Matt. Sofia was silent when she finished. When she spoke, her voice sounded stronger.

"My parents have a vacation home, smaller, six kilometers from the estate. They're there now with Catalina. I told them I'd stay here until I heard from you. We should meet up there. This place is a madhouse right now – the police said they would need to be here most of the night and part of tomorrow."

"I'm not surprised."

"I'll give you directions and meet you."

"Sofia…is it safe? Are you sure that if anyone got it into their head…"

"Nobody knows about it, and my dad called in additional security. It's probably the safest place in Argentina at the moment." Sofia gave Jet the address and instructions on how to get there. "I can be there in half an hour."

"That's perfect."

Jet hung up and thought about what she needed to do. She would only have one opportunity to save Matt and it would involve traveling to Buenos Aires and arriving before the bank opened. That Tara and Matt would be going to the bank was a certainty, and Jet's money was on them doing so immediately – which meant nine a.m., or in roughly six hours. How she would get across the country and into position was only part of her problem – she'd also need logistical support once there, including weapons and transportation.

But first she needed her daughter to be in a safe place so she could concentrate on taking Tara out before she could discover that Matt only had a handful of the diamonds she was after – at which point she'd probably kill him, torturing him first to learn the whereabouts of the rest of the stones. An unthinkable outcome, and one that only Jet was in a position to prevent.

The road to Sofia's estate was even more rustic than the last one, the inky vineyards on either side rushing past as she drove further from civilization, the air heavy with the smell of wet earth and condensation. The moon bathed the landscape in an eerie pale light, lending it an otherworldly quality, as foreign to her as any she'd seen. Hannah sat quietly in the back seat, her eyes heavy as they bounced gently along, and Jet felt a stab of regret at having to leave her with Sofia, if even for only a few short hours. After a lifetime apart, it seemed that circumstances conspired again to separate them, a state of affairs she found intolerable, albeit necessary. Jet made a mental note to make Tara pay for that too.

She watched the odometer and, when she'd come six kilometers, she spotted a road, barely more than a footpath, between rows of grapevines and stretching into the night. She'd been checking her rearview mirror religiously and was confident she wasn't being followed – that mistake had been a costly one and she wouldn't tolerate any more sloppiness on her part. Careless slips could be the difference between surviving the next hours, and not.

She arrived at an iron gate and coasted to a stop. Two men with assault rifles materialized out of the darkness with their weapons pointed at her, their faces seasoned with the battle-hardened chiseling that only veterans had. Jet rolled down the window, careful to keep her other hand on the steering wheel where they could see it, and smiled when the first of the pair neared the window, his companion standing several yards away. The red dot of his laser sight danced on her forehead through the windshield.

"I'm here to see Sofia. I'm her friend, Rebecca," Jet said quietly. The man glanced into the rear seat at Hannah and grunted.

"Open the rear cargo door so I can make sure you're alone," he said, his voice flinty, his tone flat. Jet did as instructed and after a few seconds the man returned and nodded to the other guard. "Let her through." He turned to Jet. "Keep going straight. It's about half a kilometer further. Drive slow. Even though I'm radioing ahead, everyone's jumpy, and you don't want any accidents to happen."

Jet nodded and left the window down, the cool air refreshing on her skin.

"Will do."

The gate creaked open on corroded hinges and she drove on, reassured by the guards' demeanor that they were taking their duty seriously. A two-story home appeared on her left, lights on downstairs, the walled entry filled with vehicles. Four men stood by the oversized wrought-iron gate, all with rifles, and all looking well versed in their use. Jet stopped, and the questioning and search were repeated before she was allowed into the compound. She parked next to the Land Cruiser's twin and detected movement to her right as she shut off the engine. Sofia approached, looking frayed, and offered a fatigued smile.

"You found it."

"Yes. The directions were good."

Sofia looked through the window at Hannah. "Hello, darling. You look so sleepy. Come on – let's get you some warm milk and put you to bed."

Jet stepped out of the car, opened the rear passenger door, and unbuckled Hannah, who was barely conscious, the day's events having caught up with her and her body's demands for sleep shutting her down. Jet picked her up and followed Sofia into the house, past two more stern guards with dead eyes and granite countenances.

Sofia's father was standing in the dining room, a glass of wine in hand, regarding them with the patrician superiority of an elder statesman. He nodded in greeting but remained quiet as the two women moved past him and up the wide stairway to the second-floor bedrooms. Sofia helped Jet get Hannah ready for bed after issuing instructions to a housekeeper for warm milk, and soon Hannah was comfortably ensconced in a spare guest bed next to where Catalina slumbered, unaware of the new arrival.

Sofia pulled the door closed, leaving it open a crack, and they walked softly to the stairs and joined her father in the living room, where he was sitting, a bottle of wine open, two empty glasses next to it, his in his hand.

"Please. Sit. Have some wine. This is my private reserve Malbec – I only make a few barrels every year from the oldest vines on a half acre I tend to personally. I find it therapeutic to keep my hand in it, feel the earth between my fingers, prune the vines myself, oversee the crush and the winemaking. You know, before I entered government service, I was a simple farmer, which I still am, at heart."

"Oh, Papa, you've never been a farmer. Or simple," Sofia teased, pouring the two glasses full of the purple wine and handing Jet a glass. Jet took an appreciative sip and smiled.

"This is extraordinary. It's the best Malbec I've ever tasted."

"I'm glad you think so. I was fortunate that year – nature cooperated. I only have a few more of this vintage left, but it gives me nothing but pleasure to share it with my guests. Especially in celebration of good news. Your daughter back, safe. Sofia's–"

"Yes, but, Papa, there's been a wrinkle," Sofia said.

Her father studied Jet, his expression placid. "A wrinkle?"

Jet told him what had happened with Matt, omitting the details of why Tara would want to kidnap him, preferring to leave it at being about money and extortion. When she finished, she sat back, her emerald eyes flashing as she held his gaze.

He set his glass down. "I told you that anything I could do was yours for the asking. It would seem the time to ask is here. Sofia, would you excuse us? You must be tired." Not so much a question as an order, and Jet got a brief insight into what Sofia's upbringing must have been like.

"Oh, of course, Papa. I'll leave you two to your plotting. Rebecca, thanks again for everything. Hannah will be as safe as if she were my own daughter. I promise." Sofia rose and moved to the stairs, taking her wine with her. When she was out of earshot, Sofia's father took another drink of his wine.

"What can I do for you?"

"I need to get to Buenos Aires."

He nodded. "Yes, it sounds like it. I'll make a call and see about having my friend's jet ready as soon as possible. Although it could take some time to get the pilot out of bed."

"That would be incredibly helpful of you."

"What else do you need?"

She told him about Dante and Tara's likely objective – the bank, in only a few short hours.

"I could use a few experienced men to help. There's only so much I can do alone."

He studied her. "I find that difficult to believe. But think nothing of it. Again, I'll wake some people up. I know such men."

"I figured you might."

"You are perceptive."

"I'll also need some weapons. And ammunition."

"I would expect so. Tell me what you want and I'll arrange for it."

"I have a Glock 9mm I took off the men who attacked your house, but I could use some more ammo. And a submachine gun. Whatever you can get your hands on."

He stood and carried his wine into the dining room, where his jacket was hanging on the back of an antique chair. He felt in the pocket, retrieved a cell phone, and began making calls. Jet took one more sip of wine and set the glass down in front of her. She stretched and closed her eyes as he held a hushed discussion in the other room. She felt like she hadn't slept for a week. She could feel her legs and arms bruising from her brushes with danger, and her muscles ached from the demands she'd placed on them.

She jolted awake to find the lights dimmed, Sofia's father in the dining room, his calls finished. She glanced at her watch and saw she'd been asleep for almost an hour. Not good, with valuable time slipping away. She rose and joined him at the dining table, where he was now drinking water.

"I took the liberty of allowing you some much-deserved rest. The jet won't be available until six for takeoff, so there's no point in staying awake while you wait for it," he reported.

"You got it?"

"Of course. I also did a little checking. This Dante is a very dangerous man – well known in certain circles, one of Buenos Aires' most notorious gangsters. If the woman is mixed up with him, you can expect her to have infinite resources, especially on his home turf."

"That's what I was afraid of. Then again, it didn't do their Mendoza contingent much good."

"Hmm. I got a report from a colleague at the police. Apparently there was a massacre at a warehouse in town."

"If one lives by the sword…"

"Yes, quite. I just find it remarkable that you have been able to be so…effective, in such a short period of time. I've never seen anything like it."

"Every hunter knows not to get between a mother bear and her cub."

"Indeed. Wise words. But still, remarkable."

"I appreciate all the help. The jet will be a godsend."

"Ah, and the other piece of good news is that one of my relatives will be accompanying you. His nickname's Paco, which is all you need to know, other than that he was a commando with the Argentine Special Forces for years and is now in the private sector providing security. The men here are from his group. I've asked him to take a personal interest in your difficulties, and he assured me that he'd have not only the weapons you need, but himself and four of his top men, at the airport by six. These are serious players, young lady. Hopefully they will be able to narrow your odds."

"That's great news. And what about logistical support on the ground in Buenos Aires?"

"Paco knows everyone. You'll want for nothing."

Jet couldn't help looking at her watch again.

Sofia's father frowned. "You still have several hours. I would advise you to get some sleep. It sounds as though you need it. Don't worry. I'll see to it that you're woken with plenty of time to spare to make the plane. You're half an hour away, so…say, a five o'clock wake up?"

Jet sighed. "That would be perfect."

"You'll find two empty guest bedrooms upstairs at the end of the hall. Take either one. And sleep well."

Jet managed a smile. "You really have thought of everything. I can't thank you enough."

"No, it is I who can't thank you enough." He looked away. "Ah, and I got some unfortunate news from the hospital. Tomás passed away during the night. His injuries were apparently too serious."

"Poor Sofia."

"Yes, although my private opinion is that she'll be better off without him. But still, he was the father of my granddaughter and my daughter's husband, so I'll speak no ill of the dead."

"I'm so sorry to hear about it."

"As am I – mainly for the pain it will cause Sofia. If she is up before you leave, please don't say anything. I'd like to break the news in my own way."

"I understand."

Jet trudged up the stairs, bone-tired but her mind churning. So much had changed in just a few short hours, and would continue to. The reverberations from Catalina's kidnapping continued to cause fallout, like the surface of a still lake after a stone is thrown into it. She understood Sofia's father's dislike for Tomás – he hadn't been the most gracious host she'd ever met – but still, was saddened for Sofia and the grief it would bring.

She crawled under the thick covers in the nearest guest bedroom and was out within seconds of her head hitting the pillow, her sleep restive as her body prepared for the ordeal to come.

Chapter 21

The Gulfstream streaked down the runway, turbines whining as it accelerated and lifted into the sky, the first amber rays of dawn still several hours away. The jet bounced as it climbed, but the passengers didn't seem to notice. Carl and Isaac reclined in the sumptuous leather seats, behind where Tara sat, Matt beside her, his free arm cuffed securely so as not to pose a risk in the air. The pilots were well versed in clandestine missions and didn't question the presence of a captive in the cabin, any more than they questioned the weapons the group brought on board, clearing customs no longer an issue now that they were flying within Argentina.

Matt closed his eyes, his mind working at hyper speed even as his expression betrayed nothing but fatigue. Tara was a sociopath, but she was also brutally logical, which made her uniquely effective at her job. She'd learned to hide her absence of any remorse well, aping those with genuine emotions, having intuited from an early age that others actually felt things even if she didn't.

It had taken Matt over a year to figure out what he was dealing with when they'd been romantically involved and another six months after to understand that there was no changing that particular dysfunctionality, no therapist to see or pills to take. Tara simply didn't have any emotions, other than her consuming sense of self-interest and self-preservation – and a paradoxical sensitivity to rejection that could have made a psychiatrist rich, and no doubt had its roots in her childhood.

None of which changed that she was as dangerous as a black mamba, and held her grudges. Matt had no doubt that hers against him had been festering like an open wound for years – she'd never been dumped by anyone, and when he'd walked away from their pairing, she'd taken it badly. The irony that he'd probably achieved the near-impossible and engendered in her a genuine emotion – albeit the fury of a woman scorned – wasn't lost on him, but it had given him no pleasure at the time, and even less now.

The plane quickly ascended to cruising altitude for the hour and a half trip to Buenos Aires.

Tara turned to Matt and nudged him. "So, did you miss me?"

Matt grunted, not wanting to engage.

"I'm sure you did. Although I see you took up with one of the local peasant girls. How charming."

"I'm taking you to the diamonds, Tara. What more do you want?" he asked, eyes still closed.

"I want you to understand that if you cross me, I'll kill not only you, but that bitch and her kid, too. I'll do it just for practice."

"Doesn't seem like you need any practice killing innocents, Tara. You've always been good at that."

Tara snorted. "Innocents? There are no innocents. There are obstacles and targets and collateral damage."

"Spoken like the woman I'd hoped to never see again."

"You screwed over the wrong people, Matt. That's your bad."

"Yeah, shame on me for not wanting to participate in a global drug-trafficking network being operated off the books from within the CIA."

"No, shame on you for not being smart enough to stay out of things that don't concern you."

"I'd say my country's intelligence service, to which I devoted twenty years of my life, turning out to be the world's biggest drug cartel made it my business."

"That's where you're wrong."

"Whatever, Tara. If you think working as an enforcer for these scum is anything honorable, you're welcome to stay deluded as ever. You're nothing more than an expensive hired killer working for dope dealers."

"Very noble sentiment. So you stole their quarter billion in diamonds…to punish them?"

"No, to help destroy their network."

"Ah. I see. You know Arthur is no longer with us?"

Matt played dumb. "What a shame. I guess Satan had an opening for operations manager, or master of dirty tricks."

"You don't seem surprised."

"He was a parasite. It never surprises me when parasites are killed."

Tara paused. "I never said he was killed."

"He's dead, isn't he? What happened? Did he slip on a bar of soap and hit his head? Fall down some stairs? Have a heart attack?"

"He was killed."

"Like I said, what a shame. The kingpin of an international drug-dealing network was killed. What are the odds? I mean, who knew that could be a dangerous line of work? I'm sure the scarfaced bastard will be deeply missed by whatever cockroaches he worked with. Other than that, the world's a better place."

"Your righteous indignation is touching. But it doesn't change that you took that which doesn't belong to you."

"Ha! Really? That's the moral approach you're taking? 'You stole money that was made by selling addictive poison to children all over the world, so you're a bad man'? You've got to be kidding me."

"You picked the wrong guys to rip off."

"Yeah. Bloodthirsty thugs. Who've hired you to be their hatchet man. Woman. Whatever."

"Who is she?"

"Who?"

"Your friend. The mother of that brat."

"What does it matter? I'm on a plane to nowhere. You're going to kill me as soon as you get the stones. Isn't that how this is going to work?"

"Nice deflection, but you didn't answer my question," Tara said.

"She's a woman I met here. Nothing like you."

"Something tells me you're not being entirely truthful. She laid waste to Luis' crew. I saw the footage from the casino. She's a professional."

"You're not the only one who's ever been in the game, Tara. There are people like us all over the world."

"That's reassuring if I ever want to open a theme bar. But it again dodges my question."

Like a seasoned politician, Matt decided to lie early and often.

"She's ex-SIDE. The Argentine equivalent of the CIA."

"Impressive. I had no idea they were that well trained. How did you meet her?"

"We shop at the same gun store." Matt sighed. "What does it matter? We met. That's it."

Tara studied his face. "If you try to pull a fast one with the diamonds, I'll skin her kid alive and make her watch before I kill them both."

"So you said." He sighed again. "How would I pull a fast one? I already told you. The diamonds are in a box at the bank. By the way, that was impressive in Bangkok. Nice to see that the CIA isn't above bank robbery in foreign countries to get back its ill-gotten gains."

"Thanks. That was my op."

"I kind of figured when I saw you here. How did you track me to Argentina?"

"NSA tap on the bank server. When the president sent you the email, it was child's play to track the IP to Mendoza when you logged in. That narrowed it down."

"And to the bank in Bangkok?"

"You were followed."

"Ah. Low tech. Whoever it was did a good job. I never noticed."

Tara shook her head. "Did you really think you'd get away with it?"

"I can see your confusion. For you, it's all about making away with the diamonds. But that was never my motivation. I wanted to put a bullet in a criminal network, not steal some stones. Because you don't know the difference between right and wrong, you can't imagine what I'm talking about. Besides, I accomplished everything I was trying to do. I crippled the network. Made everyone connected to its life miserable. The diamonds were just a means to that end. Nothing more."

She eyed him skeptically. "Yeah, right. All those millions and you didn't really care about them."

"Hard as it might be for you to believe that people might do something for any reason besides money, that's correct. Although keeping that money out of the cabal's hands definitely gave me a lot of pleasure. But you'll note I'm not living on a hundred-foot boat or in a beachfront villa."

"That's because you're an idealistic fool."

"Perhaps. But looking at you, I'd say it beats the alternative."

"We'll see how you feel about that in a few hours."

"Nothing will have changed. You'll have the diamonds, and you'll have killed me. Other than that, the bad will still be bad, and the good will be good. And you'll still be working for the black hats, doing damage to everything you touch."

She leaned back in her chair. "I'm tired of this discussion. You sound like a broken record. I feel like I'm listening to a cut-rate preacher on some redneck cable channel."

"Always nice seeing you again, Tara. Wake me up when we get there."

Matt closed his eyes again, knowing that when the bank opened the jig would be up. He hoped and prayed Jet would stick to their agreement, which was that if either of them ever used the 'end of the road' code, the other would run, not walk, for safety, and not risk themselves for a lost cause.

Unfortunately, he'd come to know her too well, and his fear was that she'd toss that to the wind and come after him – which knowing Tara, would be the last mistake she ever made.

He took several deep breaths as they winged their way over the pampas and prayed that they would be as sloppy with him as they'd been so far. It was only a slight advantage, but they'd slipped up and, if they didn't realize their mistake, he still had a chance. That kind of blunder was out of character for Tara, but everyone got complacent at times, especially if they believed their mission was almost finished, their goal attained.

Matt shifted, trying to get comfortable, and thought about when he'd make his move. Possibly in the vault, when he and Tara were alone. He'd have to play it by ear.

But her belief that it was all over but the shouting couldn't have been more wrong.

Which, if he had any control over circumstances, she'd soon discover the hard way.

Chapter 22

Jet blinked sleep out of her eyes and rolled over to look at the housekeeper, who had tactfully knocked on the door and then, when she didn't answer, cracked it open and called out before turning on the light. She shook off the grogginess that was a byproduct of only getting three hours of rest and glanced at the time: precisely five a.m., leaving her a half hour to shower, say her goodbyes to Hannah, and gulp down some coffee and breakfast.

The hot spray was like scalding needles against her scalp as she rinsed the prior day's grime from her hair. Had it really been only fourteen hours since she'd been waiting at the zoo with Hannah? It seemed like a lifetime.

She toweled dry, pulled a brush through her hair, and dressed, wasting no time on any further niceties. A floorboard creaked as she walked down the hall to where Catalina and Hannah were sleeping. She grimaced at the noise, slight as it was. Thankfully the bedroom door opened silently, and she stood for several seconds by Hannah's sleeping form before reaching down and softly touching her hair. She looked so innocent and untroubled, a small rivulet of dried drool staining her pillow, unaware that her mother was right beside her.

Downstairs, Sofia and her father were awake in the dining room, watching the early morning news on the television in the living area; a group of angry men were onscreen, holding placards in front of a dark square, the broadcast apparently in real time.

"Good morning, young lady. I trust you got at least a little rest?" Sofia's dad asked, holding up his coffee cup. "Coffee?"

"Yes, please," Jet answered as she moved to Sofia to kiss her cheek. "How are you doing?" she asked her.

"I feel beat, but better now that Catalina's safe. I just hope that Tomás had a good night. I got up early to say goodbye – I wasn't really sleeping, anyway."

Jet caught her father's eye but said nothing, the warning clear in his gaze.

The housekeeper entered carrying another place setting and a cup and saucer, and soon Jet had a steaming cup in hand as she waited for a plate of eggs. "What's on TV?"

"Ah, there's a big strike. Been going on since yesterday. The bus driver's union. It's always something there. As the economy has deteriorated, there's a strike or a protest every week. It's insanity," Sofia said. "All it does is cause gridlock. Nothing changes. I don't know what they expect marching is going to accomplish."

"It's the Argentine way," her father said.

"Has there been anything on the news about...the attack on the house?"

"No, not yet. But there was a breaking report about an industrial site on the outskirts of town. Apparently it looked like a war had been fought there," Sofia said.

"Anything besides that?"

"No, but it's still—"

The program changed to a shot of the outside of the casino, police lights everywhere, and an earnest brunette woman holding a microphone described the scene from the prior day. Sofia's father rose to get the remote, but before he could, the woman announced that everyone in the shootout had died, including an off-duty police officer and his brother. Sofia froze, her mouth working silently, her eyes bouncing from the screen to her father to Jet as though their reassurance could change the reporter's words.

"No. That must be a mistake. It said everyone's dead..."

"I'll contact my friend with the police and see if anything's happened, my love. Don't worry. It's probably just a mistake," her father said.

Jet looked away.

"Call the hospital," Sofia demanded.

"It will be impossible to get a straight answer at this hour."

"Then I'll call," she said, her tone edging toward panic.

Jet rose. "Would you excuse me? I have to use the bathroom." She didn't wait for an answer, preferring to get out of the line of fire. If Sofia's father wanted to mislead her, buying her just a little more peace of mind, then he'd done so, but she didn't want to watch the fallout and certainly didn't want to be a party to the deception. She studied her face in the downstairs powder room mirror and wondered whether she would have done the same thing if it had been Hannah instead of Sofia, and decided she was glad she didn't have to make that call. It was far easier to disapprove of someone else's approach than to have to decide yourself, she knew, and it was far too early in the day to play Solomon.

She gave them five minutes and when she returned Sofia was nowhere to be seen. Her father stood by the ornate stone fireplace, his coffee untouched on the table.

"I was hoping to spare her this. Perhaps I should have told her the truth last night. I only wanted her to get some badly needed sleep before having to face reality…" His voice sounded defeated.

Jet didn't say anything and was relieved when the housekeeper arrived with her eggs. Sofia's father shook his head and his demeanor changed. He looked convinced of the correctness of his actions, as only those accustomed to making difficult choices every day could be.

"The plane is waiting. I called this morning. Carlos will drive you to the airport when you're done with breakfast."

"And the weapons?"

"Taken care of. They're already on the plane."

"Good. I'll be ready in a few minutes."

"I wish you luck. I've spoken to some others about Dante. He's well known to the authorities, but never seems to be targeted by the law directly. His subordinates and businesses, yes, but never the man himself. He has cultivated powerful ties in the Buenos Aires government, obviously, so you'll need to be very careful approaching him."

"That may be true, but my experience is that even the mighty die just the same as the weak and poor."

"I'll defer to your understanding. I have the feeling you have considerably more experience than I'll ever have in that regard."

"It's not something I'm proud of," Jet said, standing.

"Our past is what makes us who we are. You've obviously served some government, and with honor, I have no doubt. You have no reason to be ashamed of your skills. If anything, we all owe you a considerable debt for putting them to good use during this unfortunate episode."

"I appreciate the plane and everything else."

"As I said before, think nothing of it."

"Will Sofia be all right?"

"Of course. She'll need some time to grieve, but she comes from strong stock. Don't worry. I'll see to it that your daughter is cared for as if she were my own."

Jet moved to him and shook his hand, then he walked her to the front door, where Carlos stood talking to one of the guards. When they neared, he turned, nodded to Sofia's father, and motioned for Jet to follow him.

Carlos could have been carved from marble. On the drive to the airport, he didn't say a single word until they arrived, when he gestured to the private charter terminal as they pulled to the deserted curb.

"Manuel will meet you inside. He's one of the pilots. You shouldn't have any issues with security."

Inside the small building, Manuel greeted her with an impassive expression on his face and deferential courtesy. She followed him out onto the tarmac where a Hawker 125 business jet waited, its interior illuminated, its fuselage stairs lowered, awaiting her arrival. Manuel welcomed her aboard as she mounted the steps. Inside, four men looked up at her as she entered the narrow cabin. The oldest gestured at the seat facing him.

"I'm Paco," he said.

"Rebecca."

"Nice to meet you. This is Sergio, Arman, and Roberto." The men nodded. "We're at your disposal," Paco said.

"Great. Who are you?"

"Whoever you need us to be."

"Do you have the equipment we discussed?"

"Of course. For you, a Glock 17 and an H&K UMP40, each with two spare magazines." Paco unzipped a green canvas duffle bag and handed her the pistol and the magazines. "We'll want to wait until we're on the ground and underway before we hand out the rest."

"That seems prudent," Jet agreed, checking the Glock before slipping it into her pocket. "Seriously, though, what's your background? I need to understand your abilities if I'm going to formulate a plan."

"We're all former special forces. Now in private security." He leaned in close to Jet. "I have some history with Dante Caravatio. You could say we go way back. So this will be more enjoyable than my typical job."

Jet's eyebrows raised. "History? Will that be a problem?"

"No. But there's no love lost."

"You'll have to be more specific."

"Once we're in the air," Paco said with a glance at his men.

Manuel closed the fuselage door and took the copilot's seat. Within minutes they were taxiing down the runway before lifting off and banking over Mendoza as they headed east.

"So what's your beef with Dante?"

"Twelve years ago, he was involved in the death of my fiancée."

"Involved? How?"

"Her father had a gambling and drinking problem. It got out of hand. The police suspected that she got in the middle of an altercation between Dante and her father. Both were found, shot execution style, at his home in the Recoleta district. Nobody heard or saw anything."

"How do you know it was Dante?"

"She'd confided in me weeks before that she was worried about her father. She mentioned debts. Dante Caravatio has run Buenos Aires for thirty years. If her father had that big a problem, it would have to have been at the Dante level. We're talking millions."

"Couldn't it have been someone else?"

"It was Dante. One of my friends on the police force said they suspected him – it's his trademark, the execution-style killing, one round to the back of the head. But of course they couldn't prove anything, so no charges were ever pressed." He eyed her. "If your goal involves taking down Dante, I'm your man."

"I don't know that it will necessarily involve him. I only know that he's helping my enemy. A woman. American. She kidnapped my boyfriend and is holding him hostage."

"How are they connected? Dante and this woman?"

"She's a professional killer. Her objective was my boyfriend. She's going to force him to give her the contents of a safe deposit box in Buenos Aires." They hit a bumpy patch of air so Jet waited until it had smoothed out before continuing. "And then she's going to kill him. So we only have one shot at this, and that's at the bank. We need to stop it from happening."

"How?"

"I don't know. My initial thought is we ambush her when they go into the bank."

"Where's the bank located?"

"It's Banco Ramirez Popular."

"The main branch?"

"Yes."

"That's in the heart of downtown. Ambushing anyone there isn't going to be easy. And we'll only have seconds before every police car in Buenos Aires is on its way to stop us."

"That is why I need your help."

"And Dante?"

"He's behind the kidnapping of Sofia's daughter. And he's provided this woman with his full support. He's part of the problem."

"Sounds like it. But he's going to be almost impossible to get to."

Jet fixed him with a cold stare. "Nobody's impossible to get to."

Paco nodded. "True. But he'll be as well protected as a visiting head of state – he's got a lot of enemies."

"There's an old saying. The higher they fly, the harder they fall."

"I'm familiar with it."

"Then why don't you tell me everything you can about the area around the bank? How you would do this if you were running the operation, and what sort of defenses Dante is likely to have, if it comes to that."

Chapter 23

Dawn's pale light warmed the partially cloudy sky over Buenos Aires as the Gulfstream circled the city on approach. The city's vast sprawl stretched as far as the eye could see, countless smaller buildings giving way to myriad skyscrapers jutting into the heavens. In the distance the Rio Plata shimmered as the first of the sun's rays reflected off its sparkling blue surface, the coast of Uruguay barely visible from the plane's windows as it executed a long curve.

The water transitioned to brown as they neared the Jorge Newbery Airport, built on the riverbank just north of the city, close to some of the most expensive homes in the country as well as the most dangerous shanty town south of Rio de Janeiro. Gusts of wind off the river made the final descent bumpy, air pockets causing the plane to seem as though it was freefalling as it closed on the runway, and then the jet was on the ground, decelerating as it reached the midpoint of the long black cement strip and turned toward the private plane terminal.

Tara glanced at Matt, who was staring through the window at the gray outline of the buildings in the near distance, and checked the time.

"Seven twenty. That should give us plenty of time to get to the bank. I checked, and it doesn't open till nine."

"You've obviously never spent a morning in Buenos Aires rush hour," Matt said, his tone sour.

Tara ignored his comment. "When we reach the terminal, I'm going to uncuff you, but if you try anything, we'll use a stun gun, so save us all the drama and play nice."

The plane stopped near the terminal a few minutes after landing. Then they had to wait almost ten for the ground crew to give them permission to deplane. Once the cabin door was open and the stairs lowered, Tara nodded at Isaac, who unlocked the handcuffs while Carl stood nearby with the stun gun, looking like he was hoping Matt would try something.

The air smelled like jet fuel and exhaust and open water. Gusts from the river blew across the open field, carrying with them the dank aroma of the marshes. Tara and her men led Matt to the building, presenting him with his first opportunity to take them – a chance that quickly became obvious was a mirage when he saw an older Argentine man standing near the entry doors with six hard-looking men in overcoats. The man held his arms wide as they neared, a predatory smile on his deeply tanned face.

"Maria. Welcome home," he said theatrically.

Tara moved to him and gave him a kiss on the cheek, then pulled away from his embrace. "Dante. You look wonderful. Something about Buenos Aires is magical for you."

"And you are magnificent, as usual. Although not nearly as convincing a liar as I need in my old age."

"Thank you for meeting us at this early hour. It was unnecessary."

"My pleasure. How could I resist greeting you on one of your infrequent visits? It would be rude, no?"

"I'm touched that you would go out of your way for me."

"As always."

"And I'm sorry about the unpleasantness in Mendoza."

Dante's demeanor changed to a more somber mood. "Yes. I lost many good men yesterday. I'm still trying to ascertain what happened."

"It wasn't my doing, but I still feel responsible. Like I brought misfortune upon you when I touched down."

"It's nothing. I'd been meaning to make some changes there, anyway. Saved me the trouble, although admittedly, in a very messy manner." Dante turned to Matt. "And this is the unlucky object of your attention?"

Matt didn't say anything, preferring to let Tara expend her energy. "Yes. Do you have the vehicle I requested?"

"But of course. With a driver. Are you sure you don't want some of my men to accompany you?"

"That's very generous, but it won't be necessary. I don't want to cause a scene or arouse undue attention." Tara hadn't told him where they were taking Matt, nor would she. Even though Dante was an ally, he was also a scoundrel and she didn't want to chance him getting curious as to why they'd gone to so much trouble to get one man to a bank. The same went for his men – and she'd leave Isaac and Carl in the vehicle so the driver couldn't make a phone call and tip anyone off.

"Ah, well, your business is your business, and you know it well. However you like. The driver has instructions to take you wherever you need to go."

"Excellent. Do you have a private location for me, as we discussed?" She'd asked Dante to line up a deserted warehouse somewhere Matt's tortured screams wouldn't be heard.

"Of course. Extremely remote. You could fire a cannon off inside and nobody would be the wiser."

A cell phone chirped. One of the men murmured into his phone and approached Dante. They had a whispered discussion and Dante turned back to Tara. "I just received a report of a private plane departing Mendoza a half hour after you left. According to the flight plan, it's headed here. My contact says it was a most irregular occurrence, and that the men that boarded looked…professional."

"Really? Well, they're too late, aren't they?"

"Perhaps. But they also had bags they brought aboard while they waited for the final passenger, who showed up shortly afterward. A woman."

Tara's pulse quickened. "Interesting. Do you have a flight manifest?"

"The passengers are listed as the Garibaldi family. Sofia, Hector, and his bodyguards. Hector Garibaldi is a very powerful man with the federal government. But my contact knows him, and he tells me that none of the men on the plane were Garibaldis. So that was just for the paperwork."

"Anything else?"

"Yes. It was a last-minute arrangement. A rush. People had to be pulled out of bed. Apparently it was imperative that the plane leave as soon as possible. It flew in from Córdoba just to make this pick-up."

"Then it's safe to say that it's pursuing us?"

"That's my assumption."

"Can you do anything about it?"

"Yes. I'll arrange for it to be dealt with in a manner that will send an unmistakable signal to Garibaldi to stay out of my affairs, and to avoid crossing me. Ever."

Tara eyed Dante, who returned her gaze with a smile that never reached his eyes. She nodded. "Then I can cross that off my list of things to worry about."

"My dear, you're in my town now. Trust me when I say nothing will happen that I don't want to happen." Dante signaled to Tara to follow him into the terminal. "Come. Your chariot awaits."

Isaac and Carl framed Matt as they made their way through the building to the front entrance, where a line of Land Rovers sat in a row. The first in the line rolled forward. Dante pulled the door open for Tara. "Maria, this is Eduardo. He knows the city like he knows his backyard. You're in good hands."

Eduardo nodded. "A pleasure."

Carl swung the back passenger door open and leaned in to Matt. "You'll sit between us. Make one wrong move and I'll blow your kneecap off."

Matt shook his head. "Little grumpy today, aren't you? Not a morning person?"

"Laugh it up, tough guy. But try anything and you'll find out just how fun I can be."

"I believe you."

Isaac climbed into the rear seat first and Matt followed him, sliding on the leather until he was scrunched next to him. Carl took up position on Matt's other side and closed the door. Tara gave the driver an instruction and he put the car in gear. Dante waved a gloved hand lazily at her before retrieving his cell phone from his overcoat and placing a call as he watched them pull away.

"It's a go."

He punched the line off and moved to his vehicle, his driver waiting patiently to take him to his office for another long day running his criminal enterprise.

కోలా

Lieutenant Hernandez of the Mendoza police department uploaded the security camera footage from the casino and watched the entire attack three times through. When he was done, he froze several frames and increased the resolution until he was able to get passable enhanced stills of the mystery man and woman who had appeared out of nowhere, joined in the brief battle, only to vanish like fog from the surface of a mountain lake at first light. He tapped out a set of instructions, printed the screenshots, then called his superior at home. The captain was an early riser, he knew, and wouldn't want Hernandez to sit on anything due to the hour. When he answered, his voice was alert.

"Captain, we finally received the casino footage."

"Took them long enough," the captain complained.

"Indeed. You'll want to view it for yourself, but we've been thrown a curve on this one."

"What do you mean?"

Hernandez gave him a brief description of the gun battle, ending with the discovery of the man and woman.

"And you say they were both unarmed?"

"Yes. The man took a gun away from a sentry. And the woman took one from a security guard."

"But then they both joined in the shooting…"

"Correct, sir. It makes no sense."

"Have you run them through the databases to see if we get a match?"

"Not yet, sir. I was going to suggest that this changes what we should be looking for at the crime scene. For one thing, we should be trying to get fingerprints from any area they might have left them."

"Good thinking. But obviously it will be hit or miss. That place probably has thousands of prints on any given area, so it's going to be a mélange of smudges, at best. Still, worth a try." The captain paused, thinking. "Put the photos into the system. Let's see if that expensive feature-recognition hardware we got from the Americans is worth anything. Do we have a link with immigration for it?"

"Not that I know of, sir."

"Damn. Well, send it off to Interpol, too. You never know what will pop up. They might not be local."

"Will do. I just wanted to get your approval before I did so."

"You have it. I'll be there within a half hour. Let's plan to look the footage over when I arrive." The captain hesitated. "Have you been there all night?"

"I ducked out for a few hours and got some rest. I'm fine."

The captain cleared his throat. "What a night, huh? I reviewed the call logs from home this morning. Seems like all hell broke loose at once. Another shootout at that warehouse, and the attack on the villa… Have you spoken with the army yet?"

"Yes, sir. They're standing by if we need them on the road, patrolling."

"I hate to get them involved, but I think we'd better. When news of all this hits, the citizenry's going to be justifiably nervous. Seeing that the government's out in force should go a long way to reassuring them."

"That'll be my next call."

"You know that if these are related, we have a real problem on our hands, don't you?"

"Yes, sir. Of course, it's too early to say. But it is suspicious that so much violence has taken place in such a short period. There might be more to this than a failed robbery attempt."

"That occurred to me. Get the photos out into distribution. I'll see you when I get in."

Lieutenant Hernandez entered the information on his terminal for Interpol and pressed send, watching as the large image uploaded, the green progress bar on the interface seeming to take forever. When he was done, he repeated the process in the domestic system and, for good measure, sent it to the Americans as well.

Finished, he sat back in his swivel chair and exhaled heavily, the long hours having taken their toll during one of the most violent twenty-four-hour periods in Mendoza's history. He pushed back and rubbed his eyes, then stood and went in search of another cup of the strong black coffee that was fueling him for his second consecutive day at his station.

Chapter 24

Two men stepped out of the brown Volvo station wagon, each toting a golf bag, one loaded with two Russian-manufactured Igla-S infrared homing surface-to-air missiles and the other with the shoulder-mounted launcher. They had arrived ten minutes earlier after receiving Dante's call and one of the pair was on the telephone with his contact at air traffic control, who was tracking the incoming aircraft as it made its final approach to the airport.

At that hour the inbound air traffic was lighter than usual, with planes landing every five minutes instead of the every sixty seconds the larger international Ministro Pistarini airport saw. Both missiles had been purchased on the black market in Brazil, where the Igla-S was deployed with the military, as it was in Venezuela – those nations preferring the less expensive Russian devices over the more costly, and accurate, American-made Stingers.

The area was deserted, the parking lot of a waterside disco that was a quarter mile from the airport now empty in the light of day, the sins of the prior night washed away by the early morning cloudburst that had hit just before sunrise, passing as quickly as it had arrived. They stopped near a large pile of construction debris that rose in a mound in the next lot and left the Volvo's engine running for a speedy getaway.

"How much time do we have?" Efren, the driver, asked nervously as his partner, Ricardo, listened on the line.

"How long until it's in range?" Ricardo spat into the phone as he set down his bag.

The air traffic controller responded immediately. "It's nineteen miles out. Over the river."

"How many planes ahead of it?"

"One. Commercial. Aerolíneas Argentinas. No way to confuse the two. Watch for that one to land, and then the next one on the same flight path will be your plane."

"Fair enough. This call never happened. Payment will be via the usual method."

"I don't know what you're planning, but I can't have—"

Ricardo hung up, uninterested in the man's nervous warnings – he'd served his purpose, and they had work to do. Efren glanced around the area, confirming they were alone, their only company a few squabbling seagulls near the water and a few uninterested fishermen too far away to be an issue. Ricardo raised a pair of binoculars and studied the sky, then pointed at the pale blue expanse, where white puffs of scattered clouds moved west, driven by the Atlantic wind.

"There. I see it. About nine o'clock."

Efren nodded and pulled one of the missiles from the sack and slid it home, seating it into the launching tube. He hefted it, familiar with devices like it from his years in the military, and grinned. "Keep your eye on the prize. Our baby should be right behind it."

"We're going to have to wait until it's pretty close. The western approach is a problem."

"We'll wait until it's within a couple of miles. Piece of cake."

෯෧

Jet leaned back in her leather seat and gazed out the window at the Buenos Aires skyline in the distance as the little jet did a slow turn over the river and slowed in preparation for landing. Paco shifted next to her, his eyes closed, trying to snatch a few more moments of rest before they were on the ground and he had to perform. Cool air drifted from the overhead vents recessed into highly polished walnut panels. Jet wondered absently what a plane like the one she was on cost to operate annually. She did a quick mental calculation and decided it had to be at least a half million dollars a year, possibly as high as a million. Even with her newfound riches, she couldn't imagine burning money like that.

Out further from the coast, cargo ships steamed south toward the port, carrying the population's necessities as the city went about its business, largely blind to the extent it depended on the sea traffic. She watched as a large ship, probably one of the ferries that departed from near the airport, plowed through the morning waves on its way to Uruguay, and remembered Alan's near miss aboard one, which now seemed an eternity away. An image of his face flitted through her memory and she closed her eyes, sad for his passing but glad for the life she'd built with Matt. You could never go back, she knew from harsh experience, and you had to enjoy the time you had, because there were no guarantees.

She shook off the maudlin mood and directed her thoughts to more productive matters, namely freeing Matt and neutralizing Tara so she could never jeopardize either of them again. Paco had arranged for a vehicle when they touched down, and with any sort of luck, they would be able to get into position at the bank before it opened and thwart whatever Tara had in mind. Jet didn't want to occupy her limited mental bandwidth, made more so by fatigue, with concerns about what they would do once Matt was free again. Maintaining her focus on the task at hand was what her operations discipline had taught her was the best approach and she wasn't about to give in to emotionally driven tangents – especially when Matt's life hung in the balance.

Manuel's voice boomed over the public address system, disrupting her reverie.

"We'll be on the ground in five minutes. Make sure you're strapped in, although I expect a smooth landing."

Paco opened his eyes at the announcement and checked his seat belt, then glanced at Jet as she did the same.

"Almost show time," he said.

"I know. Let's hope they're careless."

"We have the element of surprise."

"In my experience, that can turn on a dime. We can't be complacent."

Paco nodded.

"A philosophy to live by."

❧❦

Ricardo lowered his spyglasses and pointed at the blip in the sky. "That's it. You see it?"

"Of course. What would you guess the distance is?"

"No more than three miles."

"So fifteen more seconds and we're game on."

"I'd say fire when ready."

Efren peered at the plane and shouldered the drab green launch tube, aiming the forty-two-pound device at the distant dot in the heavens. He counted in his head. When he reached ten, he closed his left eye and gently squeezed the trigger.

The missile shot from the tube and streaked skyward, leaving a white smoke trail as it quickly accelerated to eight hundred miles per hour.

☜❧

Paco cried out in alarm when he saw the flash from the ground and the smoke as the projectile tore through space, locked onto their engine heat signature. His yell startled Jet, but she didn't understand what he was trying to warn her about, his words nonsensical to her ears. All she knew was that the color had drained from his face as he craned his neck to look out the window.

One moment Jet was taking a final gulp of water from her plastic bottle and the next the plane jolted violently as the missile exploded near the right engine, blowing most of the turbine to pieces as shrapnel tore through the jet motor and the fuselage. The plane yawed at a sickening angle and a hole in the rear of the plane appeared. Two of Paco's men died almost instantly as shards of metal cut through them.

Then the little jet was spinning as Manuel and his copilot struggled to keep it aloft, the plane in near freefall as it veered toward the surface of the river three thousand feet below. The remaining engine's warning alarm clamored from the cockpit as they dropped, the craft's aerodynamics inexorably altered by the loss of most of the tail section and the sudden absence of power.

Jet barely had a chance to brace herself as the surface raced up to meet them. The nose collided with the river and crumpled with an explosive force that tore one of the seats behind her out of the floor. The hapless young man strapped into it hurtled through the tiny cabin and nearly decapitated Paco before he slammed into the cockpit wall.

And then their forward momentum died and the cabin was nearly filled with icy water. Jet unclasped her seat belt and crawled toward the rear of the plane, where the tail section had torn free on impact, creating a massive emergency exit. Water reached her neck as she sensed Paco behind her, and then the plane was sinking into the depths, pulled lower by the current and gravity as she took a final gasp of air and propelled herself through the gap, ignoring the last of Paco's men beside her, his head lolling at an unnatural angle, his neck snapped on impact.

❧❦

Efren and Ricardo watched the detonation as the explosive charge blew the jet's engine off. They could see the fireball even with the naked eye, and when the plane, belching a long trail of black smoke, flamed out into the river, they high-fived each other. They gathered up the remaining missile and ran for the car. Their instructions were to ditch the automobile once they'd dropped the weapon back at Dante's building, so even if it had been spotted, they weren't worried. By the time the police had a coherent description of the vehicle, it would be getting stripped in the nearby slums as desperate residents fought amongst themselves for the privilege of dismantling it.

Ricardo slid behind the wheel and gunned the engine as he called Dante on his cell. When he answered, Ricardo said only two words before disconnecting:

"Mission accomplished."

They were already ten minutes away when emergency vehicles streaked by on the freeway, a helicopter in the air over the river flying toward the wreckage. All air traffic to the airport was closed for the remainder of the day. The evening news would call the incident a terrorist attack of enormous proportions, further evidence that extremists were at work in the Americas, the only positive being that they'd mistaken a private plane for a commercial airliner, where the casualties could have been in the hundreds.

Dozens of suspected Muslim agitators were rounded up in the following days, and Iran was roundly implicated as being behind the savage attack. Nobody believed its denials, and, although eventually most of the suspects would be released for lack of evidence, the press continued to flog the story until another atrocity filled the airwaves: the mass murder of an entire family by a twelve-year-old boy, high on drugs, who had been disciplined by his mother that afternoon for poor grades on his latest report card.

Chapter 25

A symphony of horns sounded an atonal contretemps in the gridlocked Buenos Aires traffic. The SUV containing Tara and Matt sat immobile several miles from their destination in the financial district. Eduardo had the radio on; the primary topic of conversation between the two pseudo-comedians who had the top-rated morning show was the huge strike and protest being staged that had caused the city to grind to a halt – a common occurrence in Buenos Aires.

Tara's phone rang. Eduardo turned down the radio so she could hear the call.

Dante's distinctive baritone boomed at her. "Maria, the plane situation is handled. But you owe me a rather large amount of money for the ordnance we had to use."

"That's great news, Dante. But what happened…and how much is a lot of money?"

"Apparently there was an attack. A missile. Blew it out of the sky."

Tara smiled. "Wow. That *is* rather final. I like your style."

"Yes; however, the missiles are rather expensive."

"As I would expect them to be. How much are we talking?"

"We had to use two. The first one didn't home in for some reason," Dante lied.

"Hmmm. So how much?"

"A hundred fifty thousand."

Tara pretended surprise, but had expected a number in that range based on her knowledge of the cost of the devices.

"Are you joking?"

"My dear, that was the acquisition price. I covered the cost of the…errand…myself."

Tara hesitated. "That was very generous of you."

"I'm confident you'll think of a way to make it up to me."

"Fine, then. I'll have my group wire you the money. Can you email the account information?"

"I'd prefer to give it to you in person. I don't like that sort of thing floating around, what with the American NSA spying on all email messages. No offense."

"None taken. That's very prudent. When will I see you?"

"That depends on how your day goes. Where are you?"

"Stopped dead in traffic."

"Ah, then you must be trying to get downtown. The protest is all over the news. Nothing's moving."

"How long is it anticipated to go on for?"

"Another hour. But it will take several more for things to get back to normal."

"I honestly don't understand your country sometimes. Why do they allow this sort of thing?"

"It's called freedom. The population is rather sensitive to being able to voice their disapproval now that the days of the secret police are over. It's a mechanism to ensure those dark times don't return."

"Still, it's inconvenient."

"Everyone's in the same boat. Try to relax. Hopefully you aren't on a tight schedule."

"No. I'll be fine."

"Very well, then. Call me when you're done, and then come by my headquarters."

"I can probably do that. What's the address?"

Dante gave it to her, and she repeated it back to him. "I'll call first."

"Perfect. Good luck with whatever you're planning to do. Hopefully it's not overthrowing the government. Although I wouldn't be opposed to running them all out of town on a rail," Dante said, fishing for information.

"Nothing so dramatic. Just a few mundane errands."

Tara disconnected as the radio switched from the laugh track that greeted every other utterance of the radio hosts to a breaking news bulletin. Tara reached forward and switched it off as she heard the first words about a terrorist attack and turned to Eduardo.

"How long do you think it will take to make it to the bank?"

"If the protest disperses when it's supposed to, maybe another hour after, as traffic moves again. So two hours, at least."

"Damn."

"But remember that everyone is equally disrupted, so the chances of many of the bank workers having gotten there before we do are low. Everyone takes it in stride. On a day like today, nothing is going to run on schedule." He shrugged in defeated acceptance. "You get used to it. Just another headache."

Matt leaned forward. Carl pushed him back into the seat. "Easy," he warned.

"Why did you turn the radio off?" Matt asked.

"I'm tired of the noise. Not that I need to explain anything to you."

"It sounded like something big was happening."

"There's always something big happening. If I were you, I wouldn't worry about anything but getting into the lock box and retrieving the diamonds."

"I'll get you into the vault."

"Then that's all you should be concerned about."

❧⋅❧

Leonid paced in front of his desk, the Moscow skyline in the background. The picture window was double-paned bulletproof glass – purely precautionary, given that his private security company headquarters was located in one of the better neighborhoods near the Kremlin. He was on the telephone with Lyon, France, speaking to his contact at Interpol, who had called him as the day was winding down.

"We got a match on the woman you're looking for," the Frenchman said.

Leonid grinned wolfishly. "Really? That's great news. Who is she?"

"Well, we don't actually know."

"Then what kind of a match did you get?"

"We were sent images of two people, and she was one of them. I had your woman programmed in when you first sent me the information, and an hour ago the system alerted me to a match. That's all I have."

"Who sent you the image? Where did it come from?"

"Not so fast. I wanted to discuss the bonus situation you alluded to when I did this for you."

Leonid sighed. Of course. Now that the petty bureaucrat had something to negotiate with, he was going to put the screws to Leonid. "It's very difficult to know what the information is worth until I know what the information is, my friend," Leonid said.

"It's an image of your woman, who participated in a robbery and was caught on film. The robbery occurred less than eighteen hours ago. Is that current enough for you?"

Leonid stopped pacing. "I'd say so. What do you have in mind?"

"I was thinking a hundred thousand euros would be a nice way to say thank you."

"I'd argue that fifty thousand euros is a princely expression of gratitude for a location. Where the woman might no longer be, I might add. Obviously, if she'd been arrested and was being held, that would be more definitive, or even if you had an identity. As it is, you're going to tell me a city, I presume, where a robbery took place, and from where she well might have already fled. Come on. A city isn't worth a hundred thousand euros."

"If you have some other way of locating her, then you're correct. If, however, this is your only lead...well, who am I to tell you what something is worth?"

"Be reasonable. That's all I'm asking. A hundred thousand is robbery."

"Perhaps you should take some time to think about it. I must have misjudged how urgent this was. We can discuss it later, if you like. Take the rest of the day to consider my suggestion..."

They settled on seventy-five thousand euros, to be wired to the functionary's account that day.

"I appreciate your continued generosity, Leonid."

"You got what you wanted. Now where is she?"

"Mendoza. Argentina. The other side of the world. She was involved in a shootout at a casino there."

"A casino? Odd. But no matter. Send me the images you have along with any details. The sooner, the better."

"It will be in your email box within a few minutes. Pleasure doing business with you, Leonid. I'm always delighted to help a fellow traveler."

Leonid's next call was to Filipov. "Your woman surfaced. The Grigenko matter. It's time to formalize our agreement."

Filipov paused, and Leonid heard him muttering in the background before returning his attention to the discussion. "Excellent. I have appointments for the rest of the afternoon, but perhaps tomorrow?"

"This is time-sensitive. I can be at your office within an hour. I'll need one million transferred today for operating expenses. This will be expensive."

"A million up front! That's preposterous. What guarantee do I have you'll perform?"

"I want the other nine, not the million – that's my incentive. But we're under time pressure. And it will take a lot to get my team to where she's located."

"Where is she?"

"Where I can find her. Do we have a deal?"

Filipov considered Leonid's demand. "Fine. With the caveat that if you aren't successful, you refund fifty percent."

Leonid thought about it. "No deal. It will cost me at least two hundred thousand just to get my men deployed. And easily three times that much to source weapons there and enlist the cooperation of the necessary officials."

"Then we both have something at risk."

Leonid paused. "Eight hundred thousand. I just had to pay a hundred to a source to find out where she is."

"Six."

"You know what? Maybe you should contact some other providers and negotiate a better deal with them. My normal contract terms are a hundred percent in advance, with a performance guarantee and a full money-back policy. Perhaps you'd like to do this deal like a normal contract? Because, no offense, but I'm getting tired of horse-trading with you, and every minute I waste on the phone is one I could be preparing to get this woman."

Filipov was silent for a few seconds. "All right. Eight."

"Today. Before banks close. You only have a few hours. Same account you sent the half mil to."

"Very well. But Leonid? We can't afford a failure here."

The tension on the line was palpable.

"Is there anything else?" Leonid asked softly.

"The wire will go out within the hour."

"Good. Oh, and I need a sample of the blood for DNA purposes. Just to avoid any confusion in the field."

"The photo's not good enough?"

"I like to be thorough. And frankly, appearances can be deceiving. They can be changed. There can be cases of mistaken identity. I don't want to blow ten million terminating the wrong target. So just arrange for it to be available, and I can have someone pick it up. Today."

"Will do. It will probably take until the close of business."

"See if you can get it within three hours. I want to be in the air as soon as possible, and every minute I'm waiting is another she could be slipping away."

"Understood. I'll make it happen."

Leonid placed the handset back in the cradle and stopped in front of the window, taking in the cloudy sky and the rush of humanity on the street below. Filipov was a weasel, but that was his role, and likely his nature. He couldn't help it any more than a dog could help barking. But Leonid would have to watch him at the end, to ensure that he didn't try anything slippery. The DNA was part of his proof that he'd successfully performed. With most clients, it wasn't an issue, but Filipov was a special case, and Leonid didn't trust him as far as he could throw him.

He depressed the button of his intercom and called to his assistant. "Please get Team Alpha ready to go. ETA three hours. And I'll need a private jet that can hit Argentina with only one fueling stop in Dakar."

"Yes, sir."

Leonid's next call was to his contact with the SVR – the Russian foreign intelligence agency. The discussion was short and sweet.

"I need an asset in Argentina," Leonid said.

"We have several. How highly placed?"

"As high as possible."

"It'll be expensive."

"I expect it will be."

"When can you meet?"

Leonid considered how much time he'd need for the Filipov meeting. "Give me two hours."

"The usual place?"

Leonid checked his watch. "I'll be there."

Chapter 26

Jet blew water from her nose and mouth as her head burst from the surface of the river. Paco popped up next to her after several seconds, coughing as he gasped for breath. They treaded water as they got their bearings.

She pointed to the shore. "Are you injured? Think you can swim that far?"

"Just bruised, as far as I can tell. Nothing feels broken," Paco said, speaking with the authority of someone who was more than passing familiar with breaks. "What do you think, about a mile?"

"About that. Let's get going. It's only a matter of time until helicopters and boats make it here, and I want to be long gone by then."

"Right. Don't want to get hung up for days dealing with the authorities."

"Exactly. Do you know this area?"

"Sure. I spent many years in BA. That breakwater should be a marina."

"I can't believe they shot us out of the sky."

"I know. That's a first for me. They must really want to stop you."

"I'd say that's the understatement of the year."

They began swimming, pulling hard for the shore. The fifty-eight degree water temperature leached into their bones, tiring them even as they neared the rocky slope. The Rio de la Plata sports stadium loomed in the near distance, its red and white striping like a monument, making it easy to stay on course. A helicopter tore over the water from the airport; Jet gave silent thanks that they had put sufficient distance between themselves and the crash site to be undetectable – at least from the air. The inevitable search and rescue boats were a different issue; she expected them to be deployed at any minute, which spurred her on to greater effort.

They passed a buoy marking the entry to the channel that led into the Puerto Nunez marina and shortly after were hauling themselves up onto the gray rock beach, their clothes dripping mocha-colored streams.

"We need to get out of here and find a vehicle," Jet said, winded from the exertion. She felt in her pocket, retrieved the Glock, and drained the water out of it. "Good thing these are waterproof."

"Shit. I lost mine with all the excitement." Paco paused and looked around. "There's a parking lot for the marina over there. If there are any cars in it, I can get one open in no time." He extracted his iPhone from his pocket and looked at it ruefully. "I think it's safe to say my cell phone isn't going to be working any time soon, or I'd call my contact and have him come get us."

"Do they have payphones in Buenos Aires, like in Mendoza?"

"They still have some, but there's no telling whether there will be one at the marina."

"What about guards?"

"Probably a parking attendant. But we can always run the barrier if we get a car."

"I'd rather not have the police looking for us from the word go. Let's look for a phone first. You remember the number?"

"I'll give it my best shot."

"At least it's warm out. Our clothes should dry in twenty minutes or so. Maybe half an hour. But we won't freeze."

"After surviving a missile strike and a crash landing, that would be a lousy way to go."

Jet moved behind a clump of nearby bushes and shrugged out of her top, taking care to wring as much water out of it as possible before pulling it back on and repeating the process with her pants, after dumping out her shoes. Paco did the same out in the open and they were relatively dry within two minutes, if slightly more wrinkled.

"You ready?" he asked.

"We look like vagrants."

"No argument. But once we're dry, it shouldn't be too bad."

They set off for the marina, where masts bobbed above several long buildings on the nearest bank. When they arrived at the nearest, they walked along the perimeter, noting a few cars in the lot. At the far end they came to a pay phone. Jet gave Paco a smile. He fished in his pocket for a coin and dropped it into the slot. He closed his eyes, searching his memory for the number, and finally dialed. The conversation lasted twenty seconds, and when he hung up, he looked relieved.

"It'll take a little while for him to get here. The airport's a madhouse. The police have shut down the roads leading to it and are searching all the vehicles coming and going."

"That makes sense. How long did he think it would be?"

"Maybe half an hour."

"That's too long."

"He also said that the protest has closed down the city center, so nobody's going to be getting near the bank for a while. Your target will be contending with the same issues we are, so there's no point in agonizing over it."

"I want him to get us as close as possible, and then we'll make it the rest of the way on foot, if we have to. I don't want to assume they didn't make it. How far do you think we are from the bank?"

"Maybe ten kilometers."

"Too far to walk," she said, running the numbers in her head. "Even if we jogged, it would take over two hours."

"Let's see how near he can get us. We won't know until we try."

"Fair enough. Where does he want us to wait?"

"We can walk over to the main access road."

The guard eyed them distrustfully as they neared his outpost. Jet took Paco's hand so they looked like a couple out for a morning tryst. The man's curiosity seemed to extend more to Jet's skin-tight damp clothes and the way they hung off her curves than anything, but they both exhaled sighs of relief once they were at the main frontage road, the freeway only a few yards away. Traffic inched along it as rush-hour crush clogged the metropolitan arteries with glass and steel.

"That doesn't look promising," she commented as she watched the procession of cars.

"Congestion in Buenos Aires is infamous. We'll be taking back roads and side streets. Of course, so will most everyone else. But there's no other choice."

"There are always options. Maybe we can steal a motorcycle."

The sun beamed down through shreds of clouds and soon their clothes were dry, if somewhat brown, soaked with a fine silt that had permeated every square inch. Jet's hair felt stiff to her touch, but there was nothing to be done for it.

"I'm sorry about your men. Obviously I had no idea that these people would blow a plane out of the sky. I'm actually surprised they even figured out we were on it. They must have considerably more reach than I thought," she said. She eyed Paco's left hand, which was swollen. "Looks painful."

"Probably tore some ligaments. I've had worse."

"So have I. But it still looks bad."

Paco stared off into the distance. "Who are they? Shooting down a jet is way over the top."

"An American black ops team. Unsanctioned. Freelancers. But clearly desperate, in addition to being well funded."

"If Dante is helping them, we have our work cut out for us. Dante's extremely powerful. He can get away with whatever he wants."

"He might have been the one who took down the plane, then. Their jet wasn't that far ahead of us, so it had to be someone on the ground who could move fast."

Paco nodded. "Dante's definitely got the connections to do it. This should serve as a lesson to us – one we'll need to remember when we go up against him."

"Which brings us to a practical concern. Can you get any more men to help?"

"All of my people are in Mendoza. I can have a couple of them hop on a flight, but they won't have weapons…"

"Can you source any here?"

"Not quickly. I mean, we can try to do a street buy in La Boca or Villa 31, but there's no telling what we'll get, and it will be dangerous…and time consuming."

A forest green nineties-era Chevrolet Suburban rolled toward them on the frontage road from the direction of the airport. Paco waved.

"There's our ride."

"How much do you trust him?"

"His name's Julian. I've used him before. But we're not that close. He's also a freelancer. But reliable."

"There's no chance he'll sell us out?"

"Before the missile attack, I would have said no. But if they want you that badly…I'd keep our discussion to a minimum. Just tell him what he needs to know."

Julian turned out to be a lanky young man in his thirties with a shock of unruly long hair and a sparse medium-brown beard. An unlit cigarette dangled from his mouth, which seemed perpetually about to smirk. Jet climbed into the back seat. Paco took the front. To his credit, Julian didn't ask what had happened, or why he was picking up two people who looked like they'd rolled down a muddy mountain.

"Where to?" he asked, his voice quiet.

"Banco Ramirez Popular. The main branch."

"Near the congress building?" Julian asked, eyebrows raised.

"That's the one."

"That whole area is closed down. Hope you're not in a hurry, because there's no way we'll be there any time soon."

"Get us as close as you can," Paco said. "Do you have a gun?"

Julian glanced at the glove compartment. "Beretta. But that'll cost extra."

"Fair enough," Paco agreed.

"What happened to yours?"

Paco opened the dash compartment and extracted the pistol, noting its serial number had been filed off. He checked the magazine before glancing back at Julian with a somber expression on his face.

"Long story."

Chapter 27

Leonid entered the restaurant and scanned the bustling dining area, mostly businessmen lingering over cocktails after a long lunch, the bottles of vodka on their tables half-drained – an unexceptional sight in a nation with the highest alcoholism-related mortality rate in the world. Leonid's eyes roamed over the diners' faces until they settled on his SVR contact, sitting in a booth toward the back, a bottle of beer on the table and a look on his face like he'd just swallowed a mouthful of cockroaches. Leonid approached him and sat down with a wince.

"Pavel. It's been too long," Leonid said.

"Yes. It's always a pleasure to hear from you. Beer?" Pavel offered, his face an unhealthy grayish color, his eyes the color of rusting iron.

"Sure. Why not?"

Pavel signaled to the waitress and pointed to his bottle. She nodded and threw him a beaming smile. Pavel sat back and waited until Leonid's drink arrived, taking sips from his glass that Leonid noted barely lowered the level of the beer. When the waitress set his bottle down and poured two-thirds of it into his glass before departing, Leonid raised it in a toast.

"*Na zdarovya!*" Leonid toasted. Pavel lifted his beer and touched the rim of it to Leonid's before taking another miserly sip and setting it down.

"I have the contact information for my Argentine. Here," Pavel said, sliding a slip of paper to Leonid across the table.

"Excellent. Have you contacted him?"

"I did, and told him to expect you to be reaching out to him shortly."

"I appreciate the help."

"As I said, it will be expensive. And I'm quite sure the Argentine will also expect a generous display of appreciation."

Leonid took a swallow of his beer. "Of course. How much for you?"

"The usual. Fifty."

Leonid nodded, finally glad to have a transaction where he didn't have to haggle. "I'll see that it's wired today."

"I knew I liked you for a reason."

"What does this man do in Argentina? Specifically?"

"He's the third-ranking official in their intelligence service. He can get you anything you want, within reason."

"That's brilliant. Perfect, actually. And who should I represent myself as?"

"I just told him my associate would be in contact shortly. I figured you could come up with whatever story fits your requirements."

"Great." Leonid drained his beer. "Anything else I need to know?"

"Only that you can't trust the Argentines. They would sell their mother if the mood suited them."

"Good to know. But I trust he can be depended on to provide logistical support for a team, at least?"

"Yes. I just wouldn't share any operational details you don't want broadcast to the highest bidder."

Leonid slid some rubles under his bottle and rose. "Always a pleasure, Pavel, but regrettably, time is at a premium right now. Thanks for everything."

"I'll look for the wire."

"It will be there."

When Leonid returned to his office, his assistant greeted him with a checklist she'd completed in her neat script. She set it on his desk and waited for any questions.

Leonid read it and glanced up at her. "What kind of plane?"

"Global Express. That was the best I could do on short notice."

"Would have preferred a Gulfstream."

"There are none available."

Leonid grunted his approval. "And the men?"

"Everyone will be at the airport in two hours, as you requested. All with passports that will hold up to any scrutiny."

"Excellent. I'll also need a hundred thousand dollars in cash for incidentals."

"I anticipated you might. Dmitry at the bank will have it waiting in…one hour."

Leonid studied the sheet again and nodded before rising. "Good. Then I'll be leaving to pack a bag. See you in a few days. I'll be on my sat phone if you need anything."

"Are there any special requests?"

"No. Hopefully this will be routine."

Leonid owned a three-bedroom penthouse in one of the most expensive buildings in Moscow. He stopped in and, after glancing at the weather report for Mendoza, packed appropriately and was on his way to the bank ten minutes later. His private banker met him in his office like a long-lost relative and ran the stacks of hundred-dollar bills through a counter for Leonid, who packed them into his briefcase.

When he arrived at the airport, his men were already waiting in the private charter lounge – five ex-Spetsnaz commandos who had been with him for years and had successfully executed dozens of difficult missions in countries around the globe. Leonid approached them carrying his briefcase and shoulder bag. He set both down, walked to the window, and looked out at the slate sky. An arctic wind was blowing from the north and the air felt heavy with approaching snow. He turned and faced his men.

"Ivan, you speak fluent Spanish, right?"

Ivan, a blond man in his mid-thirties, nodded.

"Who else speaks it well enough to communicate?"

Two others raised their hands.

"Good. We're going to Argentina. I'll fill you in on the mission in the air. Figure it will be no more than a week. Is everyone ready?" His eyes met each man's in turn. Seeing nothing but determination, he nodded. "Then let's go."

The men followed Leonid out to the waiting jet. A flight attendant stood by the stairs with a down jacket and fur hat on her head, the wind biting as they neared. They were ready for takeoff in five minutes and in the air in another ten, the first leg of their long journey begun. When they reached their cruising altitude of forty-seven thousand feet, Leonid opened his briefcase and passed out mission sheets with Jet's photograph and filled his group in on everything he knew about her, which wasn't much.

"I've already called our Argentine contact on the way to the airport, and he'll have everything we need by the time we land. He's also circulating the woman's photograph. However, he has instructions not to attempt to take her – surveillance only. He seems competent, but I've been warned that the locals are less than reliable, so we'll operate on our own as much as possible."

He fielded questions from the men and, after half an hour, had finished his briefing and settled in for the long flight. He gazed through the window at the blanket of clouds stretching to infinity below and closed his eyes, hoping that this would be the easiest ten million dollars he'd ever made. After all, it was one woman, on her own, with no retinue of guards, who didn't suspect a thing. He'd taken down warlords, hired assassins, princes, heavily guarded dignitaries, crime bosses. This was a single female, who, although no doubt extremely capable, was unaware that he was coming for her.

How hard could it possibly be?

৵৹৵

Tara checked her watch again, her composure gradually eroding over the two and a half hours their vehicle had been sitting in traffic, unable to move. The surrounding cars had shut down their motors to wait for the protest to end. Matt watched the small telltale ticks that he knew so well from their days together – the obsessive smoothing of her hair, the fingering of her left earlobe, the periodic exhalations like a safety valve letting off excess pressure – and calculated how to use her discomfiture against her when the time came.

"Good God. How can this country get anything done with a bunch of thugs closing down the city like this?" she demanded for the tenth time.

"It does make kidnapping so much more labor intensive, doesn't it?" Matt asked, needling her. He wanted her annoyed. Thankfully, the Argentine labor movement was accomplishing much of that for him.

"Shut up. Just shut it," she snapped.

A vendor walked along the rows of stalled automobiles with a large plastic container, offering fresh croissants and other baked goods, and another followed and hawked coffee from a nearby café. She was about to order a cup when she lost interest. Her eyes lit up as she pointed to the traffic ahead of them. "Look. Up there. Did that car just move?"

Everyone strained to see what Tara was gesturing at.

"Hallelujah. It's a miracle," Carl declared.

Isaac nodded in agreement.

Engines started as drivers returned to their vehicles from where they'd gathered along the sidewalk to chat and smoke and commiserate. The old man in the car ahead of them tottered back to his ancient Citroën on worn dress shoes that dated back to the Perón era and crammed himself behind the wheel before cranking on the ignition. Puffs of black smoke belched from the exhaust and then the car wheezed like a death rattle and sat silent. He opened his door and climbed out stiffly to inspect his engine.

"No. No, no, no!" Tara seethed through clenched teeth. "This can't be happening. Come on. Move it. Move it!" She made a terse hand gesture through the windshield at the man, who merely grinned and stuck a half-smoked cigarette butt into his mouth and fumbled in his pocket for a match as he considered what to do next. "Can we go around him?"

"I can't back up. The guy behind me is on my bumper. And no way is anyone going to let us in, even if we could clear him," the driver complained.

"This is a nightmare," she said.

"You could always get out and try to help. Maybe offer to push start him," Matt suggested, twisting the knife with satisfaction.

Tara turned toward him, the expression on her face ugly. "You better shut up till we're at the bank."

"Or what? You're going to kill me? How? Bore me to death? Wait for me to die of old age?"

Tara seemed to realize what he was doing and a look of glacial calm replaced the barely controlled fury she'd just displayed.

"You always knew how to push my buttons, didn't you? Well, it's not going to work. Nice try, though."

"I guess we can add paranoia to your list of mental health issues," Matt offered.

The old pensioner fiddled with something on the motor, closed the hood, and returned to his position in the driver's seat. This time, the starter clicked and churned and the little motor coughed to life with an anemic clatter, emitting enough smoke to foul half the street before the driver ground the gears and gave the car gas.

"Finally," Tara said. Matt watched a small vein in her temple throb. "Let's do this."

A paunchy policeman at the next intersection waved them through while blowing on a whistle, his expression sleepy, the snarl of traffic just another day's work at a thankless job as the city's denizens went about their business, annoyed and resentful after the impossibly long delay.

Twenty-five minutes later they reached the bank as traffic finally eased to a normal flow. A block and a half away, the tall spire of the congress building jutted into the sky, its French architecture straight from the expansive boulevards of Paris. Beyond it, the large plaza where yet another group of protestors had staked out a corner stretched for blocks. Hand-painted signs had been posted among a small tent city, where the congregation of veterans were demanding benefits for their service in the disastrous Falklands conflict decades earlier, still resolute after thirty years of being ignored by the politicians only footsteps away.

"All right, lover. It's showtime. Not one false move, do you understand? Not a twitch. Not so much as a word I don't like, or you're dead," Tara warned. She handed Matt back his wallet, which she'd taken from him on the helicopter.

"I'm not sure I got the middle part, but the takeaway seemed like I shouldn't try anything funny."

Tara ignored his taunt, now completely aware he was needling her deliberately. "Gentlemen, let's get this over with. I'll get out first, and then, Isaac, you help our friend here out, and I'll escort him into the bank."

Tara climbed out of the SUV. Carl and Isaac followed, Matt between them. Tara called through her half-open passenger window to Eduardo. "Can you wait for us here?"

Eduardo shook his head. "Probably not. There's no parking along this stretch, and after a big protest like this, the transit cops tend to get jumpy. I'll circle back around every few minutes. Or you can call me." He'd given Tara his number while they'd been waiting.

"Shit. All right." She turned to Carl. "You two stay outside. I can handle the bank. Just keep an eye out. This shouldn't take too long."

"Roger that," he said as the Land Rover drove away.

Tara fixed Matt with an icy stare. "Remember what I said, Matt. Let's do this the easy way. You pull anything and I'll blow a hole through you big enough to drive a car through before anyone has a chance to stop me. So if you're thinking you'll pull some stunt once we're inside the bank, forget about it." She slid one hand inside her purse to where her pistol was. "Are we clear?"

"Like I said. I get it."

They pushed through the oversized iron and glass double doors into the bank's cool interior, as quiet as a library, hardly any customers there because of the day's events. A security guard eyed them lazily from his position in the corner and appeared to perk up when he saw Tara, whose blonde hair and taut body usually elicited that reaction from any male between the ages of ten and a hundred. Matt approached the manager, who greeted him with a polite smile, and informed the man that he needed to get into the safe deposit vault.

"Certainly, sir. If you would step over here to the hand scanner, your identity will be verified, and then you'll be free to enter." The manager indicated a stainless-steel box with a small screen on it mounted near the heavy safe deposit box vault door. He glanced at Matt's broken arm and frowned. "I hope it's not serious?"

"Oh, this? No. Just a mishap on a flight of stairs. It happens."

The banker checked Matt's ID card and they moved to the scanner. Matt held his hand against the screen. The manager pushed a button and a neon green light rolled down the length of his palm. After several seconds, the vault door clicked as the bolts drew back.

"I trust you recall where your box is located. Will you be needing any further assistance?" the manager asked.

"No, we're good. Thanks for your help," Tara said with a sunny smile that seemed to melt the little man somewhat. He returned it and gave Matt a look of thinly veiled envy as they walked across the vault threshold.

"To exit, simply repeat the scanning process on the wall unit inside the vault corridor," the banker said and closed the heavy steel door behind them with a solid *thunk*.

"All right. Let's get this over with. Lead the way. Are there any cameras in here?"

"Not that I remember."

"Let's hope you're being truthful. It won't go well for you if you're not."

"So I've heard."

When they arrived at the vault, Tara pushed Matt forward.

"Which one's yours?"

He pointed at a box near the floor in a long bank of compartments. "That one."

"Open it."

Matt approached the box and stopped. "Damn. I completely blanked on that."

"What?" Tara demanded.

"The key. I don't have it. It's back in Mendoza."

"You don't have the key? Is this a joke?" Tara hissed.

"I wish it was. I didn't have a lot of time to get my emergency kit, what with being thrown off the balcony and all. Maybe you should have thought this through better. I can't make the damn thing appear out of thin air, much as I'd like to."

"What about the manager?"

"They don't have keys to the boxes. For the clients' protection. That way they can't be accused of impropriety. If you lose your key, they have to call a locksmith and supervise the opening and re-keying while the customer's there. They warn you about that when you open the account."

"Well, that's just great." Her eyes roamed over the room, checking for cameras. She pointed to the far corner and removed her gun from her purse. "Go stand over there."

"You have a marvelous way with words, as always, Tara," Matt said, but complied.

"Don't move an inch, or I'll shoot you," she said and then retrieved her lock-picking kit and knelt in front of the box. "The good news is these boxes are really old, so the locks are fairly primitive. I can get it open."

"You'll need both hands."

"If you want to test how fast my reflexes are, Matt, that would be a great way to do it. I'm going to bet I can get my gun back in my hand and have three slugs in you before you could make it halfway across the room. Are you feeling particularly lucky today?"

"Not at the moment."

"Good answer."

She set her weapon on the concrete floor and unzipped the little kit and, after studying the lock, set to work with two of the picks. Forty seconds later, she twisted the lock open and picked up her gun. "Stay there."

"You're going to do this? Not me?"

"Just in case you have a gun in the box. Call it a hunch, Matt."

"I can't believe you don't trust me."

She slid the drawer out of the box and opened the metal lid, then nodded to herself as she pushed a Smith & Wesson double-action semiautomatic .45 caliber pistol out of the way and pulled a black velvet bag from the compartment. She hefted it in her free hand and dropped it into her purse.

"Doesn't feel like sixty-million worth of stones."

"Those are the highest value diamonds. Best clarity and color, and the largest. Doesn't take nearly as many to add up," Matt lied.

"They better, for your sake. There's an agency gemologist flying to Buenos Aires as we speak. He'll be on the ground soon, and he'll be able to quickly verify whether you're holding out on us."

"What would be the point?"

"I don't know. But I don't trust you."

"At least we've got that going for us. Maybe there's a chance after all."

"If you're trying to screw me, I'll make sure that your final hours are a hell on earth you can't imagine."

"You obviously haven't spent months in the mountains of Laos living on rats and grubs."

"What I'll do to you will make that look like a hot oil massage."

Matt silently debated making his move there, while the door was closed. Tara was likely to be more careless now that she had the stones. She must have seen something in his eyes, because she quickly replaced the drawer with one hand, keeping her gun trained on him with the other. She didn't bother to relock the box, preferring to close the door and stand, her pistol unfalteringly trained on Matt's torso as she scooped up the lock-picking kit and slid it into her purse. "Lead the way out. Nice and easy," she ordered.

"I really thought we'd built some trust here. I thought we had something special."

"Move."

Matt did as he was told. When the scanner opened the vault door again, Tara shouldered her purse strap and eased the gun back into it, finger on the trigger.

"What now?" Matt asked.

"Head for the front door. Slowly. We're in no hurry. Just a happy couple that's finished with their errand."

They walked to the bank entrance and pushed through the doors, Matt in front of Tara. Carl and Isaac were standing together at the curb, the Land Rover nowhere to be seen. Matt watched as Tara's attention shifted to them. She asked when the last time the vehicle had been by and he moved his good hand to the one in the cast, where the slim blade of the knife he'd slipped inside in Mendoza lay warm against his skin. This was his chance – it was doubtful he'd get another one – and he could make a break for it in the chaos that would greet his attacking Tara, hopefully with her blood spraying everywhere, if he still had decent moves.

A kit of pigeons alighted from the plaza across the way, all gray and white and black feathers as they flapped into the sky in alarm. His fingers felt the handle and pulled it from the cast just as a big engine roared down the street with a screech of tortured rubber. Time seemed to freeze as the wide grill of a big green SUV bore down on them, moving too fast for him to get out of the way.

Chapter 28

Jet caught Julian's eye in the rearview mirror as they slowly crawled toward the city center, the streets still sluggish. Strikers wandered the sidewalks carrying blue and white Argentine flags and signs demanding better wages and an end to government malfeasance. They'd been gridlocked for almost an hour, but for the last fifteen minutes had been inching forward as the city limped back to life, taking the disruption the demonstration had caused in easy stride.

"How much further?"

Julian calculated quickly. "About ten blocks. At the rate we're going, maybe seven or so minutes. Oh. Wait. Up ahead it seems to be moving a little better."

Paco turned from his position in the passenger seat and looked at her. "What do you want to do when we get there?"

"I think we have to play it by ear. We have no way of knowing whether they've gotten there yet."

"Or whether they've been there and gone," Paco said quietly.

"That's always a risk. But I can't see them being too much ahead of us, unless they had a helicopter drop them in front. Plus, if Matt is smart, he'll stall as long as possible once he's inside."

"Why? Do you think he knows you're coming for him?"

"He might suspect, but no, it's because once he gives them what they want, he knows they'll kill him. So the longer he delays, the longer he lives, the longer he has a chance, even if it's a slim one, to escape."

They rolled relentlessly forward, traffic thinning as they neared the bank. Jet leaned forward and pointed through the windshield. "There. Up ahead. That's her. And look! There's Matt by the entrance." She whipped her Glock from her belt.

Julian nodded. "What do you want me to do?"

She watched Tara approach the two men and made a snap decision. "Floor it and run them down."

"Are you serious?"

Paco held up the Berretta and checked his seat belt. "She's dead serious."

"I hope you two know what you're doing..."

Jet braced herself against the back of the passenger seat with her feet as Julian gave the big V8 engine full throttle. The heavy vehicle lunged forward like an enraged bull and they hurtled toward the group by the front entrance. They covered the distance in a blink and the SUV jumped the curb. The body of one of the two men with Tara flew over the hood and smashed face-first into the windshield with a wet smack, shattering the glass and leaving a bloody smear as Julian stood on the brakes.

Tara saw the big Chevrolet lurch toward them out of the corner of her eye and leapt backward just as the front fender caught Isaac and threw him over the hood. Carl fell to the side as the bumper struck his thigh, shattering his femur with a sickening crack. His face went white from shock and he went down, his arm hitting Tara as he dropped, knocking her purse out of her hands and sending it tumbling to the sidewalk.

The purse bounced once on the sidewalk. The diamond bag tumbled out and split open, loosing a shimmering wave of sparkling stones that skittered across the cement and into the gutter. She took in the disaster as she stumbled backward. She sensed Matt behind her moving toward her and spun just as a steak knife blade slashed across her torso, cutting through her jacket and gashing her side. Tara ignored the pain and brought her arm down across his wrist and hit the pressure point straight on, causing him to drop the knife as his hand went numb.

Tara debated slamming the heel of her hand into Matt's nose and driving the cartilage into his brain, but heard the door of the SUV open and opted for survival rather than a bloody last stand. She spun and sprinted toward her purse, but changed her mind when Carl's gun barked twice, followed by a volley of shots from the SUV. Tara darted into the street in front of a motorcycle with a gelato delivery box on the back and drove her elbow into the rider's throat as he skidded to avoid her. He crumpled, and the bike went sliding down the street. She dodged a swerving sedan that was standing on its horn, its brakes locked up and its tires smoking the pavement. When she reached the motorcycle, she pulled the rider off, raised it back onto its wheels, and straddled the seat as she twisted the throttle.

One of Paco's rounds hit Carl squarely in the chest and he dropped his gun. He twitched twice and then lay still on the sidewalk amidst a wash of diamonds. Jet got free of her seat belt and threw her door open just as Tara knocked the motorbike off course. She drew a bead on her back and squeezed the trigger, but a sedan blocked the shot and her round smashed through its rear window, shattering it and sending the car into a skid.

The whine of the motorcycle's engine cleaved through the mayhem as a delivery van braked to a halt behind the sedan to avoid ramming it, obstructing her view. By the time she darted past it, Tara was zigzagging down the street on the motorcycle, out of range. Jet cursed and fired several shots at her, but knew the chances of a hit were remote. One of the slugs tore through the delivery box, sending a spray of caramel gelato into the air as Tara rounded a corner, and then she was gone.

Jet turned. "Matt! Are you okay?" she asked, running to where he knelt on the sidewalk, trying to retrieve some of his diamonds with his numb hand.

He looked up at her. "Never better. Just don't ask me to try any sign language. I'm afraid both of my mitts are out of commission," he said, clumsily dropping a few stones into his pocket with barely responsive fingers.

Their heads swiveled at the sound of a siren from several blocks away. Jet moved back to the Suburban, where Paco was in the front seat, kicking the windshield out so Julian would be able to see. "Let's get out of here. Julian. Get going," she yelled as she pulled Matt to his feet.

Matt shook his head. "But the diamonds..."

"Leave them. Or get shot by trigger-happy Argentine cops. And try to explain two dead men."

Matt glanced at Carl's body and reached down to retrieve his weapon. "Doesn't look like he'll be needing this, does it?"

"Jump in the back with me. We're out of time. Julian, drive," Jet commanded as she threw herself through the rear door. Matt followed her in and Julian dropped the Suburban into reverse. Isaac's glass-covered form slid off the hood, leaving a red streak on the green metal as Julian slid the transmission into drive and put his foot into it. They rocketed away from the curb, past the stopped van and a collection of cars that had ground to a halt. Julian had a wild look in his eyes, not quite panic, but not far off.

"Where do you want me to go?" he demanded.

"Hang a right here. First thing, lose the cops. Go wherever you think we'll have the best chance of doing that," Paco said.

"I'll head to San Telmo," Julian said.

"Good idea."

More sirens joined the first. Jet and Matt exchanged worried glances. They took a left two streets farther up.

Jet grabbed Paco's shoulder. "We need to get out of this car and let Julian ditch it somewhere. It's got bullet holes in the door and no windshield. The police will have a description from the other vehicles pretty quickly."

"She's right," Julian agreed. "I'll drop you off up at the next block. Go down into the Underground and take the first train to anywhere."

Paco nodded. "All right. I'll call you later."

"You owe me a car."

"This is yours?"

"No. It's stolen. But it cost me five thousand dollars on the black market. I wanted something untraceable."

"I'm good for it," Paco said. "You know that."

"Not at this rate. You don't have nine lives."

"I said I'm good for it."

Julian skidded to a stop. "The Underground station is over a block, at Diagonal Norte. There are two lines. Good luck."

Jet, Matt, and Paco jumped out and Julian roared away as though the devil were hot on his heels. Paco led them at a trot through the crowd of pedestrians and then abruptly slowed when he saw two police officers across the street, one of them on his radio. Neither of the cops was looking in their direction, but he knew that sudden movement, different than the throng's natural flow, would attract their attention.

"What is it?" Matt asked.

"Police. Don't look. Just move along like nothing's wrong. Try to act natural."

Jet took Matt's hand and leaned her head against his shoulder, the perfect picture of an affectionate couple as Paco walked ahead of them, seeming to stride slowly but putting distance between them. He turned onto a pedestrian-only street, both sides clogged with shoppers perusing the lines of shops on either side, and stopped in front of a discount clothing store. He spun to face Matt and Jet and indicated the shop with his head.

"I'm going to get a different color shirt and some shorts. I'd suggest you find a ladies' shop and do the same. Any description will be of us wearing these clothes."

"Good idea. And hats. Oh, and Paco…can you get a cell phone? Do you have money?"

"It might be a little damp, but yes, I've got plenty. I'll meet you in ten at the Underground station."

"You got it."

Three stores down they found a suitable establishment where Jet quickly selected a brown long-sleeved blouse and a pair of camouflage cargo pants. She changed into them in the dressing room while Matt paid the teen manning the register after handing him the tags.

When she emerged from the booth, she looked like a different person.

Matt nodded approvingly. "You need a hat," he said and tossed her a khaki baseball cap. She put it on and grabbed him a black DC Shoes flat-brimmed skater hat. He donned it, inspected himself in the mirror, and grinned. "Perfect."

"Let's get you a jacket, and we're done," Jet said. They found another store and bought a navy blue Adidas lightweight jogging jacket that was a reasonable fit. He pulled on the one sleeve and pulled the other over his shoulder, leaving the cast beneath it as he zipped the bottom closed.

"What's the plan after we get to the Underground?" Matt asked.

"Put some distance between us and the scene of the crime, and figure out what we do next."

"Thanks for saving my ass, by the way. I don't think I had much longer."

"Think nothing of it."

"Who's your new friend?"

"Paco?" She explained as they walked to the station, finishing with the jet downing. Matt's eyes widened.

"Wait. So you were in a plane that got shot down? Just a few hours ago? You're not making this up?"

"Do I look like I'm in a fun mood, Matt?"

He studied her green eyes. "You always look kind of fun to me…"

"I'm better when I haven't had to start my morning swimming through muddy water after a missile strike."

"That would definitely make me cranky."

"You don't know the half of it."

"Where's Hannah?"

"At Sofia's. She's watching her for us."

Matt slowed. "You know we'll never be safe with Tara out there. We need to find her."

"I know. Any idea where she might have gone?"

"I have an address."

It was Jet's turn to look surprised. "You're kidding."

"No. I overheard her on the phone. She's working with some local criminal. Dante something or other, I heard her say."

"Dante. There's that name again."

Matt nodded. "My money says she'll be at his place, trying to regroup."

"And you know where that is," Jet said flatly.

"Yup."

She smiled. "Have I told you how handsome you look in blue?"

"Not nearly enough. What are you thinking about doing?"

"What do you think I'm thinking?"

Matt sighed as they neared the station and took her hand.

"That's what I was afraid of."

Chapter 29

Dante's headquarters was located in the La Boca neighborhood, one of the most dangerous in Buenos Aires. Matt, Jet, and Paco sat down the block from the walled warehouse complex by the river in a beaten-to-death Renault sedan Julian had obtained for them after a call from the Underground station. He'd dumped the Suburban in a side alley in San Telmo and caught a taxi back to his office, where among other sidelines he bought and sold cars of questionable origin with no questions asked, whose plates might not have matched the vehicles they were affixed to but which were always bargains. An hour later they were outside Dante's building, watching and waiting as Jet tried to come up with a plan.

"What business is he in? That looks like some sort of an industrial plant," Matt asked.

"It's a distillery. He manufactures liquor, mostly cheap knock-offs of popular foreign brands. Some of it's undrinkable and many of the lower end bars stock it, but it's also a good front for his criminal activities, because he's been at it for twenty-plus years," Paco explained.

"Well, it's built like a fortress," Jet said. "I don't see any easy way in, do you?"

"No. Those walls are at least fifteen feet high. I've seen prisons with laxer security, which doesn't really surprise me. La Boca is known for its crime and violence. Many of the families here live ten to a room. You've never seen poverty like this area, or the ones further south —brick slums with dirt streets that flood every year during the rainy season. No wonder he's built something that's impenetrable. It has to be, given the location."

"Right. And it also gives him plenty of excuses to have guards on the premises."

"Exactly. To protect his booze business. Not that anyone would question any of this too closely," Paco said. "As I said, he wields a lot of clout."

"Then how are we going to get in?" Matt asked.

"Nobody said this would be easy," Jet reminded him. "How sure are you that Tara will come here?"

"Very. He shot down a plane for her. Who do you think she'll turn to when everything goes wrong?"

Jet rubbed her eyes. "I don't see any weak points, do you?"

Paco shook his head. "No. There are no nearby buildings we could get into and drop down onto the complex's roof. The walls are concrete and, as you pointed out, high. I just don't see how we do it."

"Maybe pose as a delivery company?" Matt said.

"We'd never get past that first gate," Paco said. "Remember, we're not his only enemies, and his men are there to keep unauthorized intruders out. We'd qualify, I'd say."

"I can't believe he drives through this neighborhood every day to come to work. That seems like a carjacking waiting to happen," Matt observed.

"Could be that he's got a helicopter. A lot of the high rollers here do. For just that reason," Paco said.

Jet frowned. "All right. The only way I see to do this is to go through the front door, hard. It's not my preferred approach, but it's the only one I think can work."

"How do we do that?" Matt asked.

"We plow through the gate and into the building."

"Plow. Plow with what? This wreck?" Matt said.

"No. We're going to need something much bigger," Jet said.

"Like what?"

"Like a bus. Or a semi-rig."

Matt frowned. "Right. But I'm not sure Julian could get his hands on one of those easily."

Paco smiled. "I have an idea."

❧❦

Carson Santell sounded more agitated than Tara could recall, even across five thousand miles of phone line. She'd filled him in on the disaster at the bank and was waiting for instructions. She could practically hear him pacing, scowl in place, brow furrowed as he tried to work out what to do next.

"This really isn't what I had in mind when I sent you down there, Tara," he chided.

"I know. Do you think this is what I wanted to have happen?"

"And you recovered none of the stones?"

"Correct. They spilled everywhere. By now half of Buenos Aires is celebrating their newfound wealth."

"And the target got away clean."

Tara probed the knife cut Matt had left her as a parting gift with a tissue. The blood had clotted, but it was still painful.

"That's right. He's still out there. Which is why I'm calling. How do you want me to proceed?"

"It's just you?"

"Also correct. As I said before, my team didn't make it."

"Explain again how that's possible. I mean, you had him in your hands, you had the diamonds, and then, in the blink of an eye, some mysterious woman kills your men and frees him?"

"It's what happened. I told you. I came out of the bank. A truck rammed the men. They exchanged fire with the vehicle. At that point the diamonds were all over the street, and I was unarmed. I managed to escape. They didn't. I'm sure you'll read all about it on the news feeds tomorrow. Or better yet, check with your contacts in Buenos Aires. I'm pretty sure you can easily verify what I'm telling you."

"I intend to do exactly that."

Tara didn't like the way the discussion was going. She knew Santell and the way his devious mind worked, and he'd be suspicious that this was all a ruse created by her so that she could make off with the diamonds for herself. Which he wouldn't tolerate.

"Remember that I'm the one that got you back the two hundred million dollars' worth in Thailand," she reminded him.

"For which we're deeply grateful. But as they say, what have you done for me lately?"

Tara kept her temper in check. "Again. What do you want me to do?"

"I'd like you to go get my diamonds and kill that bastard."

"We tried. It didn't work. And now the diamonds aren't recoverable. Which leaves Matt."

"Do you think you can locate him?"

"Unknown."

Silence hung taut on the line as Santell thought. When he spoke, he sounded disgusted. "Do what you can. I still want him dead. You're down there. Finish the job."

She found herself listening to a dead phone. He'd hung up. Not good.

Tara cursed silently and tossed the bloody tissue into the trash, worried. The last thing she needed was for Santell to suspect her. That didn't make for a long life expectancy – not that she was troubled by those notions in her line of work, but still, having the most ruthless group in the CIA gunning for her...

She returned to where Dante was waiting in his office, standing by the window looking at the shipping containers in the large yard. He heard her approach from the distillation room, where she'd gone for privacy for her call, and turned to face her.

"So, my dear, a disappointing day all around for you, eh? I'm sorry. I wish there was something I could do to help."

She gave him a smile that looked as genuine as any she'd graced him with, as she seethed at the problem she'd been left with and Santell's dismissive tone.

"Thank you, Dante. It's not your problem. Sometimes these things happen." Tara had given him a sanitized report of the events, omitting the diamonds – simply indicating that the captive had gotten away after a gunfight. Dante hadn't probed and she hadn't volunteered anything.

"It's good that you can take this all in stride, Maria."

"Yes, well, what's one to do? Dante, darling, do you have any alcohol? I'm afraid I got a nasty cut I need to attend to," she said, holding her side, playing for sympathy.

"Of course, my dear. Have a seat and I'll call for some."

She did as he suggested and closed her eyes, the image of Matt's whore holding a gun on her as she mounted the motorcycle replaying through her mind, stoking the flames of her anger with each recurrence. She'd ruined everything. The stones had been in Tara's grasp, and then the woman had come along...and now Tara was disgraced.

She would pay dearly for that. Nobody humiliated Tara.

Nobody.

Chapter 30

Jet did her best sashay up the sidewalk toward the security shack, where the uniformed guard sat listening to a soccer game on a small portable radio, the street empty. He registered the motion as she neared and his eyes got big at the apparition of a beautiful young woman moving toward him with a beaming smile on her face, her emerald-green eyes almost luminescent in the sunlight as she approached. He straightened his wrinkled jacket and switched off the radio, and regretted not shaving that morning as she strode to his station.

"Ca-can I help you?" he stammered, hating the stutter that had plagued him since adolescence.

Another smile. She was gorgeous. "Maybe. I was looking for someone else."

"Who? I'm the only one here…"

The strike to the nerve meridian in his neck was so swift that he didn't realize he'd been hit. One second an angel was talking to him, the next the world was spinning and going dark, his legs refusing to obey his brain's instructions to hold firm below him.

Jet caught the man as his knees buckled and set him back into the guardhouse chair. She did a quick search and took his cell phone. Then she jerked the landline out of the wall, leaving it ruined.

She looked down the street and whistled. Matt and Paco trotted down the street to where she waited.

"Let's make this snappy. We've only got a few minutes until he comes to," she warned and turned to enter the gravel lot. Matt and Paco followed her to where dozens of cement trucks were parked next to dump trucks and pumping rigs. They eyed the massive vehicles as Jet edged over to Matt. "So which do you think are the heaviest?"

"The cement trucks probably are, but we don't want the mixer to break loose on impact. Next best are the dump trucks. Look at the bumpers on those things. And you can take cover in the back." They had discussed how to deal with breaching the gate and Matt had insisted on driving. He'd made a compelling argument – that he had one good free hand, which was all he'd need to shift and steer. "I'll leave the rear unlatched so you can jump out once we're through. It's perfect."

Paco moved to the nearest truck. He opened the door, climbed up into the high cab, and fiddled with the wiring harness beneath the steering column. He snipped two wires and stripped the ends and, after a glance at Jet, crossed them. Matt could see a small spark flash as the starter turned over, and then the motor roared to life.

Paco hopped down from the cab and nodded to Matt. "It's all yours."

He nodded. "Okay. Get in the back. You'll know when I'm through the front gate. I'll slow down once inside the compound and you two can work your magic. Then I'll take out the main building cargo door and we're game-on."

Jet eyed his face. "You sure about this? For the record, I'd still rather you sat this one out and let me drive."

Matt shook his head. "Which will reduce your odds of success, because you won't be able to shoot and drive at the same time. We already covered this."

"I know. I still don't like it."

Matt leaned into her and kissed her. "I love how you're about to go into a heavily armed compound and shoot it out with an army of miscreants, armed with only a pistol with half a magazine left – and yet you think I'm taking too much of a risk. Which reminds me." Matt handed her the weapon he'd taken off Carl. "I'll trade you. This one only had two shots fired."

She took the pistol and popped the magazine, removed four bullets, then slammed it back in place and chambered a round before handing it to Matt. She loaded her Glock with the 9mm bullets. "I'd just as soon keep this one. It's kind of a good luck charm for me now."

Matt offered a lopsided grin and slid his weapon back into his belt. "Works for me. Hop in the dumper, and let's do this."

They did so, and Matt stabbed the clutch pedal to the floor and shifted into reverse, then powered the wheel around with his one good hand until he had room to turn and get through the security gate. He shifted into first and gave the big rig gas and it lumbered forward, quickly winding out the low gear. After he rumbled through the gate, he put it into second and concentrated on cranking the wheel. His broken arm pulsed with the effort of his good one, each turn another lance of pain as he bounced over the rough pavement worn away from decades of heavy vehicles rolling across it.

The four blocks to the distillery were the longest of Matt's life and by the time he'd shifted into fourth and was doing forty miles per hour, his face was beaded with sweat from the exertion and pain. He blinked it out of his eyes as Dante's iron gate came into view. He took a deep breath and tugged on his seat belt to ensure it was secure, then stomped on the gas, sending the tachometer into the red.

The three men standing outside the gate heard the big vehicle before they saw it, the twin smokestacks belching black exhaust into the sky as it accelerated down the road. One of the men elbowed his companion and was about to make a wry comment when his eyes widened and he screamed a warning. The truck's trajectory had abruptly changed and the leviathan was now heading straight for them. The guards futilely pulled at their holstered weapons as the truck bore down on them, leaping aside when the bumper slammed into the gate, blowing it inward and knocking one of the two heavy iron panels off its hinges.

Matt coasted to ten miles per hour as the shooting started. The rounds bounced harmlessly off the thick metal of the dump truck box. He saw Jet leap from the bed in his side mirror, firing back at the guards as she ran. He shifted into third and floored the throttle as he picked up speed again and was doing thirty-five when he barreled through the main building's roll-up door, momentum carrying him well into the interior of the two-story building, knocking oversized vats over as he careened through the production area.

He collided with a bottling line, sending glass and tanks everywhere. The stunned workers stood frozen for an instant before running for the exits, unsure of what had just happened but unwilling to stay around to find out what the next surprise might be. Apparently most of the workers were legitimate employees working for the distillery and not part of Dante's criminal sideline, because dozens of men and women ran for the shattered roll-up door and only a few men with guns bucked the tide and sprinted toward the truck.

Matt's head lay on the steering wheel. The first gunman threw the door open, his shotgun leveled at Matt. Seeing that he was unconscious, the man jabbed him with the barrel.

"What the he—"

Matt's pistol barked twice as he fired across his lap, the first round catching the man in the cheek, the second blowing the top of his skull off. His partner fired his pistol at the truck, but the rounds went wide. Matt counted to three and then stood on the seat in a crouch and leaned out with his gun – at a level that was completely unexpected, judging by the surprised look on the second man's face as one of Matt's bullets drilled a hole through his sternum and into his heart.

More shots sounded from the side of the warehouse and a slug ricocheted off the cab. Matt ducked back down and fired two shots in the direction of the shooter. An answering volley of four shots in quick succession blasted into the truck's side. One of the stray rounds hit a large vat of alcohol and a stream of nearly pure, high-octane fluid spurted forth onto the floor. Matt slid across to the opposite door and kicked it open just as a spark from a piece of shattered equipment caught the pool of liquid and it flared with a blue flame. He watched in horrified fascination as the fire followed the stream up to the huge tank and ducked behind the dash just as the container exploded, setting off a chain reaction with the other nearby tanks, which each detonated in turn.

Outside, Paco and Jet made short work of the three armed men who had followed the truck through the perimeter wall gate. They were good, but not great, and the difference between highly trained, skilled shooters and thugs with guns was no contest. Four more came running from a smaller building, these with riot guns. Jet took cover behind a shipping container while Paco ducked behind a pickup truck. The shotguns boomed as the men neared, the buckshot barely denting the steel side of the container. Jet threw herself onto the ground and poked her Glock around the corner just as the first of the two men was fifteen yards away.

She squeezed off two shots. The first missed, but the second caught the nearest man in the hip, causing him to double over and drop his weapon. She fired three times at the second man, who had loosed another blast at her, but a foot too high. Her slugs punched into his chest, driving him backward, each impact jerking him off his feet slightly. He tumbled forward just as more shooting echoed from the pickup. Paco picked off his two assailants with a flurry of shots. She thanked fate that he was competent and ran to the closest downed man, who was groaning, his hip shattered from her round. She pulled his jacket open and grabbed his pistol and, with a gun in each hand, pointed the Glock at his forehead.

"Dante. Where is he?"

The man shook his head, his eyes screwed shut in pain. Her peripheral vision caught something on her left and she swiveled as she crouched, firing both weapons at another man running toward her with a submachine gun. Her bullets shredded through him and he slammed into the gravel, the gun flying from his hands.

After another glance at the wounded man beside her, she sprinted for the submachine gun, tucking the Glock into her waistband as she neared. She scooped the weapon up and shook her head distastefully – it was a Mac-10, which was only slightly better than the pistols for accuracy, although it was fully automatic, so could spit a lot more lead in a short period of time. Too much lead, in untrained hands, she knew – it would take two seconds to burn the entire thirty-two round .45 caliber magazine on full auto. She felt in the man's jacket for a spare magazine but didn't find one, and swore. Amateurs.

The front of the distillery exploded with a series of fireballs and she winced, the heat blowing over her like a fiery wind. It took everything she had not to scream Matt's name and run into the inferno, but instead she forced herself to stay dispassionate and continued to scan the area for threats, allowing the workers to run through the gates, away from the distillery.

Jet returned to the downed man and repeated her question as she eyed the flames belching from the building.

"Where's Dante? If you want to be alive in five seconds, you'll tell me."

His eyes fluttered open, glazed with agony, and looked around wildly, unfocused.

"I…"

"Dante. Where?"

"In…the back…main…build…ing…"

"Today's your lucky day," Jet said. Two more gunshots sounded from near the pickup truck. She pirouetted, the Mac-10 at the ready. Paco appeared from behind the truck and approached her. She looked at him and motioned with her head at the pump shotgun. "That might do you more good where we're going."

Paco scooped up the shotgun. "I think that's it for guards out here." He took in the flames licking from the building. "I'm sorry about your friend."

"Let's get this over with. Follow me. Dante's offices are in the back."

They jogged toward the flames, which were already dying down, and then ran along the side of the warehouse. When they reached the rear, two armed men appeared from around the corner, both also clutching Mac-10s, and opened up at them. Jet allowed them to drain their weapons shooting at the wall she'd taken cover behind and when she heard the gun bolts snap open, she leaned around and cut them down with hers, the two-stage sound suppressor bucking in her hands as she fired. She estimated that she still had half the magazine left and whispered to Paco.

"There's a door here. Cover me. I'm going in."

Paco hurried to the door and stood with his shotgun as Jet approached it. She nodded, and he reached down with his left hand, gripping the shotgun with his right, and twisted the doorknob. It turned. He exchanged a glance with her and then pulled the door open.

Gunfire boomed from inside – another shotgun. Paco leaned around the doorjamb and returned fire, pumping the gun again and again as he laid down a devastating rain of death. When the gun was empty, he tossed it aside and freed his pistol. Jet threw herself through the door, rolling on the ground as she searched for a target. A dead man's sightless eyes stared back at her from the floor, his shotgun still gripped in his hands.

Paco entered and moved to the corpse, picking up the scattergun as Jet swept the area with the Mac-10. To their right were offices and a two-story room. Jet nodded to the office door, and Paco moved toward it, wary of any further attacks. When he reached it, Jet followed and they framed the doorway. Paco repeated his move from outside and swung the door wide, but this time no shooting greeted them. After several beats he stepped across the threshold and turned down a long corridor.

They reached the end of the hall and found themselves facing another door. This one had a deadbolt on it. Paco tried the knob and shook his head. Jet made a hand gesture and he moved away. She pointed the Mac-10 at the lock and fired a burst at the deadbolt. The big slugs tore into the wood, shattering it. She kicked it in and Paco rolled into the room with the shotgun at the ready.

Dante stood at his window, a cigar smoldering in his hand. He turned to them and held up both hands.

JET VI – JUSTICE

"I'm unarmed."

"Stay where you are," Jet said.

He nodded. She cautiously approached him and patted him down. Dante smiled as she did so.

"Under different circumstances, I'd offer to buy you a drink or a Rolex or something."

"Where's Tara?" Jet asked, her tone flat.

"Who?"

"The American woman."

"Ah. Maria. Tsk, tsk. So her real name's Tara? How sad that she doesn't confide the important things in me. I thought we had something there."

"Last time I ask. Where is she?"

"I'll make you a deal. I'll tell you where she is and I'll allow you to live. In return, you allow me to live. Your fight isn't with me, I assure you."

Paco spat. "Your assurances mean nothing."

Dante eyed him as though seeing him for the first time. "I know where she is. Kill me and she escapes. Is that really what you want?"

"Where is she?" Jet demanded again, pressing the Mac-10 suppressor against Dante's crotch.

"The police are on their way. Your finite time is even now running out. Do you want her, or do you want me? Choose. Because you can't have both." Dante's voice was calm, reasoned, the words almost a purr, so velvety was his tone.

"Fine. You live. Where. Is. She?" Jet said.

"In the lab."

"Where's that?"

"Through that door, at the end of the hall." He pointed to a metal doorway on the far side of the expansive suite of offices.

"Is there another exit?"

"No. That's the only one."

Jet looked at Paco. "Stay here. Watch him. If he's telling the truth, we let him go."

"But–"

"You heard me."

Jet moved to the door and took a final look at Dante. "If you lied to me, I'll shoot you myself. And I know how to do it to guarantee unspeakable agony for the few hours it will take you to die."

Dante nodded. "You and…Tara…will get along famously. Birds of a feather, I daresay."

"Is she armed?"

"Not that I know of. But you should assume she might be. Apparently she doesn't tell me everything."

Jet inched the door open and stared down a long hallway, at the end of which was another open doorway, and beyond that a large room with the harsh glare of fluorescent lighting shining down on lab tables. Jet crept down the hall, both the Glock and Mac-10 in her hands. When she reached the doorway, she paused and listened, every fiber of her being on alert. She stood like that for several seconds, but sensed nothing other than an empty room. She swept the visible areas with her weapons, but there was no Tara, just beakers and flasks and equipment.

Once inside, she methodically checked behind the large vats in each of the corners and beneath the tables. A door on the opposite end of the room was the only remaining spot Tara could be. She approached it and called out.

"I'll give you three seconds and then I'm going to empty a full clip into that room. This is your only warning."

Nothing.

Logic told her Tara had to be in there, but her instincts were telling her that it was empty. Still, Jet stepped back and fired a burst from the Mac-10 through the door.

Her ears rang from the sound of the shots in the small space. She reached out and twisted the knob and pulled the door wide. Inside was a storage area, fifteen feet square, with boxes and canisters and lab coats, some now with smoking holes in them. But no Tara.

Jet's eyes rose to the air grids. It was a drop ceiling, but there was no evidence of any of the big squares having been pushed out of place so Tara could climb up. There would have been white dust on the floor below when she replaced them, and there was none. Jet studied the floor in the gloom and switched on the light. There, in the center, was a grid – a large drain.

She moved to it and kneeled down. The hole below the grid was large enough for someone to escape through. She inspected the corners of the drain and saw signs of scraping – recent, to her eye, on the edges of the rusty metal.

Jet heaved the grid up and set it to the side. She peered down into the darkness, where she could see a set of rungs embedded in the concrete leading into the nothingness below. Whether it was part of the drainage system or an emergency escape route didn't matter to her. What mattered was that the grime on the rungs had been disturbed where hands and shoes had used them to descend. Follow those, and she would find Tara.

She returned to the office, where Paco was holding his pistol on Dante, who looked as calm as if he were in church as he puffed at his cigar by the window.

"Ah, I trust that you settled your differences? I couldn't help but overhear the shooting," Dante said.

"Where does the drain in the storage room go?" Jet demanded.

"What? Oh. I see. It goes down a story and a half, into the sewer."

"I don't have to tell you that she wasn't in there, so our deal is off."

Dante stopped looking so assured. "She was there. If she isn't anymore, it's because she went down the drain, so to speak. That's not my fault."

"Unless you told her there was an escape route. Where does the sewer let out?"

"I…I mean, it's been many years since I was down there, but there are some other shafts that go to manholes on some of the surrounding streets."

"Give me a flashlight," she said, her voice quiet.

"Certainly. May I?" Dante asked, glancing at Paco, who nodded. Dante moved to his desk and slid the center drawer open. He extracted a flashlight and closed the drawer and then sat down behind the desk. He flicked it on to verify it functioned and held it out to Jet. "Here you go. Seems to work."

She tossed the Mac-10 on the chair beside Paco and took the light.

"If he so much as coughs, you have my permission to gut-shoot him."

Paco gave her a humorless grin and considered Dante with hooded eyes. "My pleasure."

Chapter 31

Jet returned to the lab room and, after glancing around, made her way to the storage area and the shaft. She slid the penlight into the front pocket of her cargo pants and the Glock into her waistband and lowered herself into the gap, supporting herself with her arms until her feet found the first rung.

The shaft was a tight fit, no more than two and a half feet in diameter, but it had sufficient room for her to ease downward and she had no doubt that was how Tara had escaped the closed room. When she reached the bottom of the rungs, she switched on the flashlight and freed the pistol, holding the light in her left hand as she clutched the gun in her right.

She found herself in a dank brick tunnel barely four feet high, with calf-high suspect water streaming down its black length. The smell almost choked her and she gagged before switching to breathing through her mouth. While much of the fluid in the passageway was probably drainage, it was obvious from the stench that sewage was also a big contributor. She tried not to think about what she was walking through and instead shined the light in both directions, looking for any clue as to Tara's passage.

After a pause, Jet turned left and began making her way slowly along the tunnel. Cockroaches scuttled in the darkness, startled by the beam, the unwelcome illumination glinting off their shiny brown carapaces as they raced for cover, preferring the dark crannies of the crumbling brickwork to the unexpected exposure.

A slick, furry form darted down one of the smaller tributaries, too small for a human to enter, from which mystery fluid trickled into the sludge underfoot. The rat paused to stare at Jet with curious red eyes, its nose twitching as it evaluated the intruder into its subterranean realm, and then it continued on its way, having decided Jet was too big to eat.

She rounded a bend and found herself at an old grid crafted from iron, barring any further progress. The padlock on the clasp looked relatively new, placed within the last several years, but the coating of grime on it told her that nobody had opened it in some time – certainly not within the last few minutes.

Jet retraced her steps, listening for any hint of where Tara could have gone, ears still ringing from the shooting. All she heard were faint droplets of water trickling from the overhead pipes that ran the length of the tunnel, and the splashing from the drainage ports that spewed from the sides into the river of filth she was wading through. She arrived back at the shaft and played her light down the tunnel, but saw more of the same, with an occasional recessed area along the walls, presumably for maintenance.

Fifty yards further along she came to a junction, where the passageway split into two. She peered down both branches before choosing the right, noting the increase in pipes and valves overhead, as well as along the sides. She moved carefully but with urgency, aware that Tara had a substantial lead on her and that her odds of catching the woman were decreasing with each passing minute. She was tempted to just give up, but discarded the idea, knowing that if Tara escaped, she would be back to hunt Matt down and kill him.

She continued down the branch, the Glock clenched unwaveringly in her hand as the beam of light played across the brick, and stopped when she heard a soft splash behind her. Like a rat landing in the water.

Or an ill-placed step.

She spun just in time to see Tara turning one of the big valve wheels mounted on the wall and was about to fire when the tunnel flooded with high-pressure water blasting from a two-foot-wide aperture. The surge rushed toward her, knocking her off her feet as it hit with the force of a fire hose. Her gun and flashlight tumbled away as she was carried along, unable to breathe, caught completely by surprise – and now in danger of drowning in a forgotten sewer.

⊱•⊰

Paco shifted on the sofa in front of Dante's desk, hating the arrogant crime lord with every fiber of his being. The man was a murderer, a slaver, a miscreant of the worst sort, and he lived like medieval royalty while he operated his empire. In spite of his sins, he dined at the best restaurants, had the ear of half the members of the government, and was part of the cream of Buenos Aires society. He was responsible for more misery than anyone Paco had ever heard of, yet he seemed to go free time and time

203

again while those around him suffered. Even now, with half his distillery destroyed, it looked like he was going to walk away from the episode unscathed and probably clip the insurance company for a fortune for the damage to his plant.

Dante took another puff of his cigar and smiled at Paco. He leaned forward and locked eyes with him. "You hate me, don't you? Why is that, hmm?"

"I hate what you are, and what you've done."

"Oh, really? How many men are dead outside because of you? You're a killer. You butchered them to get to me. What makes you any better than me?"

"Because they weren't innocents. They work for a monster. They had guns and were rushing to defend you. If you work for monsters, you can expect nothing better than they got."

"Interesting bit of moral ambiguity. And here you sit, judge, jury, and executioner."

"That's right."

"Your boss there told you I was to be released."

"She's not my boss," Paco spat.

"I see. And I also see that you have no intention of letting me walk away from this, do you?"

Paco glared sullenly at Dante, but didn't answer.

"Just as I thought. You plan to kill me."

"I'd like to. I didn't say I would."

"You don't have to say so. It's written all over your face."

"Shut up. I don't want to hear your voice. You sicken me."

"Have it your way."

The unsilenced blast blew half the front of the desk apart, the shotgun mounted beneath it loud in the confines of the office. Paco's chest exploded as buckshot tore into him. He dropped his gun on the marble floor as he looked at Dante uncomprehendingly. Dante rose and walked over to him as he choked, his shirt soaked with bright red blood, his gun arm ruined. He stood over him and ground his cigar into Paco's wound.

"You dumb bastard. Don't you know that you can never compete with someone like me? You're fighting out of your weight class. You're an insect, nothing more. Think about that as you die on my sofa. You're nothing."

"I...you..."

Dante sneered. "Sure thing, sport. I'll see you in hell. Now, if you'll excuse me, it's time to get out of here before the police arrive, which they should, any minute. I called my helicopter when I first heard the shooting, and it will be here shortly. As to you, my friend, enjoy drowning in your own blood and think of me as you take your last breath."

⪥∾⪥

Tara watched the torrent shoot down the pipe with satisfaction. She'd had sufficient time to test the various valves and when she'd found one that could inflict the kind of damage she had in mind, she'd closed it and darted down the other passageway. When she'd heard Jet's footsteps choose the other, she'd waited and then retraced her steps, her eyes now adjusted to the near pitch darkness and opened the valve that would flood the tunnel with river water – thousands of tons of it at the turn of a wheel.

The water rose to waist level, but she wasn't worried. She would find another shaft along the other tunnel and climb to freedom, her pursuer drowned and carried to the sea. Tara didn't have a gun, so she'd had to rely on her cunning to survive, and it had worked. Not the first time, nor would it be the last, she was sure.

She turned and took a step back the way she'd come and was shocked when something rammed into her back and knocked her face-forward with the force of a freight train. Jet had launched herself from below the surface and slammed her into the filthy water. The vile fluid flooded Tara's mouth and nose as she flailed beneath the surface, her breath knocked out of her.

Jet waited for Tara to come up so she could finish her, unable to make out much in the gloom, the only faint light coming from a shaft near the junction – a drain from a street-level gutter. Tara burst from the water, gasping. Jet delivered a series of devastating strikes to her head and neck as she fought for air. Tara's instinct kicked in and she landed several blows of her own, but the combination of being unable to breathe and Jet's skill had left her exposed, and when Jet head-butted her forehead, she saw stars.

Tara tried to kick Jet in the stomach even as her head went under again, then she felt Jet's hands around her neck, holding her underwater. She struggled and tried to free herself, but it was no good. Arching her back, she squeezed a pressure point on Jet's wrist and felt her grip relax, and used that opportunity to push herself away and come up for air.

205

Jet leapt at Tara, keeping the pressure up as Tara tried to find her balance. Tara managed to get to her feet but Jet delivered a kick to her chest that knocked her onto her back in the water. Jet advanced, blocking the blow Tara leveled at her abdomen, and dodged the strike intended to break her jaw, using the other woman's momentum to pull her past her and pound her into the brick wall. Tara grunted at the impact but kept delivering counterstrikes, sewage spraying everywhere in a cage fight to the death.

A knee to the solar plexus knocked the wind out of Jet and the follow-up karate chop to her shoulder numbed her entire left arm. Jet used the top of her head to slam into Tara's jaw and heard the crack of breaking bone as she drove home her good hand in an eye dig that blinded Tara and stopped her attack. Jet stood panting as the water continued to rise, then threw herself at Tara, using her full weight to drive her against the brick again.

Even with her jaw fractured and partially blind, Tara was a formidable adversary and landed a roundhouse that stunned Jet as they both fell against the hard tunnel wall. Tara got her hands around Jet's throat just as Jet did the same with her. Using her right elbow, Jet smacked Tara's forearm into the brick, and that hand fell away, limp. Jet squeezed with all her might, the vision of Hannah terrified on the rooftop of Luis' building, Tara with a gun to her head, vivid in her mind.

Jet kneed the side of Tara's knee joint as hard as she could, causing it to buckle. She held the American's head beneath the surface of the vile flood, her arms like steel as Tara's struggling gradually diminished and, finally, stopped. She kept Tara's head underwater for an extra minute, just to be sure, the water now reaching her chest, then released her, the contest over, Tara no longer a threat to anyone.

She moved back to the valve and turned the big wheel until the water flow eased, then turned to where Tara's lifeless form was floating in the sewage. After taking a moment to get her bearings, she moved to Tara and checked her carotid artery for a pulse.

Tara's fist struck Jet on the cheek and the skin split, and her strike using the palm of her other hand narrowly missed crushing Jet's windpipe. Jet backed up as Tara tried a kick and caught her leg, then brought her elbow down on Tara's kneecap with blinding force. Tara screamed as the patella dislocated and tore away to the side of her leg, an injury Jet knew was incapacitating. Tara slumped, incapable of supporting herself. Jet delivered a power kick that drove Tara's head back against the wall with a sickening thud as her spine snapped.

Jet watched as she went slack, her eyes frozen open, still aware but unable to move, and slowly sank beneath the sewer water, the noxious soup her final resting place, this time for eternity. Jet had seen this injury before and it was always paralyzing. In this case, drowning while unable to save herself seemed like a fitting end for Tara. Jet didn't look back as she made her way to the shaft and the distillery above.

∂∾∾

Dante watched his helicopter, an Agusta A109E, drop onto the asphalt lot next to his office. The pilot waved, and one of Dante's personal bodyguards opened the passenger compartment door and waited for him to approach. Dante took a seat and surveyed the flames licking from the front of the distillery as the man pulled the door closed and signaled to the pilot to take off.

The aircraft slowly lifted into the sky and hovered for several seconds at treetop level. Dante regarded the dead bodies of his men littering the yard near the entry and shook his head.

"What a nightmare," he muttered. His bodyguard said nothing, his reaction unwelcome. "Let's get out of here. The police will be here any minute. Call Alain and have him run interference until I'm ready to make a statement," Dante ordered. Alain was his attorney, who acted as a buffer between Dante and the authorities.

Dante was already contriving an explanation – competitors who'd hired some thugs to try to shut down his liquor production company – but he would need some time to feed the right spin to the papers and speak with his contacts in the police department, who would arrange for his explanation to be accepted without question. One of the perks of being powerful and wealthy was not having to suffer at the hands of the law when things went wrong. Dante was untouchable, but there would still need to be a story, and between Alain and himself they would come up with something plausible.

The engine's revs increased in pitch and the helicopter rose into the sky. It was just veering toward the city when Dante saw a flash from below and the unmistakable smoke trail of a missile headed straight at them. He screamed a warning a split second before the warhead detonated, vaporizing the turbine in a fiery blaze. The chopper seemed to hang in the air for a small eternity before dropping like a rock, tumbling end over end sixteen stories to the ground. The fireball when it hit the street was blinding. Paco winced even as he collapsed back inside the window, onto the office floor, a look of serenity on his face, his last living act to use Dante's own missile to terminate his miserable existence.

Chapter 32

Jet made it back to the office just as Paco fell onto his back amidst shards of glass. The Igla-S launch tube lay by his side, the window shattered from where he'd fired the Mac-10 through it to get a shot at the helicopter. She rushed to him and knelt next to him, his torso covered with blood. His gaze wandered to her, delirious, agony radiating from his eyes as his life seeped from his body.

"What did you do?" she whispered.

"He…dead…"

Paco's death rattle was like so many others she'd heard, his spirit departing his form, shedding his battered frame for the unknown. His eyes stared lifelessly at the ceiling, a look of satisfaction on his face. Jet closed his lids before standing and nodding.

"You fought the good fight. May you find peace in whatever form you can," she whispered, murky water dripping from her clothes onto the marble tiles.

A secondary explosion shook the building as the helicopter's auxiliary fuel tank exploded, jarring her back to reality. She moved to the blood-soaked couch, scooped up Paco's pistol, and made her way outside and along the side of the warehouse. The workers had dispersed, not wanting to have anything to do with the coming inquiries, and she was the only living thing in the huge yard as she jogged to the ruined gate, flames licking at the building behind her as still more vats of alcohol ignited and burned within the plant.

Jet walked hurriedly down the sidewalk, ignoring the few spectators that had gathered, and pretended to be engrossed along with them in the flaming helicopter wreckage outside the gate. When she reached the Renault, she realized she didn't have the keys – Matt did. She was just about to break the window with the gun so she could hotwire the car when she heard the distinctive sound of someone clearing their throat from the thick hedge behind her. She spun, whipping the pistol out as she did so, and then lowered it when she saw Matt, his hair singed almost completely off, his face black from soot and smoke.

"Easier if you use these," he said, holding up the keys.

"You're alive!" she said, rushing to him and hugging him.

"Woah. Careful with the arm." He hugged her back and then wrinkled his nose. "Oh…my…God. What's that stink?"

"Don't ask. Trust me; it tastes worse than it smells."

"I don't want to ask how you know that."

"I was in the sewer with your ex."

"You found her!" He saw the swelling on her face. "Nothing broken?"

"Her neck."

"And Paco?"

She shook her head. "Didn't make it."

The howl of the emergency vehicles split the air as the first wave of police and firefighters approached. Matt handed her the keys.

"You drive. But Kee-rist almighty. We need to get you into a shower and burn your clothes as soon as possible. That's just…rank."

"I guess you haven't seen yourself in the mirror lately."

"What?"

"You just saved about two months of haircut money."

He touched his head gingerly. "That's probably best now that I'm broke. Living off my girlfriend's largesse." He winced. "It's still a little delicate. Burned."

Jet started the car and pulled away, moving in the opposite direction from the distillery. "I'm thinking we find the nearest public restrooms and get your face washed so we don't look like escapees from a house fire and then rent a cheap hotel room – and I bathe for a couple of days," she said.

"Don't forget burning your clothes."

Two hours later they were in the small town of San Luis de Giles, Jet in the shower while Matt lay on the bed, after cleaning his face off. After a seeming eternity she emerged from the bathroom, a towel wrapped around her, her gleaming black hair still wet.

"You gave me quite a scare with the blowing-up-in-a-fireball act, you know," she said as she climbed on the bed next to him.

"It wasn't my intention. Just sort of happened. One second I was shooting people, the next I was in the middle of an inferno. I'm lucky I got the truck door shut in time. But some flame still got in through the other side. As you can see."

"It could have been worse. Something important could have been hurt."

"True. At least the hair will grow back. Besides, I was thinking about a change. This might be a good look for me."

She cuddled next to him. "We need to wash our clothes in the sink and get out of here once they dry. It'll probably take an hour. I'm hoping we can find some way to entertain ourselves while we wait." She sniffed. "You smell like a barbequed leather jacket."

"I was just going to get out of my clothes and take a shower."

"I'll rinse both of our stuff off. You'll take forever with the broken arm."

"Finally I get some sympathy. That and I lost all my money. Not to mention my hair."

"But you still have your health."

"Not to mention the love of my life is rich as Croesus."

She blinked. "Did you just say that I was the love of your life?"

Matt smiled, the skin around his eyes crinkling. "I figured I better suck up and be nice to you now that I'm broke."

She opened the towel. "It's about time."

They stopped on the way out of town at a family-operated car wash and had the young brothers that ran it scrub out the interior of the car. Jet studied a map as they waited for the cleansing to be finished while Matt watched the boys work.

"How far is it?" he asked.

"About six hundred miles of road."

"So ten hours of driving?"

"Maybe more. Although I don't think it's a great idea to drive at night. There are really long stretches with pretty much nothing across the pampas, and robberies aren't uncommon after dark."

"So where do you want to spend the night?"

"We can probably make it to Junín, a few hours west, without too much trouble. Assuming that wreck doesn't blow up." She stared at the car dubiously.

"It's an ugly duckling, I'll grant you that. But beauty is more than skin deep."

"If it makes it to Mendoza, it'll be a miracle. It was ancient when I was born."

"Hey. I resent that. I was ancient when you were born."

She smiled. "And you're still serviceable. If a little shopworn."

"That's a great adjective. Shopworn. I like that," Matt said.

"We should probably find a pay phone and call Sofia. Let her know we won't be there until tomorrow evening."

"There'll be one at the gas station on the highway out of town. They all have one."

The car still smelled like the bowels of hell, albeit with a pine tinge from the aroma one of the kids had sprayed through the car, but it was such an improvement over how it had been that neither of them complained. Thankfully, the weather was nice enough to keep the windows down as they motored into the sunset. The filling station indeed had a pay phone and Sofia answered on the fourth ring, sounding typically out of breath.

"Sofia, it's Rebecca."

"Oh my God, Rebecca. You're alive! I can't believe it!"

Jet silently cursed. Of course. The jet. It would have been on the news and her father would have been notified.

"Yes, I am."

"How? I heard about the crash..."

"It was a kind of miracle. I'll tell you all about it when I get back."

"My father will be so happy. He was sure that...well...we're all surprised to hear from you, naturally."

"Give him my regards. Is Hannah there?"

"She's napping. You want me to wake her?"

"No, not if she's asleep. She needs her rest. Listen, I'll be back tomorrow evening. But I'll need to talk to your father. Will he be around?"

"Let me ask." She set the phone down. A minute later her father's deep voice came on the line.

"You haven't stopped amazing me yet," he began.

"I'm so sorry about the plane. And Paco and his men."

He paused, instantly somber. "It wasn't your fault. To be honest, I thought we had just adopted a little girl..."

"Fortunately, the rumors of my demise are somewhat exaggerated."

He laughed. "I'd have to say so. But you must tell me the story. I'm quite sure I've never heard anything like it."

"It's a good one."

She heard Sofia's voice in the background.

"You're returning tomorrow?" he asked.

"Yes. Possibly late." She paused. "I want to know if I can impose on you again for one night."

"Of course. You're welcome to stay at my home for as long as you wish. Think nothing of it. I'll make sure I have a good supply of my best Malbec ready for your arrival."

"Your hospitality is appreciated."

"It's nothing. Really. Now Sofia wants to talk to you. She's practically pulling the phone out of my hand."

Sofia returned and Jet tried to field her questions without alarming her. Toward the end, the topic turned to Tomás.

"I'm so sorry for your loss, Sofia."

"Thank you. It's hard. I know he wasn't the best man…"

"But he was yours. I know." Both women were silent. Jet cleared her throat. "I'm really looking forward to seeing you, Sofia."

"And I you. It's been a rough few days, hasn't it?"

Jet shook her head and debated a thousand possible responses before saying simply, "That it has."

When she returned to the car, Matt was listening to the radio – the news was filled with accounts of missile attacks, a daring shootout and robbery attempt outside a bank, and the destruction of a major liquor manufacturing facility, number of casualties unknown. She started the engine and pulled onto Route 7, the Renault sounding as questionable as ever as they shook and shimmied down the road.

"If I didn't know any better, I'd say we leave a trail of destruction everywhere we go," she said, listening to the announcer recount the day's disasters.

"It's not like we invite this on ourselves. We've been trying everything we can to get away from this. I mean, we were on the other side of the planet from our enemies."

"Apparently that wasn't far enough."

"Colonizing the moon would be too obvious."

"Might be worth a try."

"As long as you and Hannah are with me, I'm game," he said.

"We'll have to get you a hairpiece, though."

"You don't like my new do?"

"Way too Bruce Willis."

"Hey. What's wrong with Bruce?"

"We'll at least pick you up a hat. Maybe that will help."

"I can always wear it in bed."

She smiled. "That's what the paper bag's for."

Chapter 33

The morning started well enough at dawn, salmon ribbons streaking a deep purple sky as they continued west toward Mendoza. They'd both slept soundly for ten hours after a hurried dinner – a grill of mixed steak cuts washed down with a carafe of rustic red wine. To Jet's surprise, the Renault chugged along, never in a hurry, but reliably transporting them from the humid east coast to the arid reaches near the western mountains.

The highway that stretched from one side of the country to the other was little more than a two-lane strip of asphalt, in questionable repair in many places, the drivers as reckless as in the cities but with far more space to build to insane velocities. Several times that morning they were nearly run off the road by large overloaded trucks barreling along at double the speed limit, only to encounter a fifty-year-old pickup truck with a cow in the back, limping along at barely above walking speed.

"What are we going to do once we get home? We can't stay in Mendoza. That's pretty clear," Matt said as he watched the green expanse roll by his window, the tall grass shimmering in serpentine waves as the wind washed across the fields.

"I know. I haven't thought too much about a final destination. Out of Argentina, though."

"Where, then?"

"My diamonds are in Montevideo. But we don't need to pull any out for a while. I've got a good supply of cash in the safe at the apartment – more than enough to last us at least six months."

"How about Ecuador? I've heard good things about that area. Quito. Supposed to be quiet."

"So was Mendoza, remember? Nothing ever happens there? Wine country?"

"Or Chile?"

"Maybe temporarily, but too many big earthquakes for my liking," Jet said.

"Good point. We don't need to add being buried alive to the mix." He studied her profile. "How's the face?"

"Sore, but I'll get over it. I got the better end of the deal than Tara, that's for sure."

"She really thought she was the best."

"There's no such thing. There's just better than you. I was better than she was. It's that simple."

Matt nodded. "How much exactly do we have in the safe?"

"About a hundred and fifty thousand."

"Pesos or dollars?"

"Dollars. Or as they'll soon be referred to, American pesos." Jet smiled. "We've got plenty of money, Mr. I'm Broke Boy."

"Well, I am."

She rolled her eyes. "You'll never want for anything as long as you're with me, doll face."

"That's reassuring."

"Really. Stop worrying about it. We're rich."

"You are."

"I'll give you half my stash if you want. Easy come…"

He shook his head. "Thanks, but I prefer to hang out with you and earn my keep."

She slid her hand onto his thigh. "I was hoping you'd say that."

They reached Mendoza at six p.m. as the sun dropped behind the craggy mountains and waited until dark to return to the apartment. Matt did two circuits around the block on foot while Jet patrolled it in the car, but neither saw anything out of the ordinary. The excitement of the robbery and the murder of their doorman had obviously waned and when they returned to the lobby area, they recognized the new man – the old doorman's nephew, who sometimes worked the day shift.

"Stefan, right? I'm so sorry to hear about your uncle," Jet said as they entered, acting as though they'd just been out for dinner.

"Oh, thanks. It's horrible. Imagine. In this neighborhood. I mean, I could understand if it was in Buenos Aires, but this is Mendoza…"

"Let us know if you need anything. Seriously. He was a good man. He'll be missed," Matt said, a Fidel-Castro-style cap masking his thermally induced alopecia.

Matt retrieved his small ring of keys and cautiously opened their front door. The apartment had been closed up by Tara when she'd left and the police had gotten the building superintendent to open it so they could recreate the robbery that had ended with Matt and his attacker plunging off the terrace. A note from the super on the kitchen counter assured them that he'd been present the entire time the police had been inside and that nothing had been taken.

Jet hurriedly packed a large bag with some of Hannah's things and another with clothes for her and Matt, choosing to leave most of their possessions behind, except for the few photographs of them together. She instantly noticed the bookshelf photo was missing. A shiver ran up her spine. Her operational instincts told her that any images of her in the world were a bad thing, but she couldn't rewind what had been taken; what was done, was done.

She hurried into the bathroom with a pair of sharp scissors and gave herself a short haircut, and was pulling a hat on over her newly trimmed pate as Matt emerged from the bedroom with a small sack.

She turned to him and nodded. "You inspired me to go short, too."

"Good thinking. Because there could be footage floating around from the casino cams…"

"Damn. With everything else that happened, I didn't even think about that."

"If the cops haven't released the images yet, they will soon enough. Then again, you know how lackadaisical they can be…"

"For all we know, every cop in the city already has our pictures," she warned.

"Good point. We should get on the road as soon as possible. Maybe even tonight."

"I told Sofia we'd be spending the night, but we can always blow that off."

"I'd say we should."

"Agreed. You have the loot?" Jet asked.

Matt nodded. "And the passports."

Neither of them experienced any regret at walking away from their home. It was, after all, only a place, filled with easily replaceable trifles. A carryover from their former line of work, they didn't get sentimental or attached. It was better that way, and they both knew it.

"Poor Hannah. She's going to be so bummed that she's being uprooted again," Matt said.

"She's resilient. She'll make new friends. At her age, she can't remember more than a few hours. She'll be fine."

Matt packed the cash into their bag and then took her hand. "We all will be. You ready?"

"Sure."

Matt shouldered their heavier bag and Jet hefted Hannah's. After a final glance at the apartment, they closed and locked the front door for the last time and made for the stairs. At the ground floor, they bypassed the lobby and took their car from the garage, leaving the Renault to the vagaries of the Mendoza traffic police. The security barrier slid to the side and Jet pulled onto the street and headed for the highway, making sure they weren't being followed, both of their senses now in operational mode after the events of the past day and a half.

☙◦❧

Leonid sat with his men in the bar of the Park Hyatt Hotel, nursing a beer as they endured the worst part of any mission: the waiting. His eyes followed a comely young waitress, a stunning waif with auburn hair and a radiant smile, as she brought an elderly couple a bottle of wine and opened it for them, taking care to pour each glass only a quarter full before setting the wine down in front of them. She graced Leonid with a coy grin and his breath caught in his throat. Perhaps the trip wouldn't be all work, after all.

He'd been assured by his Argentine contact that everything that could be done had been, and that it was only a matter of time until the woman surfaced – a glib assurance Leonid put no stock in. The man had an oily manner and Leonid didn't believe a word he said, especially after he'd named a price for cooperation that was triple what would have been reasonable. They'd negotiated, but it had left a bad taste in his mouth and he was skeptical that the Argentine would deliver.

When his cell phone rang, it startled him. He dug it out of his shirt pocket and answered, his eyes narrowing as he listened.

"Are you sure?"

More listening. Leonid nodded to himself and waved at the girl to get the check.

"All right. Don't do anything until I can rendezvous with you, do you understand?"

He listened again and grunted, then hung up. His men looked at him expectantly.

"Come on, boys. Time to earn our keep."

⤟∘⤞

When Jet and Matt arrived at the villa, security at the house was heavy and the guards looked like they meant business. Sofia and her father came out onto the porch with Hannah in tow when they heard the car pull into the grounds. Jet stepped out of the car and her little face lit up, then she ran to her mother as fast as her chubby child's legs would carry her.

"Mama! Mama back!"

Jet gave her a huge hug. "I am, sweet pea. Just like I promised. How have you been?"

"O-tay."

"Did you play with Catalina a lot?"

"Yeth."

"Wow. You must be tired."

Hannah shook her head no.

Jet stood and approached Sofia while Hannah repeated her greeting ritual with Matt. Sofia's father looked her over as though he'd never seen her before, his eye immediately taking in her new haircut under the cap and the fading swelling near the cut on her cheek.

"Welcome. I have the wine open and ready, and dinner prepared. Come in, please," he said as Sofia and Jet embraced.

"Thank you so much, but I'm afraid there's been a change of plans. We're going to get going tonight."

Sofia and her father exchanged a look of concern. "What? Why?"

"There may be some complications I can't discuss. Suffice it to say that I think it's for the best," Jet said.

"But surely you have time for dinner!" Sofia protested.

Matt approached with Hannah. "It would be rather rude to say no, wouldn't it?" he said, extending his hand. "Nice to meet you all. I'm Greg."

They shook hands, and Jet relented. "If you don't mind us eating and running, we'd love to have dinner with you."

"No problem. We all do what we must. But at the very least you can do so on a full stomach," Sofia's father said.

The meal was Italian, oversized portions, each dish delicious, their private chef having pulled out all the stops, and Jet was glad they'd made an exception. For all they knew, this was the last quality meal they'd have for some time. Both Jet and Matt sipped at their wine sparingly, painfully aware that they'd be on the road late into the night in order to put as much distance as possible between themselves and Argentina. Their plan was to make it to Valparaiso, on the coast of Chile, bypassing Santiago for the more tranquil beach city, where they could take stock and develop a more coherent strategy for their future.

"So...wait. You survived the plane crash after it had been hit by...a rocket?" Sofia asked, awe in her voice.

"It was random chance that I made it. A matter of where I was sitting. If I'd been just a little more toward the rear of the plane, I would have been...it would have been unfortunate. Further forward, like the pilots, same thing. Just lucky," Jet said.

"And you swam to shore?" her father asked. "A mile or more of the river, after plummeting out of the sky."

"It didn't seem like there were many alternatives at that point. And I'm a good swimmer."

Sofia's father grunted his agreement.

"I'd say so," Sofia said. "You know, on the news there was a huge special feature on a distillery that was attacked. The owner was Dante Caravatio. He was killed in a helicopter crash at the site that's still being investigated. Eyewitnesses reported seeing something like a missile blow it out of the sky."

"Sounds like poetic justice," Matt said, offering a toast. "Live by the sword..."

Sofia's father raised his glass along with one gray eyebrow. "Indeed."

The housekeeper cleared the dinner table when they finished eating and they bantered pleasantly for ten minutes before Jet glanced at the time and leaned forward, hands folded in front of her.

"Thank you so much for all the hospitality, but I'm afraid we need to get going."

Sofia shook her head. "I wish you would spend the night. The roads can be dangerous at this hour."

"I know. But I'm afraid we can't." Jet looked at Matt. "Would you take Hannah out to the car and strap her in?"

"I'd be delighted," Matt answered and picked Hannah up, her eyes already drooping as she nodded off, full and ready for her night's sleep. Catalina ran to them and said good-bye to Hannah, who waved, neither of them realizing it would be the last time the best friends ever saw each other. Matt carried her through the front door as Jet rose to hug Sofia, who embraced her like a sister. When they parted, Sofia's eyes were moist. Jet turned to Sofia's father.

"The dinner was delicious. Really amazing," she said. "You've been far too kind."

"As I said, it's the least I can do. Anything you need, any trouble you have, please, call me. Do you need any money?" he asked.

"No. We're self-sufficient, thankfully."

"Are you sure? I kept a hundred thousand dollars from the money I returned to the bank today, just in case."

"No, really, although I appreciate it."

"Please. I insist. Really. Think of it as my way of saying thank you."

Jet decided not to fight him on it. "You're more than generous."

"Nonsense. Oh, and I took the liberty of getting a cell phone for you and programmed in my number. Remember. I'm absolutely sincere about my offer to help – although I'm not sure you really need it," he said, giving her a long, appraising look. "I'll be right back with the phone and the cash."

Jet watched him mount the stairs to his study and returned her attention to Sofia.

"You're father's a good man, Sofia. Remember that when you're angry with him. He has a good heart."

"I'll try. But sometimes it's hard." She hesitated. "You know he knew about Tomás?"

Jet shook her head. "Nobody's perfect, Sofia. He was just trying to protect you. That's what fathers do."

"I understand. But it still feels like a betrayal."

Jet had no words of wisdom to impart. She stood with Sofia, waiting as her father's heavy footsteps moved through the house. They both looked up when he came back down the steps, a small phone and charger in a white box in his left hand, a bulging brown plastic shopping bag in his right.

"Here you go. Use it well," he said, handing her the phone and the bag.

Sofia nodded. "Yes, and call us as soon as you arrive wherever you're off to. To let us know you made it safely."

"I will," Jet said – another in a long string of promises she had no intention of keeping. She hated misleading Sofia, but she had no choice. Her father's flinty eyes told her he already knew the truth, and understood.

Jet took a final look over her shoulder as she neared the front entrance, her heart tugging at her. The sight of a home, a real home, with a real family in it, now seemed like an impossible dream she'd never attain, instead doomed to being on the run, always only one step ahead of whatever threat was after them, a normal life light years away and pointless to wish for.

She sighed and pushed open the door, and nodded at Carlos standing guard on the porch. He offered a small tilt of his head in acknowledgement. She descended the steps with a heavy heart and walked to where Matt was approaching her from the car, his shoes crunching on the gravel as he neared.

"What is it?" she asked when she saw his face.

"I've got something to show you."

Chapter 34

The Chevrolet rolled south on Route 73, headed from Mendoza to San Raphael, cutting through the high desert at moderate speed, the stars overhead a tapestry of light at the high elevation with no pollution to cloud the view. The moon silvered the landscape with an otherworldly light, the barren brown soil nature's cruel joke after the lush vineyards of Mendoza stretching to the horizon.

A spotlight blinked into life overhead and traced along the freeway until it landed on the little burgundy sedan. Half a mile ahead a roadblock barred the road, two military vehicles pulled across it. A contingent of armed soldiers faced the oncoming vehicle, pointing their guns at the oncoming car.

The Chevrolet slowed as it neared and coasted to a stop, the soldiers illuminated in the headlights. A second group of older, harder gunmen stood by the side of the road, Leonid at their head, a machine pistol in his hand. A uniformed officer approached the vehicle with two of Leonid's men flanking him, their weapons pointed at the heavily tinted driver's window.

"Turn the engine off and get out of the car. Now. This is your only warning. Fail to comply and we'll open fire," the officer barked.

The engine died, the automatic locks deactivated, and the door slowly opened. An Argentine man wearing a black windbreaker and brown slacks stepped out, his hands over his head.

"What's this about?" he demanded, eyeing the gunmen, his tone puzzled.

The officer looked confused and peered into the car before he marched back to Leonid's position and had a hasty discussion. They returned to the car together and the officer ordered the driver to open the trunk. The driver complied and Leonid found himself glowering at a spare tire and a few half-empty oil containers.

"Where is the woman?" the officer growled at the driver, but Leonid had already seen enough. He turned to leave, the outcome already obvious to him.

>°<

The forest green Ford Explorer sat in line at the border crossing, waiting for the vehicles in front to move. The Argentines seemed completely uninterested in doing much besides waving the cars through, but the Chileans were actually checking passports, seemingly randomly, based on how the immigration officials felt about the occupants.

Brake lights flashed ahead and they inched forward. Hannah slumbered behind Matt, her car seat transferred from the Chevrolet to the Ford, their bags in the cargo area, their cash distributed between Jet's cargo pant pockets and Matt's. Jet had kept the Glock, but had disassembled it and put the various parts in the tool kit, the glove compartment, the spare tire compartment, and her pocket. In her experience there wouldn't be more than a cursory look at their bags, worst case, but she wanted to take no chances and had almost left it at Sofia's until Matt had ventured that it had come in handy so far.

The burner cell phone Sofia's father had thoughtfully provided rang. Jet answered.

"Hello," she said.

"The car was stopped at a roadblock just outside of San Raphael. It was the Argentine security service – the SIDE – and some unidentified third parties," Sofia's father reported.

"Is Carlos okay?"

"They roughed him up a little, but didn't have any reason to detain him. He had the signed title for the car you left, so he'd broken no laws. They didn't seem amused."

"No, I suppose they probably weren't."

He grunted. "It's a dangerous game you're playing. I suppose after the missile strike I don't need to tell you that."

"Nope. Can you get any information on who the third parties were?"

"I can try. I've found spreading money around never hurts, but it could take some time."

"Will you be okay?"

"I have enough guards, and now a contingent of police, to defend a prime minister. Nobody will mess with us. We'll be fine."

"Good. Again, thanks for everything."

"You're welcome. I'm glad you didn't tell me where you're off to. That way I can't tell anyone, even if they asked. Which they might."

"It was the only reason I didn't tell you."

"Very wise. Enjoy your trip, and be careful."

"I will. Take care of Sofia and Catalina."

She hung up and removed the battery from the phone before handing it to Matt, who put it in the glove compartment. He caught her eye and she relayed in hushed tones Sofia's father's account. He nodded.

"I wonder who that was? Maybe some of Tara's people?"

"Has to be. But we cut the head off that hydra, so they'll eventually give up."

"Let's hope so."

Matt had done a last-minute search of the Chevrolet at the villa and found a homing device stuck to the underside of the car, and they'd quickly come up with an alternate plan to driving it to Chile. Sofia's father had given them the aged Ford Explorer he used for low-key visits to his vineyards, when he wanted to do unannounced inspections without alerting the winery staff to his arrival, and had instructed Carlos to drive to San Rafael in the Chevrolet and spend the night there, pending further instructions. Anyone following Jet would be led on a merry chase while Matt and Jet slipped away undetected.

The air was icy at twelve thousand feet even as the South American summer approached. The Chilean border guards' breath steamed in the arctic breeze as they motioned for Jet to drive forward. She did, and a young man held up his hand for her to stop and approached the driver's side window. She rolled it down and offered a tired smile that wasn't hard to fake.

"Where are you headed?" he asked, his tone indifferent.

"Valparaiso."

"How long will you be in Chile?"

"A week. A beach vacation for the family."

The guard peered into the darkened interior of the cab and saw Hannah slumbering in her seat.

His tone softened. "How old?"

"Coming up on three."

He smiled. "Mine's going to be four next month."

"Tell me it gets easier from here."

"You're over the worst of it." He paused, taking in Matt, who was sitting with a neutral expression.

It could have gone either way. The guard looked like he was going to ask for their papers, which in and of itself wouldn't have been a big deal – assuming that there were no warrants out for a couple matching their description – but if they didn't have to furnish ID, so much the better. Matt reached into his breast pocket and extracted his passport, as if anticipating the man's request. The light went out in the guard's eyes as he backed from the window and signaled them to proceed.

Jet smiled again and raised the window, taking care not to accelerate too quickly and wake Hannah.

"That went well," Matt whispered.

"I think we pulled it off," she agreed. "Next stop, Valparaiso."

<<<<>>>>

To be alerted to new releases, sign up here:

RussellBlake.com/contact/mailing-list

About the Author

Russell Blake lives full time on the Pacific coast of Mexico. He is the acclaimed author of the thrillers *Fatal Exchange*, *The Geronimo Breach*, *Zero Sum*, The Delphi Chronicle trilogy (*The Manuscript*, *The Tortoise and the Hare*, and *Phoenix Rising*), *King of Swords*, *Night of the Assassin*, *Return of the Assassin*, *Revenge of the Assassin*, *Blood of the Assassin*, *The Voynich Cypher*, *Silver Justice*, *JET*, *JET II – Betrayal*, *JET III – Vengeance*, *JET IV – Reckoning*, *Jet V – Legacy*, *Jet VI – Justice*, *Upon a Pale Horse*, *Black*, *Black is Back*, and *Black is The New Black*.

Non-fiction novels include the international bestseller *An Angel With Fur* (animal biography) and *How To Sell A Gazillion eBooks (while drunk, high or incarcerated)* – a joyfully vicious parody of all things writing and self-publishing related.

"Capt." Russell enjoys writing, fishing, playing with his dogs, collecting and sampling tequila, and waging an ongoing battle against world domination by clowns.

Visit Russell's salient website for more information

RussellBlake.com/

CPSIA information can be obtained at www.ICGtesting.com
Printed in the USA
LVOW10s2154081014

407962LV00001B/188/P